WALLS

Also by L. M. Elliott

Suspect Red

Under a War-Torn Sky

A Troubled Peace

Across a War-Tossed Sea

Hamilton and Peggy! A Revolutionary Friendship

Give Me Liberty

Da Vinci's Tiger

WALLS

L. M. ELLIOTT

with a photo essay by Megan Behm

Algonquin 2021

With great admiration for all "military brats,"
who serve as surely as their parents do.

And, as always, for Peter and Megan,
who embody all that is wondrous and poetic
in free thought.

Published by Algonquin Young Readers
an imprint of Algonquin Books of Chapel Hill
Post Office Box 2225
Chapel Hill, North Carolina 27515-2225

a division of
Workman Publishing
225 Varick Street
New York, New York 10014

This book is a work of fiction. While the historic, contextual facts
of 1960–1961 and the Berlin Wall are real, the characters and their
dialogue in this novel are products of the author's imagination.

LIBRARY OF CONGRESS CATALOGING-IN-PUBLICATION DATA

Names: Elliott, Laura, 1957– author. | Behm, Megan, photo essayist.
Title: Walls / L. M. Elliott ; with a photo essay by Megan Behm.
Description: First edition. | Chapel Hill, North Carolina : Algonquin, 2021. | Includes bibliographical
references. | Audience: Ages 12 and up. | Audience: Grades 7–9. | Summary: In the days before the
treacherous overnight raising of the Berlin Wall, teenaged cousins Drew, an American army brat
in West Berlin, and Matthias, a young communist in East Berlin, become wary friends on opposite
sides of the Cold War. Interspersed throughout the story are captioned photographs from the era.
Identifiers: LCCN 2021009295 | ISBN 9781643750248 (hardcover) | ISBN 9781643752310 (ebook)
Subjects: LCSH: Berlin Wall, Berlin, Germany, 1961–1989—Juvenile fiction. | Berlin (Germany)—
History—1945–1990—Juvenile fiction. | Cold War—Juvenile fiction. | CYAC: Berlin Wall, Berlin,
Germany, 1961–1989—Fiction. | Berlin (Germany)—History—1945–1990—Fiction. | Germany—
History—1945–1990—Fiction. | Cold War—Fiction. | Children of military personnel—Fiction. |
Military bases—Fiction. | Cousins—Fiction.
Classification: LCC PZ7.E453 Wal 2021 | DDC [Fic]—dc23
LC record available at https://lccn.loc.gov/2021009295

10 9 8 7 6 5 4 3 2 1
First Edition

It is only when you meet someone of
a different culture from yourself that you begin
to realize what your own beliefs really are.

—GEORGE ORWELL,
AUTHOR OF *ANIMAL FARM*
AND *NINETEEN EIGHTY-FOUR*

WALLS

Berlin is . . . a showcase of liberty . . .
an island of freedom in a Communist sea . . .
a beacon of hope behind the Iron Curtain.
—JOHN F. KENNEDY

Berlin is the testicle of the West.
When I want the West to scream,
I squeeze on Berlin.
—NIKITA KHRUSHCHEV

In 1960, Berlin is an outpost of democracy marooned deep inside East Germany, a communist police state controlled by Russia's Soviet Union. Why? After WWII, the Allies occupied Germany to restore order and purge it of Nazism. The United States, Great Britain, and France oversaw Germany's western zones to establish a new democracy. Russia took the country's eastern half, officially named the German Democratic Republic (GDR). Because it had been Hitler's capital, Berlin was also divided. The city quickly became a poignant and dangerous microcosm of West versus East Germany and its tense, nuclear-armed Cold War standoff. Within Berlin itself, residents could still cross its internal sectors—from communist to democratic and back. As such Berlin became an escape hatch to freedom. If East Germans could evade the GDR's secret police, cross the barrier encircling the city, and make it into Berlin, they might then be able to slip into the city's American sector to beg political asylum. Hundreds tried every week.

During WWII, the Soviet-American alliance had been a wary but necessary one to defeat Hitler. As US, British, and French soldiers landed on Normandy beaches and battled their way inland across France, the Russians marched through Belarus, Ukraine, and Poland to reach Berlin first, raising its Soviet hammer-and-sickle flag over the city. In 1960, the Red Army remained in East Germany, 400,000-strong, against which a mere 11,000 American, British, and French soldiers stood post in West Berlin.

Soviet Russia drops an "Iron Curtain" of oppression across Europe after it swallows up countries its Red Army liberated from the Nazis. Some—Estonia, Latvia, Lithuania, Belarus, Moldova, Ukraine—are simply absorbed. Others are turned into a band of "satellite" Soviet Bloc nations, including Romania, Bulgaria, Poland, Czechoslovakia, Hungary, and the GDR. Any resistance is quickly put down.

Isolated inside Soviet-controlled East Germany, American troops stationed in West Berlin rely on supplies brought in by air or along the GDR-operated rail line running 110 miles through the communist zone—if the Russians keep the tracks open. In the spring of 1948, incensed that West Berlin's economy is booming under American support, the Soviets order a blockade, determined to starve Western troops into evacuating and West Berliners into submitting to Russian rule. The U.S. responded by launching Operation Vittles, airlifting fuel, medicine, and foods to West Berlin, landing cargo planes every 30 seconds at Templehof Airport, no matter how perilous the weather. Hungry Berliners waited beside

the runways. Seeing children below, pilots began tossing out parachute bags of sweets for them. The "candy bombers" became much-beloved legends among young West Berliners.

After 14 grueling months, Russia relented and reopened roads, canals, and trains to West Berlin. But in answer to the blockade and the Soviets' continuing iron-fisted control of Eastern Europe, twelve Western democracies create NATO (the North Atlantic Treaty Organization), pledging to support one another against Russia's territorial aggression and attacks on democracy.

The GDR seized family farms, broke them apart, and gave parcels to loyal Communist Party members to form agricultural collectives, forcing owners to till land that no longer belonged to them. They also enforced backbreaking production quotas on laborers. In June 1953, when the GDR demanded a 10 percent increase in worker productivity without any raise in pay, workers finally had enough and took to the streets in protest. They asked for decent wages, more humane and realistic quotas, and the right to vote. The demonstrations started in East Berlin and spread to 700 other cities and villages. Within days, Russian tanks rolled into the communist sector of Berlin to crush the uprising. With nothing but rocks to hurl, the protesters were quickly overcome. Perhaps as many as 300 died in the fighting and 4,270 were imprisoned. Attempts to escape to the West skyrocketed.

By 1960, the differences between the American, British, and French sectors in the West and the Eastern Russian sector are stark. In West Berlin, bombed-out buildings have been rebuilt. Its commercial district bustles with shoppers. A vibrant nightlife features restaurants like the Kranzler, where horse-drawn carriages await elegantly clad revelers.

The Kurfürstendamm's shops offer chic fashion equal in creative individualism and sophistication to New York City's famed Fifth Avenue.

In East Berlin, rubble left by Allied bombs remains. Children play in ruins under communist slogans. Shortages of bread, milk, meat, and soap are constant.

GDR children are seen as the "best human material" for building a lasting workers' utopia. Strict discipline, standardized possessions and opportunities, and unquestioning faith in the Communist Party's authority begin early, with toddlers being potty trained to go together in state-run daycare.

Preteens join the Pioneers, proudly parading to honor communist martyrs. Youth who seem unenthusiastic, or more religious than patriotic, are reported to school authorities or called into tribunals of their peers to be interrogated. At age 14, East Germans participate in *Jugendweihe*, a formal "youth consecration," pledging their allegiance to the "great and noble cause of socialism" and to defend the fatherland. They attend after-school courses and camps teaching Marxism and basic soldiering to qualify for the FDJ (Free German Youth, ages 14–25), a requirement to advance to university.

AUGUST 1960

In the summer of 1960, the Soviets shoot down an American U-2 spy plane and capture its pilot, Francis Gary Powers, who was photographing Russian military installations. The CIA had believed the plane flew too high (at 70,000 feet) to be detected by Russian radar.

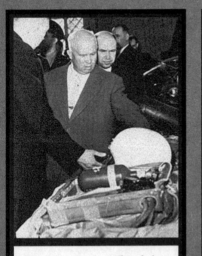

Russian premier Khrushchev gloats over the U-2's recovered wreckage as proof of Soviet superiority in technology.

Tried in front of 2,000 Russian spectators, Powers is sentenced to 10 years for espionage. Americans fear what top secret information the Soviets might extract from him in prison.

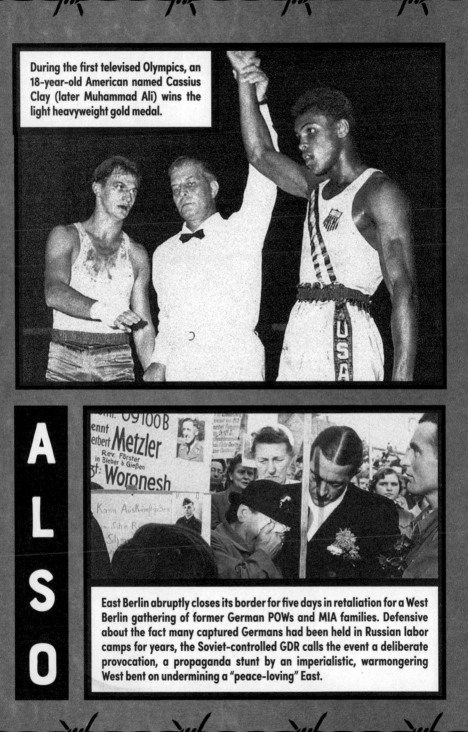

During the first televised Olympics, an 18-year-old American named Cassius Clay (later Muhammad Ali) wins the light heavyweight gold medal.

A L S O

East Berlin abruptly closes its border for five days in retaliation for a West Berlin gathering of former German POWs and MIA families. Defensive about the fact many captured Germans had been held in Russian labor camps for years, the Soviet-controlled GDR calls the event a deliberate provocation, a propaganda stunt by an imperialistic, warmongering West bent on undermining a "peace-loving" East.

Frank Sinatra and the "Rat Pack" star in *Ocean's 11*, and American families line up to swallow sugar cubes infused with a new pink-syrup polio vaccine, finally stopping worldwide epidemics that had left millions paralyzed for life.

CHAPTER ONE

AUGUST
1960

Standing in the doorway, Drew hesitated, his freckles burning crimson like a thousand flares of anxiety. Any minute, his red hair might burst into flames.

Snap out of it, man, he reprimanded himself. *You've done this before.* Five times already in his fifteen-year life—California, New York, Italy, North Carolina, and Virginia. It wasn't as if he was trying to invade the Soviet Union. All he had to do was walk through this measly door and into a party, introduce himself to a room of strangers, win them over with breezy chitchat and the gutsy bravado and pitch-perfect manners expected of "army brats." All the while knowing that in two years tops, he'd most likely be pulling up stakes and saying goodbye again.

No problem.

"Go on, soldier," his big sister Joyce nudged him. "Remember what Dad always says?"

Keeping their voices low, they recited, "To take a wall, you have to march straight and fast to it. He who hesitates . . ."

". . . is lost," whispered their little sister, Linda.

Drew and Joyce glanced down at the eleven-year-old. She'd barely spoken since they'd crossed the Atlantic Ocean and taken the military duty train through Germany to Berlin. Their family dog, Blarney—Linda's constant companion and protector—was too old for the voyage and had been left behind in the States. She'd been pretty darn shaky ever since.

Joyce kissed the top of Linda's strawberry-blond head. "Full speed ahead, sweetie," she chirped.

But the trio remained frozen.

Their hosts of this welcome party had left the door open for guests, and the swirl of army folk inside hadn't yet noticed Drew and his sisters hovering there. A chance for a quick reconnaissance.

From his family's prior postings, Drew knew this apartment would be the same layout as their new quarters across the stairwell. He assessed the living room. Yup—pretty much the same army-issued furniture arranged in pretty much the same way, minus his mom's piano. In the far corner of the living room, his father and the other non-commissioned officers guffawed over some military-blunt joke. Dressed in off-duty polo shirts and crisp-pressed civilian khakis, the men were ringed in pipe smoke and held tumblers full of straight-up, no-nonsense drinks. Drew caught the smell of lasagna baking in the galley kitchen just off the big room. Bowls of Fritos and onion dip, quartered oranges, celery sticks stuffed with Palmetto Cheese, deviled eggs, green bean casserole, and a stack of Rice Krispies treats were already laid out on the dining room's starched linen tablecloth. Typical potluck welcome-to-post dinner.

Another "little America" in a foreign land.

Except this time, they were living a hundred miles behind the Iron Curtain in a divided city—half free, half communist. Being sent to the Cold War's epicenter—to stand post in a small fort of democracy, outnumbered ten to one, surrounded by Russian-backed East German secret police and Soviet troops—was an assignment that had made Drew's dad whoop with pride. But this sure wasn't a place for his kids to screw up.

As Drew mulled all of this over, Joyce took Linda's hand and whispered, "Here we go."

Squaring his shoulders and sucking in a deep breath, Drew followed and stepped over the threshold.

Time for man-to-man introductions. Drew trooped toward the NCOs encircling his dad. But he stopped when he overheard them discussing Francis Gary Powers—the American U-2 pilot who'd been shot down by the Russians while taking photos of them. Drew knew better than to interrupt serious shoptalk.

"Think he'll hold up under questioning?" one of the men asked.

"He better."

"How much has this increased tensions here in Berlin?" Drew's dad asked.

"A lot."

"Khrushchev sure is making hay of capturing one of our guys. Gotta be a dream come true for that KGB bastard."

"Yeah. He's supposed to address the United Nations this fall. Wouldn't it be tragic if one of those crazy New York cabbies hit him?"

The men laughed.

"Drew!" His dad spotted him and waved him over.

As Drew approached the group, he caught a low wolf whistle coming from down the hall. *A-hole, six o'clock.* A tall teen Hercules with a fresh buzz cut had just come out of the bathroom and stopped mid-zip, eyeing Joyce.

Lately, more and more idiots like this guy were ogling his sister. With a pixie cut and enormous blue eyes, she was a redheaded lookalike of Leslie Caron in *An American in Paris* and seemed to make teenage boys' knees knock. Drew bristled.

"Drew, say hello to our host." Drew's dad demanded his attention. He'd deal with the a-hole later. With a made-to-order smile, he greeted Sergeant Jones. "Hello, sir," Drew said, shaking the man's hand. "Andrew McMahon."

"Hear you've got a hell of a pitching arm, son," the sergeant replied.

"Yes, sir." *Damn straight*, Drew wanted to shout. His high school coach in Virginia had promised he'd start in the lineup this year, even though he was just a sophomore on a state championship team.

"He's a southpaw, too," said Drew's dad.

"Excellent!" Sergeant Jones clapped Drew on the back so hard Drew staggered forward. "We're in need of an ace. Our Little League team just went to the world championships, but the high school–aged players act like chickens in a rainstorm."

Traded from state champions to a dodo roster. *Grrrreat.* Drew simmered. He just loved the army life.

"Have you met my boy?" Sergeant Jones asked.

"No, sir."

"Bob!" the sergeant roared.

Of course. It was the wolf-whistling jerk. He took his sweet time sauntering over.

"Glad to meet you." Bob friendly punched Drew's chest. Well, sort of friendly. It actually hurt. Drew felt his freckles roasting again.

"Paperweight boxing champ in Youth Club," his father bragged. "Box any, Andrew?"

"No way," Drew's dad answered for him. "Protecting that pitching arm."

"Right. Well, Bob can explain what's happening during the match tonight. One of our own—Eddie Crook—is taking on a guy from Poland. Eddie's an all-round all-American. He even played quarterback for the Berlin Bears when he was stationed here. So the brigade's juiced that the Olympics are being broadcast. There's no way we all could have made it to Rome to see him."

With that, the boys were dismissed. They went straight for the Fritos.

"Don't worry about having to babysit me during the match, by the way," said Drew. "I'll just listen to the commentary."

"Speak German?" Bob asked through a mouthful of corn chips.

"A little. My mom's fluent. Why?"

"Because the match will be broadcast in German. We've got a whopping two channels here, and everything's in German."

"All in German? Even *Gunsmoke* and *Alfred Hitchcock Presents*?"

Bob snorted. "Who said we got those? Get used to listening to the radio for stuff like that. AFN is pretty swell, though. They broadcast *Fibber McGee*, *What's My Line?*, and *Johnny Dollar*. Great jazz programs, too. So good, East Berliners tune in all the time—drives the commies in charge over there crazy."

Joyce would be glad to hear about the jazz. But the fact that there was no American TV was annoying news—Drew loved *Alfred Hitchcock*. And Linda lived by *Lassie*.

Where was Linda, anyway? Drew did a sweep of the room and found her in a corner, her face covered by an outstretched *London Times* Sunday magazine—reading, or hiding?

"I'll show you around tomorrow," Bob said. "Everything's a quick walk—school, fields, Outpost movie theater, teen club."

Drew nodded. "Thanks."

"No sweat, Mac."

Drew winced. He'd known Bob for all of two minutes, and the guy had already tagged him with the nickname he most hated. That stereotypical play off his last name made Drew even more self-conscious about his full-body splatter of Irish freckles and carrottop. But Bob was his host. Drew buttoned up about it—for the night, anyway.

Carrying a steaming lasagna, Joyce approached the table. Raised to have perfect army-post party manners, she had made a beeline for the kitchen to help. "Excuse me, boys." Her wide skirt and petticoat swung round her gracefully and brushed against Bob as she set the Pyrex dish down.

The guy purposefully hadn't moved out of her way. Drew felt his hackles go up again, but Joyce spoke before he could say anything.

She extended her hand to shake Bob's. "Hey, I'm Joyce. Thanks so much for having us tonight."

"Hey, I'm bewitched." Bob didn't let go. "I was just giving your brother the lay of the land." He went on as if he'd been in the middle of reciting a list: "Lights out—in the stairwell and the fourth-floor laundry room—at midnight." He winked. "Two best places for necking after that."

Jeez Louise.

Joyce burst out laughing. "Bewitched and a dreamer, too. How nice. I'm grateful for the warning. I'll be sure never to go up there past ten p.m." Blessing Bob with a practiced rejection—a warm, polite smile that still radiated *you're a bozo*—Joyce pulled her hand away. She headed back to the kitchen for another dish of lasagna, rolling her eyes at Drew as she turned.

Drew grinned. Cool as a cucumber, his big sis. If only he could learn to be like that.

"Dang," Bob muttered. "No offense, Mac, but how is that doll your sister?"

"Yeah, she's definitely in the better end of the family gene pool," said Drew. "Joyce looks more like my mom."

"Where is your mom, anyway? I heard the hens whispering that you might not have one. Or that maybe there was trouble at home, disagreement about coming to Berlin in the first place." Bob nodded to the growing crowd of military wives chatting in the living room.

"What?" First impressions were everything to a military family. Drew rushed to set the record straight. "Mom's coming. She's meeting her cousin for the first time and bringing her and her son to the party. Your mom said it was jake—that it would be nice for them to see the Olympics coverage." Drew's own opinion was that it wasn't okay—not at all. What the heck was his mom thinking, springing German cousins on him and his sisters the same night they had to enter their new world and try to befriend guys like Bob? But he just added, "Your mom invited them."

"Yeah, Mom's like that." Bob nodded. "Bighearted." He was quiet for a moment as the boys watched Mrs. Jones come in with an enormous bowl of ginger ale punch. Petite and fresh-faced, she staggered a bit under the weight and slosh, and then gave a nervous little laugh as she mopped up a small spill. Bob sighed and searched for more conversation. "So . . ."

"So . . ." Drew echoed, and trailed off.

Grabbing another handful of Fritos, Bob said, "Your mom's German?"

"Half. Her mother immigrated to the United States right after World War I. Her sister stayed here, though. That'd be my great-aunt, I guess."

"So . . . you have Nazis in your family."

"What? No! We're no Nazis. My dad fought on D-Day!"

"So did mine," countered Bob. "Omaha Beach. But we don't have any Germans in our family tree."

Drew had been ridiculed before for his obvious Irishness. But no one had ever accused him of being a Nazi! He felt his hands ball into fists and shoved them into his pockets.

The Olympic fight saved him.

"Match is on in ten minutes," Sergeant Jones called out as he flipped on the TV set and adjusted its antenna. "Grab some dinner and get seated! On the double, everyone! We don't want to miss a single one of Eddie's jabs."

✦

Mittelgewicht Ed Crook steht heute als Vertreter der Vereinigten Staaten Polen's Tadeusz Walasek gegenüber . . .

Just as the match was announced and the fighters appeared on the flickering black-and-white TV screen, Drew's mom appeared at the door like an actress ridiculously late for her cue. Mrs. Jones hurried over. "Come in, come in, my dear!" She fluttered her hand in the direction of a female guest, announcing, "Emily McMahon, this is—"

Ding! The fighting began, and the cheers of a room full of men drowned out Mrs. Jones's introduction. "Atta boy, Eddie. Take it to him!"

Getting up from the floor where he'd settled cross-legged with his plate of food, Drew picked his way through the crowd while eyeballing his new extended family. The woman standing next to his mom looked eerily like her—older, grayer, thinner, but with the same unusual teal-colored eyes, pale complexion, and high cheekbones. But while his mom's eyes were merry and inquisitive, her cousin's were wary. The woman's overall somberness was a stark contrast with the pastel-clad perkiness of the army wives waiting to meet her.

Behind her was her son, a gangly male replica of his mother. Drew knew that he and his cousin were the same age, but the kid looked too scrawny and small to be going on sixteen. He had to be at least two or three inches shorter than Drew, who wasn't exactly tall.

"Hi." He stuck out his hand. "Drew."

"*Guten Tag.* My name is Matthias." He shook Drew's hand. Strong grip, at least.

"Weird way to meet."

The boy cocked his head, hesitant. "Yah."

Oh, right, Drew thought. *This kid only knows so much English.* He searched his elemental German vocabulary for something equivalent to *weird.* He turned to his mom for help.

His mom explained, "*Seltsame Art sich kennenzulernen.*" Matthias nodded, solemn. "Yes. It is."

"I am very pleased to finally meet you, Drew." Matthias's mother gathered Drew into a brisk hug. "Please, call me Cousin Marta." She said the same to Joyce and Linda as she embraced them. Then the women were enveloped by a wave of welcoming military wives as the boys stood silent and awkward.

"Awwww, c'mon, ref! What was that?" the dads shouted at the TV.

"Boxing match. Olympics," Drew explained to Matthias. "You box?"

"*Nein.* You?"

"Naw. I play baseball. You?"

"Football."

"Oh, great! Maybe we could throw the pigskin around later. I brought one from home."

"Not American football," Matthias said. "Foot-ball. Soccer."

"Oh. Well, maybe we could toss a baseball instead. You like baseball?"

Matthias shrugged. "Not much. A slow game."

Okay, was there any guy his age in Berlin who wasn't a jerk? Drew sighed.

Matthias sighed.

At Drew's elbow, Linda sighed, startling Drew. He hadn't noticed her inch out of the flock of moms. His heart sank at the nervousness fogging her face.

"Hey, sis." Drew put his arm around Linda's thin shoulders and gave her a squeeze. She still held the newspaper. "Whatcha reading?" he asked, knowing that question always opened her up.

"Oh! This a-mazing article by Ian Fleming! He was just here in Berlin!"

"Ian Fleming? Whoa."

Matthias looked at them blankly.

"You know, James Bond. *Casino Royale, Live and Let Die, Goldfinger.*"

Matthias shook his head. "I have not heard of these."

Say whaaaat? Drew thought.

Linda held up the paper. "Look at the headline—'Spying Is Big Business in Berlin.' And look at these photos. This is the Great Tunnel. Right here in the city. The British discovered that the Russians and East Germans had run their underground telephone cables to Leningrad only three hundred yards from our sector's line. Not very far from where we're standing now. The Americans and the Brits dug this secret tunnel to tap into the Russians' telephone lines so they could hear everything the communists were saying! For three whole years! Just like something out of an Ian Fleming spy novel, don't you think?"

"Until we discovered you," Matthias muttered.

"That's right!" Linda said. "It's right here in this picture." She read the caption aloud: "One of the East German 'People's Police' examines a cable the Americans had tapped into and monitored from the U.S. radar station. Now that the tap is cut, both sides are again equal in the espionage battle." She looked up and smiled at Matthias.

Linda hadn't noticed the way Matthias had said *we*. But Drew sure had. For one thing, this guy clearly understood English better than he let on. And *we* meant that Matthias and Cousin Marta came from the Russian sector of the city, from *East* Berlin. Drew had just assumed they lived on the democratic Western side, where the British, French, and American forces held the line against Soviet incursion.

What was his mom thinking? This kid might be a card-carrying commie! And here he was at a party swarming with American sergeants. Some of these men had to be intelligence officers. What would they think of Drew's family being cozy with the enemy?

"Excuse me a sec." Furious, Drew wove his way through the party toward his mother. Maybe he could convince her to retreat with Cousin Marta and Matthias across the hall to their own apartment before anyone else figured out what Drew just had.

But he was too late.

"Oh, you're from *East* Berlin!" one of the moms was saying. "You know, our maid comes from there, too, every day. She has that special work permit. She's one of those . . . oh . . . what's the slang word you East Germans use for laborers who go back and forth?"

"*Grenzgänger*," said Marta. Her wary look turned defensive.

"That's it. *Border-hopper.* The term's rather derogatory, isn't it? Anyway, my maid says it's most economical for her to work in West Berlin, where the pay is better and the money more stable, but to live in the city's eastern sector, where things are so much cheaper." The woman lowered her voice to a conspiratorial hush. "She smuggles meat back across the line for her children. I know you can't get fresh meat over there—if you can get meat at all. So awful, the way the Russians plunder East Germany and take most everything good for themselves."

The woman tut-tutted as she crossed her arms and concluded, "You know, Mrs. Schneider, there are plenty of military families looking for housekeepers, if you're interested. We all say the same—of all the help we've had in our postings overseas, the best maids are German."

Drew stopped in his tracks seeing his mother turn as red as he did when he was mortified.

"Thank you for the"—Cousin Marta paused and seemed to choose each of her next words very carefully—"kind concern. Everything you say is true. Our life in East Berlin is much harder than it would be here. But I am already employed. I am a nurse at Charité Hospital, where they are training me to be a doctor."

"A woman doctor?" The woman stared at her in amazement.

"Yes," answered Cousin Marta. "One of the good things about the socialist state is the equality of opportunity. Women who are found capable are trained as readily as men to be doctors. Almost half the doctors delivering babies at Charité are female."

Drew's mother slipped her hand through her cousin's arm, artfully cutting off the conversation. "Are you hungry, Marta? Your buffet looks wonderful, Mrs. Jones."

"Goodness, call me Judy, please." She gestured to the table as Drew's mom and Cousin Marta separated themselves from the klatch.

The other women took their seats, trying in vain to quiet their husbands, who were shouting at the TV, telling Ed Crook how to punch and the ref how to call the match.

As he turned to follow his cousins to the food, Drew noticed Matthias pocketing cookies and oranges. His mouth dropped open. "Mom," he whispered, pointing toward the table.

Appearing out of nowhere, Joyce playfully slapped at Drew's hand. "No more Rice Krispies treats for you, mister. Save some for the rest of us."

"But, Joyce, he—"

"I know. I saw him." Joyce kept her voice soft. "I heard an interesting joke tonight from one of the girls. Want to hear it?" She didn't wait for an answer. "What nationality were Adam and Eve? Why, they were Russian, of course. How do you know? Because they were both naked, had only an apple to eat, and thought they were in paradise."

Drew turned to face her. "That's not funny."

"No. It's pitiful. People in the Soviet Bloc and East Germany always seem to be on the verge of starvation while they march and sing about the joys of communism." Joyce paused. "You better get used to the fact Mom wants us to be friends with these cousins, maybe even convince them to flee the East. You know how she is when she sets her mind to saving someone, even if they have no interest in being saved."

Yeah, he knew it. Cousin Marta and Matthias were in for a full-on Emily McMahon campaign. But Drew wasn't so sure he wanted to be drafted into this do-gooder mission of hers—it was already starting to feel like a nightmare.

"That's the ticket! Ed-die! Ed-die! Ed-die!"

The dads jumped out of their seats and raised their glasses in a toast. Ed Crook had just won the middleweight gold medal for America. "First army boxer to win the Olympics," crowed Sergeant Jones.

"Hey, what in blue blazes? Look at that." Drew's dad motioned to the TV. "The crowd is heckling him!" Drew turned to see people throwing programs and shaking their fists.

"Are you kidding me?" Sergeant Jones exclaimed. Now the crowd in Rome was stomping in protest. "Bunch of Italian communists and their anti-American bull! Poor Eddie. Look at his face. He fought a clean fight. What gives? Wait . . . *shhh . . . shhh . . .* he's stepping up on the podium to get his medal."

In Rome, the crowd continued to jeer. But as "The Star-Spangled Banner" began playing, the Berlin Brigade men snapped to attention. Everyone in the apartment rose and sang, drowning out the booing on the TV.

Everyone except Cousin Marta and Matthias.

The kitchen phone began to ring. The Joneses ignored it—the national anthem was playing. But it rang again. Sergeant Jones snatched up the receiver. "Sergeant Jones's quarters, Sergeant Jones speaking. Whoever this is, you better be calling about Eddie winning!"

His attitude instantly sobered. "Yes, sir. Understood, sir." He turned to the room. "Sorry, gentlemen. Go home. You'll be receiving your own calls. It seems the Russians and their GDR lapdogs are shutting down the city's East-West border for five days, starting in a few hours."

"Why?" Mrs. Jones gasped.

"Why do the Russkies do anything?" he answered curtly.

But after letting out a sigh that reeked of impatience with his wife, he added, "According to the Politburo, it's a precaution against West Berlin"—he paused to make quote marks in the air—"'provoking potential unrest' by hosting a reunion of German POWs and relatives of those still missing in action. So many German POWs died in Soviet work camps before Stalin finally released them; the reunion touched a guilty Russian nerve, I guess. The border closure is a typical Soviet redirect—accusing the West of making trouble to distract from their own inhumane policies."

Sergeant Jones retreated to his bedroom, and all the other men left, quickly kissing their wives goodbye before they exited. "Don't worry," Drew's dad said to his mom with a grin. "This is what I came here for!"

Sergeant Jones reemerged in uniform with a sidearm on his belt. "Sorry, ma'am," he said to Cousin Marta as he passed. "You better go back across right away if you want to make it home before the border shuts." He put his hand on Bob's shoulder. "Help your mother. No screwing around." Then he was gone.

Without comment, the women began gathering dishes and cleaning.

Drew's mom stared at the door, looking dumbfounded. "How long will they be mobilized?"

Mrs. Jones shrugged. "Your children are wearing their dog tags, right? And you have an emergency bag packed and your water-sterilizing tablets, just in case?" She stopped picking up plates to give Drew's mom an apologetic smile and a sympathetic pat on the arm. "Welcome to Berlin."

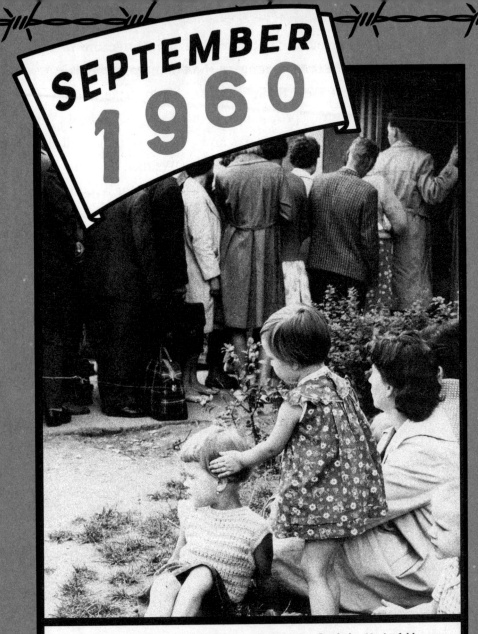

SEPTEMBER 1960

East German refugees from Russia's communist zone flood the Marienfelde camp in Berlin's American sector. They must flee quickly, secretly, before their absence is detected, leaving behind homes, bank accounts, pets, bringing little with them since suitcases would give them away. If caught, refugees are arrested for *Republikflucht*, a crime considered treason and punishable by "reeducation" in GDR labor camps.

Refugees enter under a sign proclaiming: THE FREE WORLD WELCOMES YOU. They are assigned bunks in dormitories, awaiting relocation to jobs and housing in West Germany.

The camp provides two full meals a day. This refugee girl reacts with delight to being handed a banana. She'd never tasted one before.

Back in East Germany, the Communist Party counteracts the increasing defections by trumpeting 17-year-old Ingrid Krämer's two gold medals in diving. The *Neues Deutschland* claims Krämer owes her success to her "joyful life in the socialism of the GDR." She's flown to East Berlin for a parade and autograph-signing with the slogan: "With Ingrid Krämer's will for victory, we can fulfill the plan."

ALSO

The GDR outlaws rock 'n' roll and its "provocative" dances like the twist. East German youth who defiantly tune their radios to AFN (American Forces Network) risk being reported by paid informers the Stasi secret police install in every East Berlin neighborhood and charged with *Kulturbarbarei*, "culture corruption."

Chubby Checker's song "The Twist" hits #1 on America's pop charts and becomes a dance sensation in the U.S.

the flowers that kill in the Spring
TRA-LA

THE FUNNIEST
PICTURE
THIS YEAR!

The Little Shop of Horrors plays to packed theaters in the U.S.

CHAPTER TWO
SEPTEMBER
1960

"**V**ictory, victory, is our cry!"

Sitting in the gym of the Berlin Brigade's American school, Drew was watching cheerleader tryouts and feeling like a dope. He'd been in Germany for almost three weeks. He should have gone to the PX to buy a maroon crewneck or something so he could dress in school colors like everyone else for this September opening assembly—especially since Joyce was out on the floor, auditioning.

Whenever Drew felt like grumbling over being uprooted again, he reminded himself how much this new deployment stunk for his big sister. She'd been head cheerleader back in the States, the lead in almost every play, and a soloist in all her choral groups. As a senior, she would have totally ruled their old high school, probably even been prom queen. Instead, she was here, starting all over again.

Joyce was a shoo-in for this squad, though. The other girls were good, too, but Joyce was . . . *well, look at her*, Drew thought. *She's Joyce.* He turned to Bob, who'd announced he was going to be Drew's designated escort for the first week of classes. "We actually vote on who makes the squad?" he asked.

"Yup," grunted Bob. "Although teachers have the deciding vote." He gestured dismissively toward some of the older teachers standing along the wall of the gym and added, loud enough for everyone around them to hear, "But I bet they don't remember what makes a guy stand up and cheer."

The girls sitting next to them made faces and squirmed as far away as they could get on the crowded bleachers.

Drew wasn't so sure Bob was the guy he really wanted as his wingman.

Clap-clap, clap. "Ber-lin Cubs!"

The crowd echoed. *Clap-clap, clap. Stomp-stomp, stomp.* The bleachers swayed.

Four boys picked their way through all the bodies jammed onto the hard wooden seats to crowd around Bob. Without taking his eyes off the cartwheeling girls, Bob said, "The gang's all here," then introduced Drew. "This is Mac."

"Drew," he corrected, shaking hands with interchangeable juniors Larry, Gary, and Steve, plus another named Charlie, who seemed more promising. "Glad to meet you."

"Where'd you transfer in from, Mac?"

"Drew. A tour at the Pentagon. My dad is glad to be back to what he considers real duty."

"Mac lives across the stairwell from me . . ." Bob began.

"Drew."

The boys nodded.

". . . and according to his dad, Mac is a primo left-handed pitcher."

"Drew."

The boys nodded again, this time with more interest, saying, "Swell" and "That'll help us big-time."

"Mac's also got a babe sister, down there . . ." Bob pointed toward Joyce as she gracefully slid into a split.

The boys nodded with even more enthusiasm.

". . . and some commie cousins."

The nodding stopped.

Drew no longer needed a maroon sweater—his face was the color of school spirit. "I do not!" he protested.

"Don't they live in the Russian sector?"

"Yeah, but—"

"I rest my case." Bob smirked. "See, I'm a regular Perry Mason." He sighed. "Man, I miss watching that show."

"Listen, Bob," Drew started, but everyone suddenly jumped up in a wave of chanting. *Ber-lin! Ber-lin! Ber-lin!*

Charlie patted Drew on the back and shouted in his ear, "Don't let Bob get to you. He razzes everybody. If you take the bait, he gets worse."

Yeah, yeah. Drew knew the type. Picking fights to establish pecking order was second nature to some military kids. Swagger first or be swaggered at. Still, he leaned over so Charlie could hear him over the cheering. "I just met my mom's cousin and her kid for the first time the other night.

I had no idea they lived in East Berlin until then. I'm sure not planning on spending a whole lot of time with them." No matter what his mom might have in mind.

Charlie shouted back, "Don't worry. I know two moms who speak German, and the CO seems pretty happy to pull them into events as unofficial translators sometimes. Bet they've got family on the other side, too."

Drew smiled. Finally, a guy who actually seemed okay.

"By the way," Charlie said, "I play catcher. Maybe we can toss a ball around some this weekend?"

Drew forced himself to stay nonchalant. "Sure, man. That'd be outstanding." But inside, he was bouncing up and down like the cheerleaders. Maybe the next two years wouldn't be a complete disaster after all.

After school, Drew found Linda and then doubled back with her in tow to meet Joyce at her locker. Linda was silent, shadowing her brother to avoid bumping into passing students, until she spotted their big sister.

"Joyce!" Linda skipped toward her. "You were so good!"

Slamming her locker hard, Joyce forced a smile. "Hey, cutie. How was your day?"

Linda shrugged and glanced over her shoulder before whispering, "Okay, I think." Then she grinned. "The best part was when the other girls heard I was your sister. Boy oh boy, did you do great today!"

"Thanks." She took Linda's hand without smiling and muttered, mostly to herself, "Glad to be of service."

But Drew heard her. "What's wrong?" he mouthed.

Joyce just shook her head. "Let's go home, okay?"

The trio walked to their apartment in a shoal of other students, all clutching shiny-clean notebooks and wearing loafers with brand new pennies in the slots. As the other kids reached their own apartment buildings, they darted away, calling out, "See ya later, alligator," until Drew and his sisters were alone. Only Bob and one other guy trailed behind them. Their apartments were in the last building on Flanaganstraße, the outer rim of the American post housing, bordering the vast Grunewald Forest and not far from where the British sector began. Drew started to ask again what was bugging Joyce, but she looked so stone-faced that he left it alone.

Stomping up the steps to their third-floor unit, she turned the doorknob. It was locked.

"Where's Mom?" Linda's eyes welled up with tears. "She's always here waiting for us after school."

"Marooned?" Bob had climbed the stairs and stood looking up at Joyce from a few steps below. "I'd be happy to entertain you for a while," he offered, leaning against the stair rail, attempting to look all James Dean cool.

Drew tried to find some clever comeback but was totally flummoxed. He couldn't remember his mom ever not being at home after school.

"Relax. I'm sure she hasn't been kidnapped or anything," Bob said.

Drew knew Bob was kidding, but Linda slipped behind him and peeked out. She'd always been painfully shy, but this move to Berlin without Blarney had left her even more apprehensive than usual.

"Oh, you just want to be careful in the Grunewald, if you go there to play," Bob said awkwardly to Linda, seeming to think that would somehow reassure her. "That's all. There have been some cases of American personnel or their kids getting nabbed by Russian agents."

"What?" Drew blurted.

Bob blundered on. "Yeah. About two hundred and fifty since the occupation started. But don't worry, most times we've gotten them back pretty quick, and just as many kidnapping attempts have totally failed! Damn commies." Bob paused to sidle up to Joyce. "Still, you need a strong man— someone like yours truly—if you go to the jazz clubs in the Russian sector, 'cause the Stasi looooove to pick up us brats and hold us overnight to shake up our dads and—"

"Bob!" Joyce interrupted sharply to shut him up as Linda's mouth dropped open. She smoothed her voice and continued, "Is your mother home? Maybe Mom left word for us or a key with her?"

As if by magic—or maybe because she'd heard Joyce's raised voice—Mrs. Jones pulled open her door, totally disrupting Bob's not-so-suave moves. "There you are, dears. Come in, come in! Your mom left a key for you. And I've got butterscotch brownies ready to come out of the oven."

If looks could kill, Bob's glare might have knocked his poor mother down dead—Drew made note of it. If Bob insisted on being his uninvited escort, Drew was going to make a mental dossier on the guy for self-protection.

As Drew bit into a chewy brownie, sucking in air to keep from scorching his tongue, Mrs. Jones explained, "Your mom's gone to Marienfelde to help out. Close to a thousand refugees managed to get past the border this week, and the usual translators were swamped." She passed them napkins.

"I've volunteered at the camp myself," she went on, "helping in the cafeteria or showing families to their bunks. But what the camp really needs is people who speak German, like your Mom. There are intellectuals and pro-fessionals among the refugees, of course, who speak better English than I do." She laughed self-consciously. "But many of them don't, especially the farmers who've fled because the state confiscated their land for collective agriculture. The poor lambs—they are terrified.

"The Russians have laid so many land mines along the border between West and East Germany, they call it the death strip. So the only real way to freedom is through West Berlin. We're the only porthole left inside a prison ship. Like that wardrobe to Narnia in *The Lion, the Witch and the Wardrobe*."

Mrs. Jones paused, thoughtful, as she poured four glasses of milk.

"If only it were that easy, though—open the door and step out," she continued. "After having to make the awful choice to just up and leave everything, they have to do it all in secret, since their own neighbors might report them. Scurrying through the night like frightened mice, faking their way into a city they've never seen before." She stopped, looking at Drew. "Can you imagine?"

No, he couldn't, really. He shook his head.

"By the time they make it to Marienfelde—if they manage to bluff their way through all the checkpoints—they're wrecks." She sighed sympathetically. "To think of all that those peasants have endured in the last twenty years—Hitler, the SS, the Russians . . ." She trailed off. "Anyway, your mom kindly offered to help when she got the call. She'll be home by dinner."

Handing Joyce the key, Mrs. Jones said, "She wants you to pop a meatloaf she's left in the refrigerator into the oven at 1730 hours." Then she knelt beside Linda, who backed herself into Drew. "Sweetie, your mom asked me to tell you that she can't wait to hear all about your day. She left this note for you." With a reassuring smile, Mrs. Jones gently took Linda's hand and closed it around an envelope.

"Thanks, Mrs. Jones," Joyce said. "This has been awfully kind of you. Come on, troops."

"Please stay, dear," said Mrs. Jones. "You haven't had a brownie yet."

"Thank you. So much. But we really should finish unpacking."

Inwardly, Drew cringed. Mrs. Jones would know that was a fib. Army families pitched camp immediately. She'd know they'd been settled in for days and days at this point.

A twinge of hurt passed over Mrs. Jones's face, but she nodded. "The door is always open for you, my dears."

"Yeah," Bob echoed as Joyce passed him, his tone totally different from his mom's.

≻///←

Shoving the key into the lock, Joyce jiggled it with some agitation.

"Odd about Mom, don't you think?" Drew whispered to Joyce as Linda stood back on the landing, reading her note. "I know Mom volunteers for everything, but it's the first day of school."

"Didn't you notice Sergeant Jones cornering her at the party? I overheard him say Marienfelde was being infiltrated by Stasi secret police posing as refugees."

"What's that got to do with Mom?"

"The U.S. sets up the refugees with housing and jobs in West Germany. Being rubber-stamped as okay by American authorities gives a Russian spy perfect cover in NATO territory." She leaned over, really working the lock. "The camp has to interview the refugees carefully, to corroborate their identities and reasons for fleeing. Someone who's truly fluent in German, like Mom, will catch inconsistencies in their stories."

Finally, the door popped open. "Poetic, isn't it?" Joyce continued. "Hard to believe, given that Bob is such a dope, that his dad is in intelligence."

"CIA?"

"I bet so." Joyce threw the key onto the table before retreating to the bedroom she shared with her little sister.

"Oh, for pity's sake, Linda!" she shouted from within. "Can you *puh-lease* pick up all these stuffed animals? I can't get to my records."

Linda burst into tears.

Drew was stunned—Joyce hardly ever lost her temper, especially with their little sister. Hugging Linda, he said, "She didn't mean it, sis." Then he headed down the hall to the girls' bedroom. "What gives? You made Linda cry."

Joyce was standing in the middle of the room, her arms filled with her little sister's stuffed bears and Peter Rabbits, her back turned to the door. "I didn't get in," she mumbled.

"What?"

"I . . . didn't . . . make . . . the . . . squad," Joyce said slowly.

"That's impossible. You're better than all of them."

Joyce turned. Her face was streaked with tears. "One of the teachers—one of the nice, young ones—pulled me aside and told me that I had been deemed a risk."

"What?" Drew sure had been saying that a lot since coming to Berlin. "What's the risk?"

Joyce hugged a huge bear. "She was nice about it, at least. She explained that the school had to be careful about which girls were on the squad, because cheerleaders travel with the sports teams—on the overnight duty trains."

"So?" Now Drew swelled up with protectiveness for Joyce. "She wasn't implying that you—"

"No." Joyce interrupted. "But I worry this will start rumors about me now—about what kind of girl I am. Especially with jerks like Bob." Joyce shook her head. "She said it wasn't my fault. That it was just because I was so . . ."

Joyce's face puckered, and her voice caught as she continued, "... so ... unusual-looking."

"You mean pretty?" Drew interrupted gently.

Joyce shrugged. "*Mature* was the other word she used." Her face flushed. "Anyway, she said that my looks would make me vulnerable to being hassled by Soviet border police as the duty train passed through East Germany. Maybe even pulled off the train at checkpoints, just ... just so the police could cause trouble and amuse themselves."

Right—there were no other American military schools behind the Iron Curtain. Any away game the Berlin Cubs played would mean traveling through a hundred miles of communist-held territory to schools in West Germany— Frankfurt, Bremerhaven, Stuttgart. During those trips, all of them would be open to the commies harassing them for fun, but a girl as beautiful as Joyce even more so.

"That's so unfair!" Drew exploded.

"Tell me about it." Joyce sighed.

They stood in silence for a moment.

"You know the other really swell thing I heard today?" Joyce added. "I'm missing a requirement at this school, and it could mean I can't graduate in the spring."

It happened all the time. Different school districts had different requirements, sometimes varying wildly. School administrators never seemed to care that the reason military brats might have missed some class was that they were serving their country. But at a post school? C'mon. They at least should cut Joyce some slack. "Can't they make an exception?"

"Evidently not."

"What are you going to do?"

"I don't know. But I sure as heck am not going to stay here for an extra semester," Joyce fumed. "Especially not after today. I'm going to hightail it back home for college the day after I graduate." She threw down the teddy bear she was holding and gazed forlornly at her records, blocked by mounds of other stuffed animals. "I forgot—I can't even play any of my music until I get my Decca converted to German voltage."

Drew looked over at Joyce's most prized possession, her behemoth collection of 45s. She'd already had to pare it down to accommodate the army's weight limit for moves. Her red-trimmed portable record player with musical notes on its lid sat open and ready, but silent.

"Hey, I've got an idea," he said. "There's a jukebox at the teen club."

"Really?" Wiping away a tear, Joyce lifted her chin and managed a small, defiant smile. "Let's go."

As if her entrance had been choreographed, right as Joyce walked into the teen club, the jukebox thundered a crescendo of rock 'n' roll piano chords. Bobby Freeman's voice sang out: *Do you, do you, do you, do you waaaanna dance?*

"Yes, I do!" Grinning, Joyce stepped forward and grabbed the hand of a girl standing just inside the door—a complete stranger—and waltzed them onto the small dance floor, slip-sliding in an easy swing. Just as Drew had witnessed dozens of times before, Joyce's example emboldened others.

Two more girls stood up from the chairs along the wall and joined in, giggling, their skirts swaying as they let the infectious music envelop them.

Do you, do you, do you, do you waaaanna dance?

Drew watched. His big sister beamed with a no-holds-barred joy, not looking at anybody or anything, not worrying about waiting to be asked to dance by a boy the way convention said she was supposed to. He leaned over and whispered to Linda, "Now that, sis, is how you take the hill."

Linda smiled.

Beyond the dance floor was a game room, loud with ping-pong and tabletop shuffleboard. On the other side, high chrome swivel seats were lined up along a diner-style countertop. A soda jerk was making milkshakes. Drew spotted Charlie playing pool and some girls Linda's age at the snack bar. He elbowed her. "Divide and conquer?"

Linda's face turned ashen, and she chewed on her lower lip. But after watching Joyce for another moment, she took a deep breath and whispered, "I could go for a root beer float."

Drew pulled a quarter out of his pocket. "Come get me if you need me. Okay?"

Linda nodded and approached the counter. Joyce swiveled her head around as she danced to monitor her little sister's advance. When Linda finally reached her objective and the other preteens seemed to welcome her, Drew and Joyce nodded to each other before turning to focus on their own tactical forays.

Drew headed for the game room. Bob was there already, shoving the shuffleboard pucks hard to obliterate his opponent's, which lay on the number three. *Sssccrr-bang! Sssssrr-bang!* His blue puck slammed into a sitting-duck red one, vaulting it into the air to zing by Drew.

"Sorry, man," Bob shouted and waved. "Just don't know my own strength!"

Suuuuure, Drew thought, admiring Bob's aim. He picked up the puck and tossed it back as he sauntered over to the pool table, where Charlie leaned on his cue. Drew could tell Charlie was getting trounced.

"Sweet," Charlie complimented his opponent as the kid managed to slam the two ball into the side pocket with a wild bank shot.

Four shots later, he'd sunk every ball before Charlie ever got another turn. Laugh-groaning, Charlie handed his cue to the next guy in line. "Good luck, man, you're gonna need it against this Fast Eddie."

"Rack 'em," the boy crowed.

Charlie rounded the table to Drew. "After that drubbing, I'm going for a BLT. Want to join me?"

Drew pulled out the change he had left over after giving Linda that quarter. Thirty-seven cents.

"That'll be enough for a hot dog," said Charlie. He headed for the snack bar, and Drew followed.

"Is there any way to make some money around here?" Drew asked. "I used to bike a paper route in Arlington."

"Bagging and carrying groceries on weekends for tips. On a good day, you can make ten bucks, easy. The really nice moms usually give you a quarter. Only downside is that you have to get to the commissary's back door to sign up around

0500 hours to beat out everyone else. I do it every Saturday there's not a game going on. The army teams are really good, by the way. The Bears play Stuttgart in football this weekend. You should come. Everybody goes together."

They sat on two stools at the end of the counter and swiveled as they talked. Half a dozen seats down, Linda silently sipped her root beer float. The girl next to her had shifted to chat up the kid on her other side, her back turned to Linda.

There wasn't any way for Drew to swoop in and save his little sister without embarrassing her. Closer in age, he and Joyce had always been able to bail each other out better. Well, Joyce had been able to rescue him. Drew tried to catch Linda's eye to give her encouragement, but her gaze was riveted on her drink.

The music stopped. As she caught her breath, Joyce walked over to peruse the jukebox's record selection, ringed by the other dancing girls. They'd all taken off their shoes to swivel more easily in their bobby socks, and now, cheeks flushed and ponytails a bit awry, they burbled happily at one another.

"Excuse me a sec," Drew said to Charlie, and he walked over to Joyce.

"Yeah, I see," she murmured before Drew could even say anything about Linda. "Drew, this is Shirley." Joyce introduced him to the girl whose hand she'd grabbed at the door. "She's new, too. A sophomore, like you. She's from Oklahoma—Fort Sill."

Shirley smiled at Drew. "That was our last post. But my family's from Chicago. I like to call that home."

Drew had never heard a brat say that before. Where would he call home, he wondered.

"It's not in here." Joyce frowned.

"You're kidding," Shirley answered. "It's the biggest thing there is stateside."

"I know!" Joyce glanced over at Linda, then back at Shirley. Drew had seen that look before, when Joyce double dared him to do something totally nonregulation. "You sing?" she asked her new friend.

Shirley's eyebrow shot up. "Do birds have beaks?"

Joyce laughed. "Here we go, then." She whirled around and shouted, "Hey, everyone! Listen up."

Shhhh-shhhh. The room quieted.

"My brother, Drew, and my little sister, Linda, and I"— she did a little curtsey—"have just come from the States. Shirley, here, too. And we want to introduce you to the dance that's all the rage back home—the twist! Any of you guys know it?"

A girl and a boy about Linda's age raised their hands.

"Come on out here, then!"

The children crept forward. Linda looked up.

"The record isn't on the box yet, so Shirley and I are going to sing it to you. And all you have to do is twist your hips and arms, almost like you're using a Hula-Hoop." Her listeners laughed. "Shirley and I will show you."

Shirley nodded. "Ready?"

"Ready, Freddy!" shouted the younger kids.

Joyce cleared her throat and then let fly the voice that

had dazzled her former high school's audiences when she starred as Laurie in *Oklahoma*.

"Come on, baby, let's do the twist." She swung her hips, leaning forward and back as she sang, her skirt singing along—*swwwiiiish, swish, swish*.

Snapping her fingers on the beat, Shirley gave Joyce perfectly harmonized backup: "Doooooooooo-wop-wop."

Joyce sashayed her way over to Linda, pointing at her and pretending to reel her in as she sang, "Yeah, you should see myyyyyy little sis. She really knows how to rock . . ."

Before Linda could fight it, Joyce pulled her onto the floor, tugging on her arms—left, right, left, right—so Linda had to twist along. And suddenly, there Linda was—for a magical moment, anyway—smack-dab in the middle of the Berlin brats' social swirl.

Drew plunged in, too. If Joyce was brave enough to sing without a band, he could forget trying to be cool. He swiveled his butt.

"Round and around and around and around."

Within seconds, Charlie was out on the floor, followed by one, two, three—more than a dozen kids in a full-troop surge, all laughing and clapping. It was beautiful—a total devil-may-care, sock-hop romp, all thanks to Joyce. She might not be an official cheerleader, but she sure knew how to muster an all-American pep rally.

That new girl Shirley was pretty darn bodacious, too.

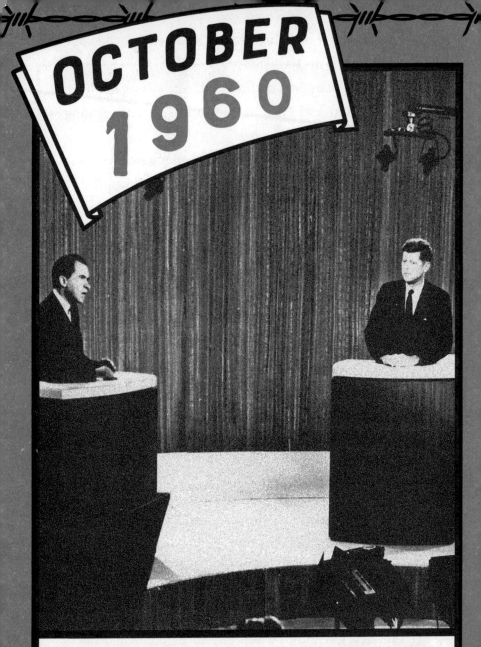

OCTOBER 1960

In the first televised presidential debates, Vice President Richard Nixon takes on Senator John F. Kennedy. Both WWII veterans, the candidates speak of the critical importance of NATO. The next president, says JFK, "in his first year is going to be confronted with a very serious question on our defense of Berlin. It's going to be a test of our nerve and will."

Speaking at the United Nations, Khrushchev shocks its general assembly by pounding his table—reportedly with his shoe—to interrupt the Philippines' delegate, who was speaking against Russia's depriving Eastern European nations of their civil rights. Having already claimed he didn't have to invade America, that he would "destroy it from within," Khrushchev calls the Philippine official "a toady of American imperialism," and later adds that communist states were "in the minority now, but not for long."

A L S O

The Andy Griffith Show—a comedy about a widowed sheriff, his young son (played by Ron Howard), and a bumbling deputy (played by Don Knotts)—premieres on the CBS television network.

Dr. Martin Luther King Jr. calls for lunch counter sit-ins as peaceful demonstrations against segregation. Despite his being arrested and jailed for four months for violating the "whites only" policy at an Atlanta department store cafe, others take up his call across the nation. In Arlington, Virginia, 15-year-old Dion Diamond waits for service at a five-and-dime store when a group of white teenagers surround and harass him, led by the founder of the American Nazi Party. But Diamond and his fellow demonstrators prevail. Two weeks later, several businesses in Washington, DC, end their segregation practices. Virginia's Arlington, Alexandria, and Fairfax counties follow.

CHAPTER THREE

OCTOBER
1960

Groggy, Drew reached for his alarm clock. *Oh no!* No ticking. He must have forgotten to wind it. He fell to the floor in a tumble of blankets, thrashing to disentangle himself. When he scrambled to his feet, he came eye-to-eye with the Kennedy campaign poster and its slogan he'd tacked above his bed: A TIME FOR GREATNESS.

Greatness? He couldn't even manage to wake up on time. At this rate, he'd have to pull off the perfect code-red scramble to make it to the commissary before all the bagging slots were filled. Drew raced to the kitchen.

His mom was at the stove. "Good morning, sir!"

Drew looked past her at the teapot-shaped wall clock: 7:15! "Mom!" he nearly shouted.

"*Shhhh.* I promised Joyce she could sleep in."

"Can you drive me to the commissary?" Normally, Drew would bike, but today, no moment could be spared. If he hurried, maybe he could be the last name on the list.

Charlie had been right. Bagging on Saturdays was a great way to make money. It had also turned out that hauling bags stuffed with Frosted Flakes, deviled ham, and Jell-O was a great way to bond with the other brats. Last weekend, the other boys had swept Drew up in a spur-of-the-moment outing to climb one of the seven mini mountains made of World War II bombing debris to watch for a glint of *Echo I*, a new satellite the Americans had sent into orbit to rival the Russians' *Sputnik*. It'd been swell.

"Scrambled or fried?" Drew's mom asked as she lifted out the last strip of bacon from the skillet.

"*Mom!* I need to go!"

"Honey, don't you remember our plans for the day?" He could hear a dash of hurt in her voice.

Drew frowned. No, he didn't. But it began to dawn on him that she was already neatly dressed in her typical going-out garb: straight skirt, pressed blouse, cardigan sweater, and sensible heels, her blond waves perfect.

Maybe he should start drinking coffee.

"We're sightseeing with Marta and Matthias. We've been here seven weeks now, and you haven't really seen Berlin—the Brandenburg Gate, the Tiergarten, the Berlin State Opera. This is the perk of these overseas assignments, sweetheart. You get to see the world."

She popped two slices of Wonder Bread into the

toaster. "We'll start in the West, take a little tootle along the Kurfürstendamm—it's like Fifth Avenue. Dad's Bonneville finally got shipped over, and he said we could take it for the day." She paused. "It's unusually warm for October. Maybe we can put the top down! Wouldn't that be lovely?"

"Mom . . ." Drew tried to slow her field trip euphoria.

"To think we'll be walking the same streets as Mendelssohn and Strauss."

Yeah, thought Drew, *and Hitler and Himmler and Goebbels.*

"Oh, and the Schumanns. To be in the same place as Clara . . ." Drew's mom gazed dreamily over at her piano. "One of the first female concert pianists, you know. And a composer!"

"Don't you have piano students on Saturdays, Mom?"

"Not this Saturday. I canceled all lessons. Today is just for us, sweetheart." She patted his face. "You and I get so little one-on-one time, especially now that I'm translating at Marienfelde. I love feeling as if I am finally doing something to help in the battle against communism—and lord knows, it's not easy to say no to the CO—but I worry I'm missing out on so much here with you and the girls." Her brow furrowed for a moment. "Besides, won't it be nice to get to know Cousin Marta and Matthias better? And"—she spoke more to herself now—"for them to learn to trust us." She turned back to the stove. "Fried or scrambled?"

Drew flopped down at the dining room table. "Fried," he muttered. Just like he'd be when Bob found out he'd spent an entire day with his "commie cousins."

Once they were out in their turquoise Pontiac—fins gleaming, top down, sunbeams spilling into the convertible—Drew had to admit it was a great day to be joyriding. He laid his head back on the dove-colored leather seat and watched Berlin's main drag slide by.

The postwar-rebuilt Kurfürstendamm sparkled with storefront after fancy storefront, designer-clad mannequins in the windows. Women emerged, fox stoles dangling about their shoulders, hatboxes and dress bags hanging heavy on their arms. Gilded glass cages along the wide sidewalks displayed smooth leather handbags, cosmetics, radios, and watches. Mercedes and Jaguars lined the streets. Neon signs hawked businesses Drew recognized: IBM, Pan American Airways. He even noticed a Coca-Cola billboard with a bikini-clad girl wearing a Hollywood smile, her hair in braided pigtails, holding up a bottle: MACH MAL PAUSE . . . TRINK COCA-COLA.

About the only traditional German thing Drew saw was an organ grinder. The guy even had a little monkey holding a tin cup for passersby to drop in coins. A stoplight brought them to a standstill, allowing Drew to examine the brightly painted, big-barreled music box as the man cranked out a tune Drew vaguely recognized.

"Ooooh! Mozart! *The Magic Flute!*" Drew's mom smiled dreamily and glanced over. "Oh. Oh dear. Poor man." He stood on one leg and a crutch. "A veteran, I guess," she murmured. A survivor of Allied firepower. Maybe even from his buddies' fathers. Or Drew's own dad.

The light turned green, and they drove on.

A little unnerved, Drew sat up and spun the dial, searching for Radio Luxembourg—the station most likely to play uninterrupted rock 'n' roll. *Splish-splash, I was taking a bath* . . . crackled out of the speakers, then pop-sputtered and disappeared into static. It was hard to pick up that signal clearly until evening.

"Oh, that's a shame. Such a fun song." Catching his doubtful look, Drew's mother smiled. "What? You think I don't know Bobby Darin? Try AFN."

As he locked on to 935 AM, the very American voice of a Berlin Armed Forces Network DJ announced the "Merely Music" hour. Frank Sinatra's "I've Got You Under My Skin" filled the air around their blue road yacht with a cloud of big-band crooning.

Drew cranked the volume.

On the sidewalk, two German teenagers shouted, "Frankie!" They raised their hands, thumbs pointed upward. *"Dufte Auto!"*

Drew gave a thumbs-up back.

Music changed to news. "Tomorrow, Vice President Nixon and Senator Kennedy will meet again to answer questions posed by four expert newsmen, broadcast live from NBC Studios in Washington, DC. We'll bring you the highlights."

Drew sure wished he could *watch* that debate. Most of his classmates were rooting for Nixon, vice president to Eisenhower, the commander of American forces in Europe during World War II. A couple of their dads had even met

Ike back then. But Drew was all-in for JFK. "Do you think Kennedy has a chance?" he asked.

"I sure hope so," his mom answered. "I really like his ideas. Forward thinking. And I love how cosmopolitan his wife is. She'd bring a lot to the position of first lady." She gestured toward the city. "God knows, with all that's going on these days, a larger world outlook would be helpful."

"Bob says JFK being Catholic disqualifies him, that he might be more loyal to the Pope than to the United States."

Drew's mom laughed. "I'm getting the sense that Bob says a lot of things. You know, honey, in the army, there's typically only one church building on post that all denominations use. So how someone worships isn't as big a deal. But stateside, some people still have a problem with Catholics. It'd mean a lot for us if JFK wins." She added mischievously, "I'm glad Mr. Nixon sweats so much under those studio lights. Makes him look a little shifty. We lady voters don't like that."

She turned the Bonneville into the Tiergarten. Replanted after the war, the park's trees were still willowy and supple, shimmying in the slight breeze. A sprinkle of golden autumn leaves salted their open car. Drew's mom pulled over near a spoke of boulevards radiating out from a grassy circle. In its center rose a tall column, topped with a gilded and winged female holding aloft a laurel wreath. Drew shaded his eyes to look up. It had to be as high as the Washington Monument. "What's this?"

"The Victory Column. Isn't it beautiful?"

Drew snorted. "A little ironic, don't you think?"

"It's not from Hitler's time, honey. It was built in eighteen seventy-something to celebrate the Prussian wars that unified the German states into one empire, where arts and philosophy flourished."

"Wow, Mom, I never knew you were so proud to be *German*." He meant it to be teasing, but his lingering irritation about being on this field trip tainted it toward insolent.

She turned off the car and faced him. "When my mother immigrated to the United States," she began, her tone frosty, "she walled off her heritage to blend in. And certainly during World War II, being German was not something to advertise. So I've never explored this part of my history. I'd like to now." Drew's mom got out of the car. "Marta and Matthias are meeting us here. Please leave your sarcasm in the car."

They found Matthias just inside the entrance to the temple-like first floor, leaning against a mosaic depicting an officer atop a massive black horse that was trampling foot soldiers. As slight a figure as Matthias was, he was copping a gigantic attitude. Okay, two could play that game. Drew shoved his hands into the pockets of his old letterman jacket from Arlington and slowed his walk to a strut, meant to convey he was totally unimpressed by both the monument and Matthias.

His mother and Cousin Marta embraced formally. They turned expectantly to the boys. Drew nodded his greeting. Matthias, too. Neither budged.

Their mothers sighed.

"Shall we?" Cousin Marta began explaining what the images depicted—Father Rhine, the defeat of Napoleon when France invaded the Germanic states—as Drew's mother *oooh*ed appreciatively.

Rolling his eyes, Matthias peeled himself off the mosaic to follow, muttering, *"Dafür verpasse ich mein Fußballspiel?"*

Drew picked his way through the German, feeling insulted by Matthias's obvious annoyance at the outing, even though he resented the forced encounter just as much. "You had a soccer game?" he asked, more to prove he understood basic German than to engage in conversation.

Matthias nodded, perhaps slightly impressed. Maybe recognizing he'd been caught being blatantly rude.

"Well, I'm missing out on making money with my buddies at the commissary."

"Ah, ein kapitalistischer Samstag."

Drew knew *Samstag* was Saturday. *A capitalistic Saturday.* What the heck, man? He bristled.

But before he could protest aloud, Drew remembered reading that in the Soviet Bloc and East Germany, doing any kind of work on your own initiative or trying to make a bit of extra money—"unauthorized gatherings for commercial purposes"—was illegal. Did this kid really believe that stuff? Or . . . Drew felt a bit of empathy tug at him. Was Matthias simply repeating the party line out of defensiveness? Was he as uneasy about an American Armed Forces cousin being foisted on him as Drew was about having a commie one?

Maybe Matthias had a Bob in his life, harassing him about spending time with some capitalist pig. The thought stopped Drew from taking his cousin's bait, and instead, he started planning his response to Bob if he found out where

Drew had been that day. *It was just one of my mom's field trips. You know moms.* Yeah, that would work.

As if on cue, Cousin Marta continued playing tour guide. "There is an observation tower at the top that lends a wonderful view of the Brandenburg Gate."

"I read that the gate is a replica of the Propylaea, the entrance to the Acropolis," Drew's mom replied. "Isn't that amazing, Drew?"

Drew forced an overly bright smile.

His mom ignored it, but Cousin Marta clearly read his mood. She checked her wristwatch. "We best leave, Emily, if you still wish to see the State Opera House before lunch. *Mutter* will have it ready for twelve thirty. She will worry if we are late."

Lunch, too? Drew turned to his mom with a scowl.

Abruptly, she took his arm, steering him toward the car. "Just think, this will be the first time I meet my mother's sister," she said, overly emphatic. "My aunt. Your great-aunt. And I will see—finally—where my mama grew up. This is special for me, honey."

Drew spotted Matthias rolling his eyes again. His sentiments exactly.

But when they reached the Bonneville, Matthias stopped in his tracks. "This is yours?"

"Sweet, right?"

"Typisch angebender Amerikaner."

Show-off American? Okay, the smidgeon of sympathy Drew had felt for Matthias a few minutes before evaporated. "You can walk, you know."

But Matthias didn't seem to hear Drew as he ran his hand along the car to the door handle, admiration in his eyes no matter what he had said. He even smiled slightly as he clambered in.

They roared onto Unter den Linden and were joined by a fleet of Volkswagen Beetles that could have fit in the Bonneville's back seat. As they neared the Brandenburg Gate, Drew counted a dozen American and British soldiers strategically posted along its wide plaza. Watchful. Standing at that unwavering military attention that Drew and all brats knew meant the men were coiled and ready to spring into action if ordered. Reassuring and alarming both.

His mom slowed to a halt beside the first American MP, who held a paddle-sized stop sign. "On the other side of the Gate, you can keep moving, ma'am," he said. "The Russian sector border guards have no right to stop you—not with your car's Occupying Forces license tag. They should just wave you through." Stepping back, he let the Bonneville motor on.

Drew felt a surge of uneasiness as they passed the final American soldier, intently monitoring the gate through enormous binoculars. A stark sign warned: ACHTUNG! SIE VERLASSEN JETZT WEST BERLIN. *Attention! You are leaving West Berlin.*

"Look how magnificent, Drew!" his mom gasped as the shadow cast by the behemoth structure washed over them, cool and dim. She gazed up at the wide, seven-story-high gate, at the reliefs and sculptures carved into its marble. Four enormous bronze horses, pulling the chariot of another goddess of victory, peeped over the edge of the gate's crown as their car slid through the massive Doric columns into East Berlin.

"Mom! Look out!"

A young Vopo had stepped into the lane—right in the Bonneville's path!

"Oh my goodness!" She slammed on the brakes, barely missing the teen guard. "He's not supposed to do that, is he?" she whispered to Cousin Marta, whose expression had turned apprehensive.

"*Ausweis!*" shouted the guard.

Flustered, Drew's mother shook her head.

"*Reisepass!*" the Vopo barked louder, putting a hand on the gun at his side while motioning for another guard to join him. An older German officer clad in the same green paramilitary uniform approached slowly, hands clasped behind his back.

Her voice shaking slightly, Drew's mom explained—in German—that she was the wife of an Occupying Forces NCO, so she did not need to show them her passport. She looked to Marta. "Sorry. We're told to do this—to remind the Russians that the Potsdam Agreement gives us just as much access to this part of the city as they have."

Matthias shrank in his seat, putting his elbow on the edge of the open window to shield his face with his hand.

"*Sie!*" The Vopo pointed to Cousin Marta. "*Sie sind schon mal durchgekommen.*"

Yes, she had come through the gate earlier.

"*Steigen Sie bitte aus dem Auto.*"

Drew's mom put her hand over her cousin's.

"It's all right," Cousin Marta murmured. "Just checking for black market items, I'm sure." She got out of the car. The young Vopo, his authority now bolstered by the older officer's presence, grabbed her black plastic purse and rifled through it, tossing pencils, a hairbrush, and a handkerchief to the cracked pavement.

When he found a lipstick, he triumphantly waggled it in front of Cousin Marta's face like some moralizing preacher. *"Sie verhuren sich mit westlicher Kosmetik!"*

Without flinching, Cousin Marta stood tall in silent forbearance as the young Vopo berated her about "corrupting herself" with Western cosmetics.

Drew had witnessed teachers back home dressing down girls for their makeup, but it was nothing like this gun-toting teenage guard doing it—and to a grown woman! It was intimidating as hell. Drew fidgeted in his seat.

Matthias didn't move, didn't say a thing, didn't even look.

Drew watched his cousin out of the corner of his eye, looking for some reaction to what was happening to his mother. But Matthias had shut down and was holding his breath, submissive, like Drew had seen brainiac boys do to survive repeated barrages of insults from playground bullies. Clearly, Matthias had been through this scenario before and knew the safe response.

His cousin's passive stance made Drew feel sick to his stomach—but what exactly would he do if these Russian-backed East Germans started hassling *his* mom? What was he *allowed* to do without causing some international incident with a nuclear-armed foe, the kind of ruckus he and his classmates had all been warned against upon penalty of their dads being shipped home, pronto?

"Genug!" The older Vopo finally brushed the younger one aside. He scooped up Cousin Marta's things and handed them back as he opened the car door for her. *"Verzeihen Sie die Umstände,"* he said, apologizing for the trouble. He bowed slightly as he closed the door after her, saying in a low voice, *"Er hofft, unsere sowjetischen Freunde beeindrucken zu können."* He nodded toward two Russian colonels standing near the guardhouse, whom the young Vopo had hoped to impress.

"I will be reporting this to our CO," Drew's mother said, regaining her voice.

"I would think so, madam," the older officer answered, stepping back.

Drew's mom gunned the engine as the young Vopo switched to haranguing a pair of bicyclists, squeezing their tires, checking for Western contraband embedded in the rubber.

"What the heck, Mom?" Drew exploded. "Why—" But his question stuck in his throat as their hopeful-blue Bonneville plunged into a world of gray. Before them stretched a wasteland of weeds and rubble, scorched brick and burned-out skeletons of once-grand government buildings. This had been ground zero of Hitler's regime and of the Allied bombing.

The buildings that were restored had bloodred banners with the Soviet hammer-and-sickle emblem slashing down their faces. Gargantuan photos of the Soviet leader, Khrushchev, framed with flower garlands, loomed everywhere. Russia's Big Brother, straight out of George Orwell's *Nineteen Eighty-Four. Jeez Louise.*

Ahead of them, a huge painted slogan wreathed the brow of a reconstructed block-long building. Drew waded through translating it: BERLIN YOUTH FIGHT FOR FRIENDSHIP AND THE VICTORY OF SOCIALISM IN THE GDR. Underneath that was a two-story-tall Russian bear pushing away a NATO soldier lugging two missiles under his arm. Wow, Drew thought, what a heavy-handed depiction of the Russians' favorite assertion: that East Berliners needed Soviet protection from Westerners, who were all warmongers.

In previous weeks, the other Berlin brats had told him how tense the standoff was between the city's halves, but seeing such Orwellian newspeak firsthand made it real. Suddenly, Drew felt pretty darn threatened. He glanced over at Matthias with some alarm.

Matthias, on the other hand, had finally straightened up and was saying with noticeable pride, "That is the FDJ headquarters where the Free German Youth attend programs about our just new society."

Drew felt a shiver run up his spine. "Have you ever read *Animal Farm*?" he muttered.

"What?" Matthias asked.

"Nothing," Drew mumbled, catching his mom's eye and the slight warning shake of her head in the rearview mirror.

She gestured abruptly out the window, like she always did to stop sibling squabbles on family road trips, and pointed to one of the few palatial buildings left intact. "Look, it's the State Opera House, all rebuilt. Isn't it gorgeous, honey?"

But it was Matthias who leaned forward to respond. "Brecht's Berliner Ensemble theater is not far from here. Near *Mutter*'s hospital."

Brecht. Wasn't he some agitating Marxist who'd had to leave the United States after being called in front of the House Un-American Activities Committee? Again, Drew tried to catch his mom's eye, but she was watching her cousin, who had not spoken since the Brandenburg Gate.

"That's Charité Hospital, Marta?"

"Yes."

"At Marienfelde, I recently met several doctors who shared some harrowing stories . . . events that pushed them to seek a . . . a freer life in the West. They said it was easy to cross over, since the hospital is only a few hundred yards from the British sector." She glanced hopefully at her cousin.

Cousin Marta stared out her window. "Yes. I know one of them. His sister is imprisoned now for at least a year. They say she helped him betray our nation by fleeing— *Republikflucht.* She will undergo reeducation." She changed the topic. "Matthias loves theater."

Matthias nodded.

Rebuffed, Drew's mom shifted to a polite, singsong voice, but he caught an undertone of disappointment in it. "Drew, too. He loved *Damn Yankees.* Of course, it's all about baseball. Right up his alley! Maybe the musical will come to Berlin. We could all go together!"

Another outing? The boys eyed each other, mutually horrified by the idea.

Their mothers sighed.

For about twenty minutes, they circled streets around the Opera House while Cousin Marta pointed out the National Gallery, the Dom, and Berlin University, all still in varying degrees of bomb devastation fifteen years after V-E Day. Then they doubled back to the Brandenburg Gate, turning south on Ebertstraße, a wide boulevard that straddled the East-West border. A white line divided the street down the middle, not for traffic but for politics—one side was in the Russian sector and the other in the British. The Tiergarten was to their right, the rubble of Hitler's palatial home and his underground bunker to their left.

Passing what once had been the Nazis' Ministry of Public Enlightenment and Propaganda—now refurbished to house Russian and East German government offices— the Bonneville reached Potsdamer Platz. There, three sectors—British, American, and Russian—collided, like three arrows thrust into a bull's-eye. On the Eastern rim of the wide circular plaza, a Russian billboard proclaimed, MARXISM MEANS PEACE! A loudspeaker brayed, *"Ami, go home! East Berliners want a free, demilitarized West Berlin!"*

Just across the street, on American-controlled ground, an illuminated billboard like a Times Square ticker tape display answered the Politburo propaganda with flashing news bulletins from the West. Drew could read: "Premier Khrushchev endangers world peace by threatening leaders at the United Nations," and "Premiering in beautiful, sundrenched Hollywood, *Spartacus* tells the real-life story of a gladiator who led a brave revolt against tyranny."

The whole scene was bizarro.

"Turn left at Zimmerstraße," said Cousin Marta. "There will be Vopos at the corner, but they know us." As promised, the two East German guards merely waved at Matthias and gaped at the Bonneville. Two West German border guards—about sixty yards away on the southwest corner— did the same. Marta smiled at both pairs of young men.

Like Ebertstraße had been, Zimmerstraße was divided down the middle between East and West Berlin, but here there was a string of distinctly American-looking cars parked on the Russian side of the street. Cousin Marta noticed Drew staring with surprise at several Chevys. "West Berliners park on our side of Zimmerstraße all the time without any trouble. In this neighborhood, at least, there is cooperation between the sectors." Marta pointed at a narrow side street. "Turn left here, please. We are one block up."

"I didn't realize you lived so close to the American line," Drew's mom said.

"Oh yes, a stone's throw away, as you say." Marta pointed again, announcing, "Here we are. "

Drew gaped again. Before him was what once must have been an elegant three-story building. Stone busts of men in long eighteenth-century wigs were tucked into ornately carved arches along the top floor, still perfectly preserved. But the building's walls were riddled with machine gun bullet holes. Its plaster facade had peeled away in chunks, revealing ancient, pockmarked bricks. The windows of the ground-floor shop were boarded up. Next door loomed the shell of another vast townhome, its roof gone and grand staircase exposed, its balusters like broken teeth.

As Matthias pushed open the building's heavy, paneled, carved-wood front door, an athletic guy about Joyce's age jogged down the stairs. He was lean and angular, swift and lithe. "*Freundschaft!*" he bellowed at Matthias as they passed in the dim hallway.

The loudness of the greeting made Drew jump a little. It sounded like the *Heil Hitler* salutes Nazis threw around in movies.

"*Freundschaft!*" Matthias replied.

"You say hello by shouting *friendship* at each other?" Drew asked Matthias, turning to eyeball the guy just as the older teen opened the outside door and a spotlight of sunshine fell on his face. He glanced up at Drew at the very same moment with an obvious frown and look of suspicion. The guy had enormous round eyes—one blue and one brown! He gave Drew the creeps.

"Yes," Matthias answered, his own voice suddenly raised. "Not like American capitalists, who exploit the worker. We are a society of friends. Of friendship." He waved at his neighbor and repeated, this time in a shout, "*Freundschaft!*"

The guy nodded and left. Drew heard Matthias take in a deep breath.

"You have tenants?" Drew's mom asked Cousin Marta with surprise as they climbed the marble steps. "Mama said the family lived in the entire building."

"We share our home with one other family now," Cousin Marta answered in a studied, matter-of-fact tone. "A man and his son. They occupy the third floor's rooms and bath—originally quarters for my grandfather's maids. It is GDR ordered. Party-led redistribution of wealth makes things more equal. More just." She unlocked a leaded stained glass door to the second floor, which had been turned into an expansive apartment. "Welcome."

Inside, Drew's mom turned around and around, taking it all in. She seemed ecstatic, oblivious to what shocked Drew—cooking pots on the floor to catch leaks from the ceiling; wallpaper streaked with mildew; cracks in the windows mended with tape. The place stank of burning coal.

Drew caught Matthias watching him, glowering defensively.

"Oh, Drew," his mother murmured, "my mother used to talk about these window seats." She wandered to the tall, wide, French-door-style windows. "She would read here and . . ." She trailed off, suddenly tearful. "I'm sorry. I still miss her so much."

Reaching for Drew's hand, she said, "I wish you'd known her, honey. She was such a gentle soul. I swear she died of heartache during the war, not knowing if her sister—Cousin Marta's mother—was still alive. Mama had pleaded with her to leave as Hitler rose to power. But who knows if Aunt Hilde ever received those letters. After Germany declared war on us, there was nothing but silence for years." She paused, filled with reverence, and whispered, "I can feel Mama here."

She sat down on the window seat, bathed in Berlin's strangely gray sunlight. "Her father—that would be your great-grandfather—had a piano showroom and studio downstairs. Mama told me she would sit here and listen to her father tune his pianos and to customers who would play as they decided which instrument to buy. It was how her love of music began." She wiped away several tears.

"My mother, the same," said Cousin Marta. "A great pianist."

"I can hardly believe I am about to meet her, finally."

"I will get her. But before you meet her, Emily, my mother . . ." She hesitated. "She has no English. But more important, she . . ."

"*Sie ist ein hoffnungsloser Fall.*" Matthias grumbled. A basket case.

"*Zum Schämen.*" Cousin Marta shot a dark look at Matthias. "*Mutter* has changed since the war," she said simply. Then she retreated down the hallway, calling, "*Mutti, Emily und ihr Sohn sind hier.*"

Matthias disappeared as well, leaving Drew and his mom alone. Her face fell. "Oh dear, how shabby this once-grand house is." She smiled wanly at Drew. "But don't say anything, honey. We don't want to offend. So much of East Berlin is like this."

Drew meandered. He perused a bookshelf stuffed with well-worn sheet music. There was no piano to be seen, though. Next, he examined framed pictures on the fireplace mantel. Drew was staring at two spitting images of Matthias when his cousin walked back into the room, now wearing a bulky turtleneck sweater. The apartment was colder than the air outside.

"My brothers. Twins," Matthias explained, noticing Drew looking at the photos. "I never knew them. My mother was pregnant with me when your Allied bombing killed them." His antagonistic tone changed a bit as he turned to a portrait of a dapper-looking man, his face kind, his smile amused, his hair thirties-style parted and slicked. "My father. I was born after he died, too. My mother calls me his last and best gift to her. She loved him very much."

He offered nothing more, and the boys lingered in awkward silence until Cousin Marta reentered, holding her mother's hand. The tiny woman, her white hair swept up in a wispy French twist, had the same enormous teal-colored eyes as Drew's mom, Cousin Marta, and Matthias, made even more vivid by her ghostly coloring and hair.

"Mutti, das ist deine Nichte, Emily."

"Aunt Hilde!" With a childlike peal of jubilation, Drew's mother darted forward to catch her aunt up in a hug. But Aunt Hilde recoiled.

Seeing his mom's face pucker in disappointment, Drew winced for her.

"I . . . I am thrilled to meet you." She reached out again, slowly this time. But again, Aunt Hilde retreated.

A deep sadness shrouded Cousin Marta's face. Drew stole a glance at Matthias, who was studiously picking lint off his sweater. Damn, was this guy made of stone? But Drew had to admit he recognized the look on Matthias's face—that universal embarrassment at an older relative's behavior. The expansive room suddenly felt crowded with untold tragedies.

During lunch, Drew made himself swallow the bratwurst and red cabbage Cousin Marta put on chipped bone china plates and wipe his mouth properly with a faded linen napkin embroidered with an ornate *B* for Becker, Aunt Hilde's maiden name. He watched his mom watch her aunt.

Finally, Cousin Marta served the coffee that Drew's mom had brought as a gift. It was only then that Aunt Hilde brightened, sipping the brew with delight.

Noting the change, Drew's mom cautiously slipped off her chair and knelt by her aunt. "Aunt Hilde," she said gently.

The tiny lady turned slightly, still drinking, shyly looking over her teacup.

"Oh," Drew's mom gasped. "You look so much like my *Mutti.*" She cleared her throat. "Aunt Hilde, I am Elsa's daughter." She repeated herself in German.

"Elsa?" Aunt Hilde looked worried.

"Yes."

"Elsa ist nicht hier." She put her cup down, her eyes anxiously searching the room. *"Nicht hier."*

"She is here, Aunt Hilde." Drew's mother took her aunt's hand reassuringly and placed it on her heart. "Here—in my heart. I am her daughter. Feel my heartbeat? It is hers."

For the first time, Aunt Hilde looked directly at Drew's mom.

"One of my first memories is Mama singing me a song you taught her when she was young. My *Mutti.* Your little sister, Elsa. She said you always protected her from danger."

As abruptly as if she'd been slapped, Cousin Marta turned her face away, frowning with a sadness Drew could see but not understand.

"The only things I have," Drew's mom continued, "that

my mama, my *Mutti*, Elsa, carried with her to the United States are wooden puppets—puppets you gave her."

A glimmer of recognition sparked in Aunt Hilde's teal-colored eyes. *"Kasper und Gretel."*

"Yes!" Drew's mother smiled. *"Mutti* would pretend the puppets were singing to me." Nodding on each beat, just as she'd done with Drew when she'd tried to teach him to play the piano, she began softly singing, "Can't you see, I love you, please don't break my heart in two. That's not hard to do, 'cause I don't have a wooden heart." She stopped, a catch in her voice. "Remember? *Erinnerst du dich?"*

Aunt Hilde nodded ever so slightly.

Mesmerized, Drew leaned forward as he saw a smile—a tiny, tentative splash of joy—slowly light up Aunt Hilde's pale, gaunt face as she whispered the words along with his mom. *"Muss i' denn, muss i' denn, zum Städtele hinaus, Städtele hinaus . . ."* She paused. "Elsa's Emily? *Du bist Emily?"*

"Yes!" Drew's mother kissed her aunt's hand as tears slipped down her cheeks. "Yes. Elsa's Emily. Your niece."

"Oh," Aunt Hilde murmured. *"Ich habe so lange auf dich gewartet, Kind."*

"I have waited so long to meet you, too, Aunt. Too, too long."

Aunt Hilde held open her arms, and Drew's mom melted into them.

Tears stung Drew's eyes. Embarrassed, he looked down and rubbed them away. He could swear he heard his seemingly coldhearted commie cousin sniffle, too.

NOVEMBER 1960

Singer Elvis Presley was drafted and drove tanks for the army in West Germany, where he also filmed *G. I. Blues*. The GDR condemns the movie and Elvis's hip-swinging "degenerative" rock 'n' roll. Its state-run youth magazine, *Young World*, writes: "His 'song' resembled his face: stupid and brutal. The guy was completely unmusical . . . and roared like a stung deer, just not so melodic." The GDR creates an alternative, government-sanctioned dance—the Lipsi—to distract youth from "the trash literature and petty-bourgeoisie habits, 'hot music,' and the ecstatic 'songs' of a Presley." A 6/4-meter dance, done in an arm's-length embrace like a waltz, the Lipsi does not catch on elsewhere.

Three days after Soviet Russia announces the completion of its first nuclear submarine, the United States launches the USS *George Washington*, armed with nuclear-tipped missiles. President Eisenhower warns Cold War foes that the sub's 16 missiles have the same destructive power as "the total of all of the bombs dropped during WWII."

ALSO

Movie star and singer Sammy Davis Jr. marries Swedish actress May Britt. Despite his popularity, his interracial marriage (outlawed in 31 states in 1960) prompts national controversy. Davis's invitation to sing at JFK's upcoming inauguration is rescinded, despite his having campaigned tirelessly for Kennedy.

The Shirelles' "Will You Love Me Tomorrow" becomes the first #1 single by a "girl group," and also launches the songwriting career of Carole King.

CHAPTER FOUR
NOVEMBER 1960

"**I** can't believe Mom made you ask him to the Sadie Hawkins dance." Drew and Joyce were setting the table, watching Matthias talk with Linda in the living room.

"Oh, I don't mind," Joyce answered. "It seemed so important to Mom, especially after you two met Aunt Hilde last month. And"—she lowered her voice to a whisper—"it's not as if I'm looking to date someone at school. You know the class I'm taking at Free University to fill that requirement?"

Drew nodded.

"There's a really interesting guy in it."

Drew stopped laying out silverware and turned to look at her.

"His father is a literature professor—one of the founders of the university, actually. He left his post at Berlin University for the American sector so he could keep teaching Goethe, Mann, and Hesse without any communist restrictions banning so-called petty bourgeoisie writers."

"He's German?"

"Fritz? Of course, silly." Joyce laughed.

"Dad's not going to like your dating a foreigner. Or a college guy, you know." Maybe Drew didn't approve, either.

She shrugged. "I'm banking on Mom's help. Fritz is an amazing musician, a pianist. She'll like that."

"Aha! That's why you invited Matthias when she asked!"

"There's always a method to my madness, brother mine." Joyce broke into a full-dimpled grin. "Besides, look how sweet he's being with Linda. I've haven't seen her talk this much all fall, ever since coming to Berlin, have you?"

Joyce was right. Linda wasn't exactly daring to look Matthias in the eye, keeping her gaze focused on the apron she was stitching for home ec class, but she was chatting. A lot, in fact. What if he was filling her head with commie nonsense?

Drew hurried over to the couch. "We'll be eating in a few minutes, when Shirley gets here," he announced. "The bathroom is by my room, if you want to wash up."

Matthias stood and retreated down the hallway.

Drew plopped down beside Linda. She was glowing. "What were you two talking about?" he asked.

"All sorts of things! Matthias said he was surprised that an American school was teaching something as useful as home economics," she explained. "I told him it's very practical and all, but I don't plan to join the Future Homemakers of America." Her freckles flared as she whispered, "What I really want to be is a veterinarian."

"Really, sis? I didn't know that."

She nodded solemnly. "Then I told Matthias about Blarney. How much I missed him. And that if I were a vet, I could have taken care of him so that he could have crossed the Atlantic with us, even though he's old. Then he'd be here now." Linda paused, her eyes welling up with tears that she blinked back quickly. "Matthias reminded me that Cousin Marta is training to be a doctor! So if I want to be a doctor for animals, he said, I have every right to. As long as I'm smart enough. I think I am, don't you?"

"For sure!" Drew answered. "If anybody tries to tell you that you aren't, you send him to me, okay?"

"Okay!" She leaned against Drew as he put his arm around her shoulders. "I asked our vet about it before we left."

"Dr. Gallagher?"

She nodded again, not looking up. "But he said he wasn't so sure that was a good idea. He said I could be a receptionist and say hello to all the animals as they came through the door, and that would be a good job for me before I get married."

Drew sucked in his breath. He knew Dr. Gallagher had only said what most people would say to a girl about what dreams she should have, but now that it was being applied to his sister, he didn't like it. Of the three of them, Linda was definitely the smartest academically. She'd gotten straight As last year. Anybody with a brain like that who was as animal-crazy as Linda was would make a great vet.

Drew pulled away a bit so he could look into Linda's face as he said, "You can do anything you put your mind to, sis."

Linda smiled. She thought a moment and added, "Matthias asked me if I had to join an official youth group to be allowed to go to university. I don't, do I?"

"Nope. Just study real hard."

Pleased, Linda went back to her sewing.

Drew watched her meticulous stitching for a moment before getting up to look for Matthias. He should thank him for encouraging Linda. Cousin Marta had probably read Matthias the riot act about getting along with Drew, like his mom had him. Or maybe Drew had misjudged the guy.

He found Matthias standing a few feet inside his bed-room. What the heck? "Looking for something?" he asked.

"You have a poster of your new president." Matthias pointed.

The subject of JFK distracted Drew from Matthias's trespassing. "Yes—I'm stoked he won!"

Matthias frowned. "*Was heißt* 'stoked'?"

"Excited."

"Ah." He nodded. "Chairman Khrushchev, too."

Drew frowned. "Why? Because JFK is smart and more of a peacemaker?"

"Because he is *unerfahren*. Mmmm…has no experience."

Matthias shrugged. "It is what Khrushchev said." He meandered back to the living room.

Misjudged? Maybe not.

><<

A knock on the apartment door announced Shirley's arrival.

"You answer, honey," Drew's mom called from the kitchen. "She's your date!"

"Don't get excited—we're only buddies, Mom," he tossed back lightly as he went to the door. But as Drew open it, he had the wind punched out of him, and not by the November cold streaking up the stairwell. Standing in front of him was not the Shirley he was accustomed to seeing around school in bobby socks and corduroy skirts.

This Shirley was . . . was . . . *wow*. With her dark hair swept back from her face, arty gold earrings carved like Egyptian hieroglyphs dropping to below her chin, and an off-the-shoulder black dress, Shirley looked like glamour-girl photos he'd seen of Natalie Wood, the star of *Rebel Without a Cause*.

"Hi!" Shirley held up a boutonniere. "I told Mom we were just going as friends, but she insisted I bring it."

"Oh gosh." Drew felt his freckles flush hot and damned his face. "I . . . I didn't get you a corsage." Strike one.

"Don't worry." Shirley smiled, waiting for him to move. Drew was spellbound by her large dark eyes, now catlike with mascara and thick eyeliner. "Drew?" She waited, then finally asked, "May I come in?"

"Oh! Sorry!" Strike two. He stepped back to make way.

Shirley's crisp skirt rustled as she swept past. Drew's heart banged against his chest.

"Oh my—get a load of you, gorgeous!" Joyce held Shirley at arm's length and turned her around, revealing a little swish of purple satin below her hem. "You wore the slip your nana sent!"

"You don't think it's too much?"

Joyce shook her head. "No. The color combination is absolutely wonderful. So mod." She introduced Shirley to Matthias.

Matthias stared—no other word for it—and kept staring as they sat down to their dinner of Irish stew.

Drew kinda wanted to punch him.

Once everyone was settled, Drew's father said to Linda, "You're official now, cutie patootie. You say grace."

"Really? Okay." Linda sat up proudly, bowed her head, and shyly recited, "Bless us, O Lord, and these Thy gifts, which we are about to receive from Thy bounty . . ."

"Amen," everyone murmured, except Matthias.

"What is official?" he asked.

"She finished her confirmation classes right before we came here in August," Joyce explained. "For Catholics, that's the big step into adulthood."

"Ah. For us, that is the *Jugendweihe*. But we pledge our lives to the state, not God. Karl Marx said religion is the opiate of the masses." Matthias took a bite of his stew while everyone else froze, their forks halfway lifted.

"What are you talking about, man?" Drew asked, incredulous.

"Our youth consecration, when we join the FDJ, marking us as responsible socialist citizens. I took classes, too—but on *Ethik*, Marx's *Philosophie*, and the . . . hmmmmm." He looked to Drew's mom for help. *"Die edle Architektur des Kommunismus, und Verfolgung des deutschen Kommunisten durch die faschistische Nazis."*

"'The noble architecture of communism,'" she translated, raising her eyebrow at Drew's dad, "'and the persecution of German communists by fascists and Nazis.'"

"Yes," Matthias continued, oblivious to the startled reactions around the table. "We took field trips, met our soldiers. When I completed all those hours, I was selected for a ceremony at the Theater of Friendship, where I repeated our official pledge." He held up a finger for each promise: "'To the workers' state, to support friendship with the Soviet Russian people, who are the best friends of Germany, and to secure and defend peace.

"'Youths who finish the classes and make the pledge are sent to attend academic high school'"—he looked to Linda—"'that prepares people for university. Those who do not, or who do church confirmation instead'"—he looked to Drew—"'go to apprenticeships.'" Matthias took another bite of stew. A big, ravenous one. "This is good." He scooped up more. "Thank you, Cousin Emily."

Inwardly, Drew groaned. Taking this dogma-spewing commie kid to an all-American Sadie Hawkins dance had the makings of a total disaster. Especially among military brats whose fathers might have to risk their lives to protect West Berlin against a Soviet Russia incursion, something Khrushchev was threatening more frequently with each passing week.

Every day it's a-getting' closer, Goin' faster than a roller coaster...

The sounds of a Buddy Holly song skipped down the halls as the foursome approached the sports center gym.

"Oh, the band's starting!" Shirley grabbed Drew's hand to dance them through the canopy entrance of maroon and white streamers and balloons. Spotting Bob just inside, Drew entered with dread. Matthias trailed along behind them in absolute bewilderment.

"Look what a great job the art class did!" Shirley said as they came to a life-sized drawing of Li'l Abner darting away from Daisy Mae Yokum, in hot pursuit.

Bob, of course, had positioned himself beside a drawing of the busty Moonbeam McSwine, Daisy Mae's main competition in the Al Capp comic strip. "Whatcha think, Mac? Now, here's a babe any red-blooded American could fall for," Bob blustered as he pointed. "Wait a minute." Bob stopped mid-ogle and shifted his point to Matthias. "What's this guy doing here?"

"He's my date," Joyce announced. "Matthias, you remember Bob?"

"Yes," Matthias answered, completely distracted by Moonbeam and Daisy Mae.

"The whole Sadie Hawkins thing started with this cartoon," Joyce explained to him. "In the comic strip, when Sadie was in danger of becoming an old maid, her father, the mayor of Dogpatch, set up a race and declared that any bachelor caught that day had to marry the woman who nabbed him."

Seeing Matthias's perplexed and slightly shocked face, Joyce burst out laughing and took his hand, saying, "It's okay. Just pretend you're here on a diplomatic mission. We'll probably prove everything the Politburo says is amoral about the West a hundred times over tonight. But maybe you can have a little fun, too. C'mon." She led him to a table holding punch and cookies to watch the band.

Drew started to follow, but Bob caught his arm. "Why would you bring him here? That kid could be gathering all sorts of intel."

"It was my mom's idea."

"Well, she's a birdbrain, then."

"Watch it," Drew snapped. "It's just a dance. It's not as if we're discussing battle plans."

"Listen, Mac, you haven't been here long enough to understand—"

"Understand what, Bob?" Charlie had crossed the dance floor and cut him off. "That you're top dog? Nobody doubts that." He clapped Bob on the back. "Hey, Drew."

Drew shot Charlie a hundred silent thank-yous as he shook his hand.

But Bob kept at it. "Listen, I could tell you some things. The Russians have totally brainwashed East Berliners into thinking we're out to take over Germany. My dad said—" He broke off abruptly, adhering to military family rules that Drew recognized. In a place like Berlin, even dinner table conversation was essentially classified. "Just keep an eye on that bozo." Bob tipped his head in Matthias's direction. "I know I will."

"Ah, maybe you better keep an eye on your girl, Romeo." Charlie elbowed him. "I see a snake coming, twelve o'clock."

The school's quarterback—a loping boy with a sunshine smile and Hollywood-dreamboat cleft chin—was asking Bob's date for a dance.

"Hey, what the—" Bob started forward, but it was too late. She took the football player's hand and followed him out to the floor just as the band switched to a Sam Cooke ballad.

Darling, you-oo-oo-oo send me . . .

The quarterback swung Bob's date into his arms and spun them around and around.

"Damn. That guy's a regular Gene Kelly," Charlie joked. "But of course, he ain't got your charm, Bob."

Bob snort-laughed in reply. "Well, that serves me right for neglecting her." He turned to Shirley. "May I?" he asked, as courtly as could be. "If Mac here doesn't mind?"

Shirley glanced at Drew.

The night had been full of surprises already. If Bob could regroup and act civilized, Drew could, too. "If the lady agrees," Drew answered, adding a little touch of flirtation with Shirley. "Just promise you'll come right back to me."

She giggled and gave her hand to Bob, who bowed low to Drew before sliding them into the swirl of dancers.

"You old smoothie," Charlie teased him. "Let's get some punch."

Drew and Charlie joined Joyce and Matthias against the wall, tapping their feet to the music. "Shirley sure looks gorgeous tonight," Charlie commented. "Brains and beauty—you better be on your toes, buddy boy."

Drew laughed at his teasing, but he felt his face flush a little as he watched Shirley dance with Bob. "Who'd you come with, Charlie?"

Charlie pointed to Betty, one of the cheerleaders, center stage in a circle of pretty girls. "We're just friends," he added. "We actually knew each other from before—elementary school at Fort Bliss. We promised to come together and to leave together, and maybe dance a few times in between. Her dad is being transferred back to Texas at the end of the school year. No use starting anything up again."

"You guys were an item?"

"Oh yeah, we were a biiiiiig thing in sixth grade." Charlie laughed. Then he grew serious, lowering his voice. "The girl I'd really like a dance with is your sister. She's . . ." He watched Joyce explaining various all-American things in the room to Matthias. "She's . . . lovely."

"Ask her." Maybe Charlie could distract Joyce from her college crush.

Suddenly bashful, Charlie shook his head. "Maybe in a minute."

"Oh, don't be a chicken." Drew shoved Charlie in Joyce's

direction. "Hey, sis, someone wants a dance with you, but he's being all Li'l Abner about it."

Joyce smiled. "Why, Charlie, I'd love to."

Speechless, Charlie let Joyce take his hand and pull him toward the band. Over her shoulder, she mouthed at Drew, "Stay with Matthias."

Drew nodded. Shirley was still dancing with Bob. Wouldn't hurt to stand post with Matthias for the next song, which turned out to be Elvis.

Oh, baby, let me be your lovin' teddy bear . . .

Matthias' mouth fell open as he watched Joyce and Charlie rock 'n' roll.

"Never heard Elvis Presley before?" Drew asked.

"I have," Matthias muttered, like he was confessing to a crime.

"On AFN?" Drew knew the signal was strong enough to waft into the Soviet sector.

Matthias shook his head. *"AFN zu hören ist in Ostberlin verboten."*

Listening was forbidden? "How can they know?" Radio was sound, floating free, like air, like imagination.

Matthias sighed. "They know. *Spitzel.*"

"What?"

"Informers. Paid by the State Security Ministry, the Stasi. Each street has one. Or more."

"What?" Matthias's life really was straight out of Orwell's dystopia. "Jeez, man, that's . . . that's awful."

Matthias remained silent a moment before hesitantly adding, "I know 'Jailhouse Rock.'"

Wow, of all things. That song was controversial even in the United States. "How, if you're not allowed to listen to our radio stations?"

"A friend. He . . . he . . . smuggles . . . he visits a cousin in the West."

"Like me?" Drew found himself smiling encouragingly. That's what his mom would want him to do, but in truth, Drew was beginning to feel sorry for Matthias. Not being able to hear Chuck Berry, Little Richard, the Everly Brothers, or Bill Haley—it'd be like starving!

Matthias turned to look at Drew. "Yes, like you." He nodded, mulling that over with a tiny hint of a smile. "He brings records to the East, but it is dangerous." He watched the dancers. Slowly, carefully, Matthias added, as if thinking aloud, "It's not as if music makes . . . my friend . . . stop believing in the needs and rights of the workers." He rubbed his forehead and murmured, "Fats Domino is his favorite. 'Blue Monday.'"

"Whoa, daddy-o! That song? That's straight-up blues. All about work being nothing more than a paycheck so you can play hard on the weekend—not exactly happy-worker, proletariat lyrics," Drew teased him.

Matthias cocked his head, baffled. "Daddy-o?"

Flushed and breathless, Joyce and Charlie came bouncing back to them before Drew could explain the slang. Joyce grabbed Matthias's hands. "Your turn!"

"*Nein, nein!*" Matthias was totally flummoxed now. He managed to say thank you—relatively politely, for him—before explaining, "FJD says free dancing is corrupting—the wiggle-hip, facing each other."

"Oh, we could all use a little corrupting, Matthias. Don't be afraid." Joyce refused to let go of him. "Besides, I asked the band to play a totally innocent line dance. No wiggling at each other. You'll see!"

The combo started singing Johnny Otis's "Hand Jive."

I know a cat named Way-Out Willie

He got a cool little chick named Rockin' Billie . . .

Oh, yeah! Clapping, cheering, everyone shouted and took to the floor, reminding Drew of the gleeful jamborees his mom used to orchestrate at the playground with a box of tambourines and kazoos.

Joyce and Drew guided Matthias through the hand-jive sequence: slapping his palms on his thighs; crossing his hands over and under; balling them into fists and bouncing them on top of each other: right on top, left on top, right, left.

Repeat, repeat, repeat, everyone on beat. Everyone happy.

The most amazing sight, though, was Matthias belly laughing.

"There you are, Mac." Bob was leaning up against the sinks in the men's room with two of his buddies when Drew, Matthias, and Charlie entered to splash some water on their faces, sweaty from dancing.

There was a faint scent of something sweet hanging

around them. Drew couldn't identify it until he got a little closer—whiskey.

Charlie whistled. "You on some kind of suicide mission, Bobby? If the chaperones catch a whiff of you, you're DOA."

Bob waved him off. "We're moving out. Heading to the Metropol. Best cabaret in Berlin. Wanna come?"

Charlie shook his head. "Nah."

Bob shrugged. "Suit yourself. Be a stiff." He glanced at Drew and then scowled at Matthias. "Enjoying our hospitality?" He took a step forward. "Our music?" Another step. "Our girls?" He stood toe-to-toe with Matthias.

"What the hell, man?" Drew instinctively stepped in front of Matthias, pushing Bob back an arm's length. In return, Bob shoved him, his hands instant fists.

"Hey, hey." Charlie moved between them, throwing his hand up against Bob's chest. "You want the teacher-MPs down on you?"

"My beef's with the commie, not you, Charlie."

"Well, see, now you've made it my beef, too, Bobby. I can't let you cause some international incident in the can. You know what our dads say."

At the mere mention of their dads, the boys leaning on the sinks stood like they'd been shoved into a cold shower. A scuffle in the men's room was the kind of thing that could get them in trouble with the principal, sure, but it could also land their dads in hot water with the CO. Teenage rebellion carried heavy penalties on post. Drew had already been warned that not stopping and getting off his bike during evening retreat and the flag being lowered for the night could bring serious reprimand.

Bob backed off. But as he exited, he knocked Matthias's shoulder with his.

"You're kidding me," Joyce said when Drew quietly relayed to her and Shirley what had just happened.

"Let's get out of here," said Shirley. "You know those horse-drawn carriages that sit outside Café Kranzler's?"

Joyce looked a little puzzled at the non sequitur, but she followed along. "Like Tavern on the Green in Central Park?"

"My dad said I could treat us to a ride around the Kurfürstendamm. Take a look at the city all lit up and lively." She turned to Charlie. "You want to come?"

"I better get back to Betty. But thanks." He put his hand on Drew's shoulder. "You okay?"

"Yeah. Thanks."

Matthias extended his hand to shake Charlie's. *"Dankeschön."*

They gathered their coats and took a military taxi to the Times Square of Berlin, thick with people all gussied up for a Saturday evening on the town.

"Here we are!" Shirley announced.

They got out at the entrance to the famous three-story restaurant ringed with red-and-white-striped awnings and awash in bright lights, waltz music, and delicious smells.

"Oh, look!" Shirley pointed down the avenue. "I see a carriage circling back already! It's like they knew we were coming." She bounced up and down on her toes.

Standing beside them on the curb, a petite, pretty young woman murmured, "*Gott sei Dank, mir ist so kalt!*" She snuggled up against her American GI date.

Wrapping his arms around her against the cold of the November night, the soldier asked, "Are you sure you'll be okay, honey? I know there's a blanket in the carriage, but if you're too cold . . ."

"*Nein.*" She smiled sweetly. "Tonight is a fairy tale. The carriage—I will feel like a princess." She gazed up at the GI adoringly.

Beaming, the guy announced to Drew, Matthias, Joyce, and Shirley, "She just agreed to marry me. I'm the luckiest guy in the world."

"*Ooooooh*—congratulations!" Joyce and Shirley sang out.

Matthias had been staring at the couple, and now he elbowed Drew. "Does this Black soldier know about Emmett Till?" he muttered. "White men killed him just for flirting with a white woman, yes?"

"How do you know about that?" Drew asked with surprise. The 1955 Mississippi trial of the Black teenager's murderers had ended with a not guilty verdict after less than an hour of deliberation by a white jury. Newspapers back home had been filled with the shameful details, but in Germany?

Matthias looked at him like Drew was a total dolt. "It is

used as proof of American cruelty and . . . mmmmm . . . *die Heuchelei.*"

Before Drew could figure out what the German word meant, two carriages pulled up at the same time, depositing a crowd of rosy-cheeked riders, bundled up and laughing. Both top-hatted coachmen looked very happy to have another fare so quickly. "*Guten Abend. Bitte komm,*" they beckoned.

"Good luck," Drew called to the GI and his fiancée as he took Shirley's hand to help her onto the carriage's narrow step.

"Thank you, kind sir," she said softly, smiling at him.

Drew caught his breath a little as she gracefully ascended. The carriage swayed and dipped gently as she nestled next to Joyce on the red leather seat, pulling a thick wool blanket up around them. After gesturing for Matthias to climb in next, Drew waved goodbye to the engaged couple, who settled into their own carriage behind them, exuding an aura of blissful romance.

That's when Drew spotted a pair of middle-aged American men stumbling toward the GI's carriage, each dragging by the hand a young German woman wrapped in a full-length mink coat.

"Hey! We've been waiting!" one of the men bellowed. He was clearly drunk.

Matthias and Drew paused, still on the ground, sensing trouble.

Now the obnoxious middle-aged man stood gaping at the couple, his mouth hanging open. He pointed angrily at the American GI and shouted at the coachman, "You're taking that Negro before us?"

Passersby froze.

The man's companion strode forward and grabbed the bridle of one of the carriage horses. "My friend asked you a question," he roared up at the coachman. This man was dead sober. He continued threatening the couple's carriage driver. "I suggest you tell this Black man to get out of your carriage. Show some respect for American rules, since we've rebuilt your sorry-ass country. Back home, it's the back of the bus for that guy. Whites up front and definitely"—he paused for emphasis—"first."

It was the GI who replied through gritted teeth, "Maybe you haven't been home in a while. The Supreme Court ended segregation on public buses four years ago." He added sarcastically, "Sir."

The man didn't let go of the horse. "Last time I checked, boy," he countered, "mixed-race couples were still *verboten* in America—in thirty states, I believe. Does the *Fräulein* know that?"

"Yes, she does," the soldier answered calmly. "*She* judges a man for who he is, no matter his nationality or his race."

He and the American glared at one another, neither relenting.

After a moment, the coachman spoke haltingly. "*Bitte.* I want no trouble." He beckoned to a pair of West German policemen standing on the corner.

The American smirked. "That's right. Call in the cops. Police respect authority."

"You can call whoever you like. I have the right to this seat and this carriage ride." The GI didn't budge. His fiancée shifted nervously.

Time seemed to freeze as the *Landespolozisten* approached. Drew was filled with dread. Police back home weren't exactly friendly to Black Americans pushing for equality.

Suddenly, Shirley's voice pealed out. "Good evening!" Drew looked up at her in astonishment as she stood and waved at the German policemen. "Isn't it wonderful? This American soldier has just proposed to this lovely lady."

"And she said yes!'" Joyce stood as well, blessing the officers with a dazzling smile.

The two German policemen were young and grinned back, totally enchanted by the American girls.

Shirley continued in a bubbly voice, "They want to celebrate their engagement with the most romantic thing Berlin has to offer—a ride through the Tiergarten in a horse-drawn carriage!"

"*Wunderbar!*" One of the *Landespolozisten* clapped in congratulations.

"There is a problem with this?" the other policeman asked the carriage driver.

The drunk American responded first. "We were here first."

"That's right," echoed his friend, who still clutched the horse's bridle. "What kind of hospitality is this for American businessmen, who patronize your Kurfürstendamm shops?"

He gestured to his date, who stroked the arm of her mink coat on cue.

"*Bitte*," the coachman repeated, "I want no trouble."

The German policemen hesitated, frowning as they considered the middle-aged Americans. They looked back to the GI, then to his fiancée, their gazes almost imploring, perhaps worrying they might be dressed down by superior officers for alienating Americans with fat wallets.

The GI saved them. He called to Shirley, "You know, now that I think about it, it'd be nice to celebrate our engagement with other Americans. I'm such a long way from home. Do you have room in your carriage for us to join you?"

"Yes, please! Come with us!" Shirley answered.

Their driver protested quietly. "Too much weight, *Fräulein*."

Shirley turned to him. "We will only ride with them around the corner. Please?"

The coachman stuck out his lower lip, considering, then shrugged and nodded.

The couple clambered in with Shirley and Joyce.

Clucking and snapping his whip in the air, their coachman urged his horses forward at a trot as Drew and Matthias hurried to swing themselves up and squeeze in beside the GI and his German sweetheart. When they rounded the corner, their driver pulled over. Drew scrambled out and helped Joyce and Shirley step down to the pavement before the second carriage, now stuffed with the middle-aged troublemakers and their dates, could catch up to them.

"Dankeschön." Matthias nodded at the carriage driver, who answered, *"Gebt Acht."* Be careful.

"Congratulations again!" they all called and waved as the carriage and the GI and his fiancée disappeared into the night.

"That was quick thinking, girl, announcing their engagement like that." Joyce put her arm around Shirley.

"Oh, I didn't do anything. It was the GI who figured out how to de-escalate the situation using nonviolent resistence." Shirley smiled, thoughtful, then added, "My nana was one of the original members of CORE—the Congress of Racial Equality. She's been in sit-ins in Chicago at lunch counters as far back as the forties. CORE would send in its members—Black and white, like my nana—together. They'd all order, and if the restaurant refused to serve the Black members, the whites handed them their plates. CORE helped integrate Jack Sprat diners that way, like Reverend Martin Luther King is leading people to do right now across the South."

Shirley pushed her coat lapels up around her face against the cold. "Nana has told me never to just stand by if I see people fighting for their rights. To get involved. She quotes the playwright George Bernard Shaw at me all the time. Somebody in one of his plays says that the worst sin toward our fellow creatures is not to hate them, but to be indifferent to them."

Shirley turned toward the Kurfürstendamm. "Maybe we can get a strudel?"

"My treat," said Joyce.

As they walked back to the brightly lit avenue, Matthias murmured, "A very illuminating night here in the West."

Drew didn't know exactly what Matthias meant by that comment. But he suddenly remembered what *die Heuchelei* meant—hypocrisy. He felt his face flame red with mortification at what he'd just witnessed fellow Americans do. Then other German words filled his head as he gazed at Shirley— *der Schneid* for guts, *die Bewunderung* for admiration, and *sich verlieben* for falling in love.

For once, Matthias was right—it had been a very illuminating night.

Back home, Drew changed into his pajamas and went to the bathroom for some aspirin. He'd danced so much his legs were actually sore. He opened the medicine cabinet and reached for the Alka-Seltzer. But it wasn't there. His toothpaste and zit medicine were missing, too. Weird.

Maybe he'd left them on his night table. As he padded barefoot around his bed, he stepped on a folded paper. His father—mostly jokingly—did a neat-and-tidy inspection of their rooms each night. Drew didn't leave scraps of paper on the floor.

Puzzled, he scooped it up. It was in German, official looking, and Matthias's signature was at the bottom.

"Wegen der Kriegsgefahr durch die NATO..."

What the heck? Drew's German was improving fast, especially since all American students in Berlin were required to take the language. He could translate, "Because of the threat of war by NATO . . ." But the rest of the document was so formal, it would take him a while to work through it with a German dictionary. Joyce, too. He needed his mom. Drew glanced at his clock. She'd be fast asleep at twelve fifteen. But this was an emergency!

Slowly opening the door to his parents' room, Drew tiptoed to his mom's side of the bed and gently touched her arm.

Instantly on mom alert, she reached for her robe and slid her feet into slippers. "Are you sick, honey?" she whispered, putting her hand on his forehead. "You don't have a fever."

"Mom, I need to show you something. Right now."

They went into the kitchen. Pushing her hair out of her eyes, Drew's mom quickly skimmed the paper, her face growing serious. "Oh no," she murmured.

"What is it?"

"Where did you get this?"

"It was in my bedroom!" Drew was beginning to put two and two together. Matthias had been snooping in his stuff! Just when Drew had kinda started to like the guy.

"This is pure Soviet propaganda, honey. Bald-faced lies about why NATO was formed in the first place—which was to protect Western Europe *from* Russian expansionism," she explained. "The Russians need East Germans to believe *we* are the problem, so they flip reality on its head to make

America look like the aggressor. These types of trumped-up falsehoods are how they do it."

"That's crazy."

"Yes," she murmured.

"What does this say?" He pointed to the paper.

"It's a pledge Matthias has signed." Drew's mom read to herself and then translated aloud, "'Because of the threat of war by NATO, it is a moral consequence of my political convictions that I, as a young socialist, help to defend the achievements gained by the sacrificial struggle of the working class even to the extent of pledging my life.'"

"Good grief," Drew muttered.

His mom continued translating. "'I give my wholehearted support to the struggle against imperialism and the politics of NATO.'" She paused, shaking her head. "'Therefore, at any time deemed necessary by the Party, I will bear arms to defend peace, my fatherland, and the workers' and peasants' government. To this end, I will familiarize myself with the use of arms . . . with revolutionary discipline and unconditional obedience.'"

With a long, sad sigh, she took Drew's hand and said, "This is exactly why I so want you to befriend Matthias."

Drew snatched his hand away. "You want me to be friends with a kid who signed this? Someone who might take a gun and shoot at me or at Dad if things get bad?"

"Of course not, honey." His mom's voice quavered at the mere thought. "Let's try to get Matthias on our side before that happens."

"What makes you think he's interested in that?" Drew

was too mad to recall Matthias's misgivings—about music censorship, at least—that he'd witnessed that evening.

"Well . . . I can tell Marta wants him to be more open to American ideas, to see us as friends instead of enemies."

"You might think you know everything, Mom, but you don't always."

Drew's mother studied him for a long, long moment. She let his impertinence slide. "I think so because—even though Marta hasn't said anything directly, since the Soviets enforce such harsh de-Nazification policies in East Germany—she—"

Drew interrupted. "That's a good thing, don't you think, Mom? Purging Nazis and anyone who agreed with them?"

Again, his mom contemplated him. "The sins of one person don't automatically define his family members, do they?" she asked quietly.

Drew chewed on that for a moment.

"What I was about to say, honey, is that although I don't know for sure, I get the sense that Marta's older sons—those twins—might have been browbeaten into joining the Hitler Youth, and . . ." She trailed off. "Sometimes, honey, you have to look beyond a person's rhetoric when it has clearly been stuffed into his head by his government. Or by political figures. Or by the people who hold the power in a society. It's brainwashing. Some people have trouble seeing past the hyperbole or conspiracy theories or hate-filled labels and stereotypes they've been fed. But that doesn't mean they can't change if they are given truth and factual information as counterbalance. That's where we come in. As living proof that the lies his country's leaders are spreading are not true. Matthias . . . beyond that wall of what he's been inculcated to believe, I think he's a boy much like you."

She folded the paper and tucked it into her robe pocket. "I better show this to CIC at Marienfelde." She kissed Drew's forehead and went back to bed.

DECEMBER 1960

Paul Newman stars in the movie *Exodus*, based on a book about the founding of the modern state of Israel after WWII. The screen adaptation was written by Dalton Trumbo, one of the "Hollywood Ten" convicted of contempt of Congress during the Red Scare and blacklisted by Hollywood. He survives financially by writing under a pseudonym, remaining anonymous when *Roman Holiday* wins the Oscar for Best Story. With *Exodus*, Trumbo is finally able to use his own name. Blacklisting people accused of being "un-American" or "subversives" because of their political beliefs comes to an end.

After communist rebel Fidel Castro seizes control of Cuba, islanders flee in droves. President Eisenhower authorizes $1 million to help resettle those who make it to the U.S. border. He also sanctions emergency visa waivers for Operacion Pedro Pan, a program run by the Catholic Welfare Bureau that brings thousands of children with Cuban dissident parents to Florida, placing them in protective foster homes.

A new band called the Beatles plays in Liverpool's Litherland Town Hall, starting a fanatical following in England that soon spills to America.

CHAPTER FIVE

DECEMBER 1960

Standing on the sports field, waiting for the military heli-copter that would bring Santa Claus to the school's annual orphans party, Drew was holding a shivering boy's hand. He could feel the child's fingers tremble through his mitten.

"Ist dir kalt?" Are you cold?

The five-year-old nodded, not taking his eyes off the ice-blue sky. *"Wird der Weihnachtsmann bald hier sein?"*

"Yes, Santa will be here soon." Drew stamped his feet, feeling his own toes prickling from the chill.

The boy mimicked him. *Stamp-stamp.*

Drew glanced down. The boy's peacoat was patched but heavy. His bright red-and-green knitted hat and scarf looked new, probably a gift from the army wives club. What the poor kid really needed was some real pants. He was dressed in the standard attire for German boys—shorts and woolly knee socks, which provided little protection for the kid's spindly legs against the bitter Berlin cold.

Stamp-stamp.

Stamp-stamp. The boy's eyes never left the heavens.

Drew surveyed the other thirty or so orphans. They were dancing in place, speculating on what Santa might bring them. Elfin girls in pointy, tasseled knit caps, their cheeks rosy from the frigid air, happily swarmed Joyce and Shirley and the other student council members who'd organized the day.

Drew's assigned orphan, on the other hand, was so still, so quiet. Drew wondered what the boy's story was. Drew and his classmates who'd volunteered to be escorts for the party hadn't been told anything specific. When he was five years old, Drew's biggest worry had been whether he was getting a tricycle or not. Instinctively, he patted the boy's hand.

Turning his enormous, walnut-brown eyes to Drew, the five-year-old asked fretfully, "*Wird Knecht Ruprecht mit dem Weihnachtsmann zusammen kommen?*"

Drew didn't know who Knecht Ruprecht was and answered that he thought Santa was coming alone. The reindeer couldn't fit in the helicopter, he joked.

But the boy didn't laugh, just added in a hushed and solemn voice, "*Ich verspreche, dass ich dieses Jahr brav war.*"

"I'm sure you have been very good," Drew reassured him, proud that his German had improved enough for this simple conversation.

The child nodded and returned his watchful gaze to the sky.

Whump-whump-whump-whump. The faint sound of rotating blades sliced the air, and the helicopter appeared in the horizon.

"He's coming! *Er kommt!*" The children clapped. The Berlin high schoolers grinned, caught up in the infectious holiday spirit. A few of the orphans hung back shyly, but only Drew's charge remained completely contained and apprehensive.

Whump-whump-whump-whump. The helicopter grew large quickly, and within a few moments, it landed in a gale of whipped-up rotary wind.

Out jumped the high school coach, pillowed and padded and dressed as Santa. The orphans broke loose and charged him, jumping up and down.

"Ho-ho-ho, merry Christmas!" he shouted through his fake, cotton-fluff beard.

A chorus of children shouted back, *"Fröhliche Weihnachten!"*

"C'mon. You too." Drew walked the boy to the line of eager children.

When Santa swung his heavy bag off his shoulder to drop it to the ground, the five-year-old gasped and stepped back.

"Don't worry," Drew reassured him, "Santa just wants to give you a gift."

Multiflavored Lifesavers, skipping ropes, kaleidoscopes, yo-yos, jacks, marbles. As each child received a present, he or she peeled off, running back to the school building for cake.

Finally, Drew's boy reached Coach Santa, who handed him a little wooden push puppet of the Disney cartoon dog Pluto. Push the button, and the mini puppet collapsed; release, and it popped back up. Still silent, the boy pushed and released the toy's mechanism all the way back to the cafeteria.

After making sure the boy had a piece of cake, Drew found Shirley. "Who is Knecht Ruprect?" he asked. She seemed to know everything.

"A terrible ogre with horns and fangs. Also known as Krampus. In some parts of Germany, the tradition is that Father Christmas is accompanied by Knecht Ruprect, who knows for certain whether children have been good or not. If they've been naughty, Krampus stuffs them in his large sack and carries them away."

"Are you kidding?" No wonder the boy had startled when Coach Santa dropped his bag.

Shirley laughed. "Nope. Have you read their fairy tales?" She darted off to mop up an overturned glass of milk.

Drew watched the boy wolf down his cake. Just like Matthias. The orphanage was in West Berlin; the boy shouldn't be so hungry.

Joyce came to stand beside him and breathe for a moment.

"Good job, sis. What comes next?"

"Singing Christmas carols. Then they go home." She smiled at Drew. "Thanks for doing this." Then she dashed away to quell the tears of a little girl whose long braids had fallen into her ice cream. Joyce quieted her by pulling a pretty clip from her own hair and tucking it into the girl's.

>///|<

Inspired, Drew went to his locker and retrieved one of his baseballs. When the children were pulling on their coats to leave, Drew knelt by the boy he was escorting and put the ball into his hands. The five-year-old was way too young to really pitch, but Drew showed him how to properly hold the ball, guided by its seams.

It was like plugging in a Christmas tree, the boy lit up so brightly.

Suddenly, Drew totally felt the Christmas spirit. Humming "O Tannenbaum," he waved as the boy got on the bus, and Joyce, Shirley, and all the other Berlin brats helping at the party clumped together to watch the German children drive away.

"That was fun," Shirley said.

"Oh man," one of the brats shouted as an earsplitting roar came from the east. "Here they come! Look out!" Drew turned to see two Soviet MiGs zooming toward them, way too low, gray contrails steaming after them like dragon tails. He and the others couldn't help ducking a bit as the jets whooshed by, dipping their wings up and down, a sarcastic salute for sure. The school building shuddered in their wake.

The brats straightened back up. "Well, at least they

waited until Santa was gone this year," said the boy who'd sounded the alarm.

Drew had heard the boom of Soviet jets buzzing their end of Berlin before. He knew they did it purely to razz American troops. But during a Christmas party for orphans? C'mon.

"Peace on earth and goodwill toward men," Shirley quipped. Then she linked arms with Joyce. They were heading to choir practice. "Merry Christmas, Drew," she said softly.

"You too," he answered, feeling his face flame a little. Joyce tossed him a knowing-big-sister smile as she turned Shirley back toward the school.

I'll have a blue Christmas without you. Elvis's holiday anthem popped into Drew's head as he turned for home.

⇥⫲⊬

Drew was still humming Elvis as he entered his apartment building and heard what was becoming a familiar sound. Shouts—muffled by cinder block, but clearly angry.

A door flew open, and a bellowed "*What have I told you?*" rolled down the stairs like a bowling ball banging along the gutter.

Feet clattered along the steps, fast and furious.

Turning his back to the stairwell, Drew opened his family's mailbox, knowing his mom would have emptied it already this late in the afternoon but figuring it would allow whoever was escaping that argument to save face. Drew was pretty sure he knew who it was. He heard the footfalls slow to fake casual.

"Hello, Mac."

Drew closed the box. "Hi, Bob."

He expected Bob to push past him into the cold, but instead, he sat down on the bottom step.

Drew made himself ask, "You okay, man?"

"Peachy." Bob assessed Drew's face.

Now, if it'd been Charlie, Drew would've let on that he'd heard the rumble, sat down, and *really* asked if he was all right. But this was Bob.

"I was talking with my old man," Bob confided.

Drew braced himself. Army dads were all demanding—that went with the territory—but given the constant arguments Drew and his family couldn't help hearing from across the hall, Bob's clearly crossed the line into harsh.

"It got me thinking about your commie cousin."

Not what Drew expected. "You know, Bob, you're getting to be a broken record. Don't you have any other tunes?"

Humphf. Bob nodded, thoughtful, a self-deprecating smile on his face like the one Drew had spotted when Charlie had teased Bob about his date at Sadie Hawkins. "You seeing him around Christmas?"

"Yeah. Christmas Eve." Drew didn't let on how annoyed he was that his mom was insisting his German cousins be included in their family holiday.

"I'm starting to think maybe it's good that you're all cozy with the guy." Bob got up. "*You* can pick up intel, too, if you're over there in the Russian sector. Isn't his mom a nurse at a hospital?"

"Yeah, so?"

"Maybe she'll let drop some info about it, how bad off they might be in terms of medicine. Maybe he'll let slip the name of the informant the Stasi is sure to have planted on his street. Maybe he'll mention the time of day when it's safest for them to tune into AFN or RIAS's Voice of America broadcasts. Maybe you'll see some of the garbage they make kids read. You never know what details might be really helpful to our guys to countermand Russian propaganda."

He stepped close to Drew, a shadow of desperation on his face. "If you get anything, give it to me, okay?" Nodding more to himself than to Drew, he added, "Then I can give the intel to my dad." Bob punched him lightly on the shoulder as he headed for the door. "See ya . . . Drew."

Then Bob left the building, disappearing into the twilight.

Hark! The herald angels sing. Glory to the newborn king . . . Nat King Cole's smooth jazz voice filled Drew's living room.

Singing along, her voice as honeyed as Cole's, Joyce sat with Drew at the table, wrapping presents for Matthias and Marta. Sweaters, marmalade, oranges, silk stockings, light bulbs, flashlight batteries, safety pins, Nescafé, nail polish. A copy of *Little Women* and women's magazines for Cousin Marta, and a new novel called *My Side of the Mountain* for

Matthias. Drew secured shiny red paper around a copy of George Orwell's *Animal Farm*.

"You know," Joyce began gently, her forehead furrowed, "Cousin Marta and Matthias could get in a lot of trouble if the Vopos find that Orwell book on them, Drew. Fritz told me his dad's entire library was confiscated." She pointed to another gift awaiting ribbons: a two-sided 45, Presley's last release during his time in the U.S. Army, "A Big Hunk of Love," with "My Wish Come True" on its flip side. "And that's really a thoughtful gift, too. I could see how much Matthias was enjoying our 'wiggle-hip' music." She and Drew laughed in bemused sympathy at their cousin being denied the music and dancing they so loved. "But," she added, "he could also get busted for that."

Drew had picked out the record himself in a Kurfürstendamm store—Matthias had seemed like such a Presley fan at Sadie Hawkins. But Drew couldn't say for sure whether he was motivated by generosity or whether he had ungenerously wanted to remind a guy who had signed a pledge to shoot at NATO soldiers that he secretly loved this American singer. As if to prove Drew's point, Elvis was pictured on the jacket in his army uniform, leaning against a building in Friedberg, Germany, where he was stationed.

Or had Drew subconsciously thought the 45 might work as a bribe to pull Matthias into Bob's minor-league cloak-and-dagger business? Did Drew imagine he could actually turn Matthias like some kind of CIA recruit?

"I suppose the paperbacks will fit into a deep coat pocket," Joyce said, pulling Drew back into the moment.

"The record will, too," Drew said defensively. It was only seven inches in diameter.

Joyce nodded "True. And hopefully, the sector guards won't be paying as much attention on Christmas." Another thought hit her. "Does he have a record player? Did you see one in his apartment?"

Drew only knew that Matthias had heard Elvis some-how—because of his friend who smuggled 45s into the Russian sector. So Drew had just assumed he did. But then again, *he* hadn't seen Matthias's room. Unlike Matthias, who'd obviously been snooping around in Drew's!

While he and Joyce wrapped at the table, their mom was opening Christmas cards that had arrived in one big shipment from the States and handing them off to Linda to tape on their door. "Oh, look, honey," their mom said carefully, "it's a picture of Blarney. That was sweet of them to send." With an encouraging smile, she handed the photo to Linda.

Before they'd left Arlington for Berlin, Linda had chosen a dog-loving neighbor to adopt Blarney. She'd bravely marched him across the street to his new family, hugged him, and managed to walk away as Blarney howled. That was the beginning of Linda's deep retreat into shyness.

Biting her lip, Linda looked long and hard at the photograph. "He . . . he looks happy," she forced out. Then she lovingly tucked the photo into the Christmas tree's branches at her eye level, so the collie could gaze out at her.

Their dad stopped fussing with the lights to give her a hug. "I'm proud of you, soldier."

Nodding stoically, Linda retreated to her room, her face puckered, fighting tears.

Joyce got up to follow.

Watching her daughters, Drew's mom stood and shook out her skirt. "I'm going to check on the girls and then change," she said quietly. "Time for you boys to get ready, too. Marta and Matthias will be here in an hour."

⇥⫼⊀⊢

The Christmas tree was glowing in their front bay window by the time Cousin Marta knocked on the door. Drew's mom threw it open with a jolly "Merry Christmas!" Then her voice caught, and she exclaimed, "Oh! How wonderful!"

A trembling, shell-shocked Aunt Hilde was with them, Cousin Marta's arm around her waist. "*Mutti* wanted to come," Cousin Marta said. She leaned forward and added, "It is a miracle, Emily. As I told you, she has not stepped out of our home for years."

"Welcome," Drew's dad boomed.

"Jimmy." Drew's mom held up her hand to quiet his we're-all-buddies-here effusiveness, but it was too late. Aunt Hilde backpedaled toward the stairs with such alarm that Joyce instinctively stepped forward to reach for the elderly woman's hand.

"It's all right." Drew's mother took Aunt Hilde's other hand to stop her. "*Es ist alles in Ordnung.* This is Elsa's granddaughter, Joyce." She gestured toward Joyce and then motioned for Linda to come over. "*Und mein* baby girl,

Linda." She nodded toward Drew. *"Du erinnerst dich an meinen Sohn."*

A faint smile of recognition glimmered on Aunt Hilde's pale face upon seeing Drew, but she did not step inside. She glanced furtively at Drew's dad. Seeing her fear, he inched back, hands up slightly, to make it clear he meant no harm.

Only then did Aunt Hilde gaze into the apartment, at its candlelit Advent wreath, the sweet-smelling traditional German fruitcake Drew's mom had just pulled from the oven, and the piles of presents by the tree. Then she spotted the piano. *"Klavier,"* she murmured. *"Ist das dein Klavier?"*

"Yes, that is my piano. Please . . ." Drew's mom held out her hand in invitation. Ever so cautiously, Aunt Hilde tiptoed inside to touch the keyboard, as reverent as the magi approaching the manger, thought Drew.

Cousin Marta followed, and then Matthias, looking slightly defiant, slightly annoyed, and totally out of whack with the situation, as always. When he spotted Linda, though, Matthias's attitude completely changed. "We have brought you something," he announced.

Drew realized Matthias was holding something wrapped in a shawl—and the bundle was squirming!

Matthias knelt. Linda approached tentatively, her eyes still red and slightly swollen from crying about Blarney.

"My mother tended to a man on our street," Matthias began. "He died two days ago. Now Heidi needs a new home. A person who can take care of her in old age—like a veterinarian." Ever so carefully, Matthias pulled open the bundle to reveal an ancient dachshund, her little snout rimmed with gray, a red ribbon around her neck.

"Oh!" Linda scooped her up. "Oh!" She buried her face in the dog's fur.

Matthias sat back on his heels, looking up at his mother with a pleased smile.

Heidi's plumy tail wagged, thrashing Linda's head. "Oh!" Linda giggled. She didn't lift her face, and for a moment, it was hard to tell where her strawberry-blond curls ended and the dog's chestnut waves began. "She's the best present ever!"

Drew's mom engulfed Cousin Marta in a hug and held on tight until her German cousin softened and wrapped her arms around her as well.

Watching, Drew needed a handkerchief. Maybe his mom was right. Maybe behind that terrifying pledge and that wall of commie dogma, there was a boy Drew could truly like.

After dinner, they exchanged the remaining presents. Linda radiated as much holiday light as the Christmas tree as she rocked the old dachshund like a baby. The dog seemed just as happy with the snuggle. Next to Linda, tucked safely in the corner, Aunt Hilde sat with her gaze fixed on the piano.

Cousin Marta *ooh*ed over the silk stockings, looking embarrassed to need them but grateful to have them. Drew's mother teared up over little wooden Christmas angels that were clearly Becker family treasures, probably hidden away for safekeeping for years. Matthias seemed dumbfounded when Drew handed him the Elvis 45. And Drew tried to look interested when Matthias presented him with a scuffed-up soccer ball.

"I don't know how to play," he blurted, then immediately regretted it. Drew felt his mother watching him. Given the night's aura of Christmas goodwill, he knew the best gift he could give his mom would be to accept Matthias's gesture. "Will you show me how?"

Matthias looked him up and down. "I will *try.*"

Say what? Drew felt himself getting indignant until Matthias's expression made him realize his cousin was joking. The commie could wisecrack! Drew laughed at himself.

Matthias laughed, too.

"Then I'll *try* to show you how pitch a baseball." Drew smiled.

Matthias grinned.

His mom sighed. Cousin Marta sighed. This time, they were pleased.

Suddenly, their moms froze and clasped hands. Drew's held her index finger to her lips and then pointed behind Drew. He turned to see Aunt Hilde creeping toward the piano.

Hushed, they all watched as the frail, skittish woman sat on the instrument's bench and touched her forehead to its empty music rack as if in prayer. Then she began to play, entranced. Drew recognized Schumann's *Kinderszenen*, "Scenes from Childhood," from his own mother's playing.

Soft and hesitant at first, but quickly gathering joy and confidence, Aunt Hilde drew out notes and chords from her memory as if pulling the sublime down from heaven, her fingers pirouetting gracefully along the keys. The air around her became poetry. With each passing melodic phrase, the tiny woman seemed to shed her earthly fears altogether, to stretch up noble and tall, like an angel unfurling its wings, preparing to ascend. It took Drew's breath away.

When she finished the Schumann, Aunt Hilde immediately began another piece—a Chopin nocturne. Then Beethoven's "Für Elise." A sonata by Schubert.

Nobody moved. They were all captivated by the metamorphosis unfolding before them.

"When was the last time she touched a piano?" Drew's mom whispered, awestruck.

"Before Matthias was born," Cousin Marta answered, her voice raspy.

"That's astounding. To play so fluidly, without missing a note, after so many years."

Cousin Marta nodded.

Keeping her eyes on Aunt Hilde, Drew's mom asked, keeping her voice low, "What happened to her piano?"

At this question, tears welled in Cousin Marta's eyes and slipped down her face—a startling show of emotion from a woman who maintained such disciplined composure. "It . . . it was after the Red Army invaded, when the city was defended by the few German soldiers left alive. Old men, the wounded, the handicapped, and boys . . . some of them no more than ten years old." She seemed to choke on the last words.

Aunt Hilde switched to the contemplative delicacy of Debussy's "Claire de Lune."

"This was one of her favorite pieces," Cousin Marta murmured. She listened for a few more translucent measures before continuing, "Throughout the war, *Mutti* turned to her piano when things were . . . the most awful. Even when bombs fell like the wrath of God. It was her way to hang on to sanity."

Playing on, Aunt Hilde was completely enthralled, her eyes closed, seeming not to hear her daughter.

"When the Russians captured Berlin, after the Führer killed himself, when the house-by-house attacks began, day after day . . . still *Mutti* played. Even after . . . after four of them . . . broke down our door and . . ."

Cousin Marta swallowed hard. "She played, even after that—perhaps even more so. Desperate to find some shard of beauty in all that cruelty. But her music called attention to us . . . which was . . . dangerous.

"One day, right after I begged her to stop, an officer suddenly banged on our door. We were terrified. He pointed to the piano. He had been standing outside, listening. He demanded that she keep playing. Oh, how *Mutti*'s hands shook . . . but she did. He arrived unannounced for three weeks. Eventually, he softened. He asked rather than demanded. He even played himself."

Once more, Cousin Marta paused and collected her thoughts, seemingly relieved to have reached this part of the story. "Eventually, the Russian command ordered him to Leipzig. He wanted *Mutti*'s piano with him there. He could have just taken it. They took everything else, the Russians. But he offered to buy it. We were starving. Matthias would be born within a few days. So she gave up her piano." She looked meaningfully at Matthias. "To feed us."

Cousin Marta glanced back to Aunt Hilde. "It is a night of miracles," she murmured as they all listened, swaddled in the rapture coming from the piano.

Aunt Hilde switched from classical pieces to carols, beginning with "Silent Night." Tremulous, in the quietest of voices, she started to sing: *"Stille Nacht, heilige Nacht, Alles schläft; einsam wacht."*

On the second verse, Joyce joined in with the English words, then Drew's mom and dad, Linda and Drew, and finally Cousin Marta, dredging up lyrics long buried inside her. German and English harmonizing.

Only Matthias refused to join, sitting rigid, frowning.

When she came to the end of the Christmas carol, Aunt Hilde stood. Slowly and gently, she closed the piano lid, caressing it. *"Darf ich zur Mitternachtsmesse gehen?"*

She wanted to go to Midnight Mass. Cousin Marta's mouth dropped open in astonishment.

"Of course!" Drew's mom popped to her feet. "We can take you to Mass, can't we?" She motioned for everyone to get up, to hurry before the spell broke. "Grab your coats."

Linda shook her head. "Mom, I can't go. I can't leave Heidi the first night she's mine."

Matthias shook his head as well. "I cannot go. The FDJ says church is superstition. A weapon of the ruling class to dull the minds of workers."

Everyone froze. The magic hanging in the air grew as fragile as spun glass.

Aunt Hilde walked to Matthias and gently pinched his cheek. He stared at her, stunned.

Then she took Linda's hand, patting it as she asked, "*Wirst du dich bei Matthias sicher fühlen?*"

Linda nodded. "I will feel safe with Matthias here."

"*Das ist gut.*" Nodding, indicating things were all settled, she took Cousin Marta's hand. "*Komm.*"

Spellbound as he was by it all, grateful as he was to Matthias for bringing Linda that dog, Drew still couldn't forget the fact that Matthias had snooped in his bedroom. If his cousin thought like Bob, that any contact was a chance to dig up intel—and who was to say Matthias didn't, given his *Jugendweihe* pledge—what might that kid be tempted to do? What might he dig up, left alone except for Linda in an American sergeant's apartment?

"Mom." Drew tugged on her sleeve. "What if—"

Slipping her arm through his, she stopped him. "I know what you are about to say," she whispered. "Have a little faith, honey. 'Tis the season."

JANUARY
1961

UNLATCH COVER
WHEN NOT IN USE

In the continuing space race with Russia, the United States launches Ham the Astro-chimp from Cape Canaveral. He survives a 16-minute suborbital flight, his vital signs and life-support system meticulously monitored in order to perfect one for the human astronauts NASA promises to soon send into space.

JFK's inauguration is one of the coldest ever recorded, after a Nor'easter dumps eight inches of snow on Washington. Seventeen hundred Boy Scouts help shovel Pennsylvania Avenue for the parade. Kennedy speaks directly to the nation's Cold War foe, Russia: "Let both sides join in creating a new endeavor—not a new balance of power, but a new world of law, where the strong are just and the weak secure and the peace preserved."

Great Britain discovers a Russian spy ring sending Allied submarine secrets to Moscow. The KGB had groomed one of them since childhood to blend seamlessly into the culture of Russia's democratic enemies. The Soviet spy had masqueraded as a Canadian playboy, selling jukeboxes and bubblegum machines and driving a large U.S.-imported Studebaker.

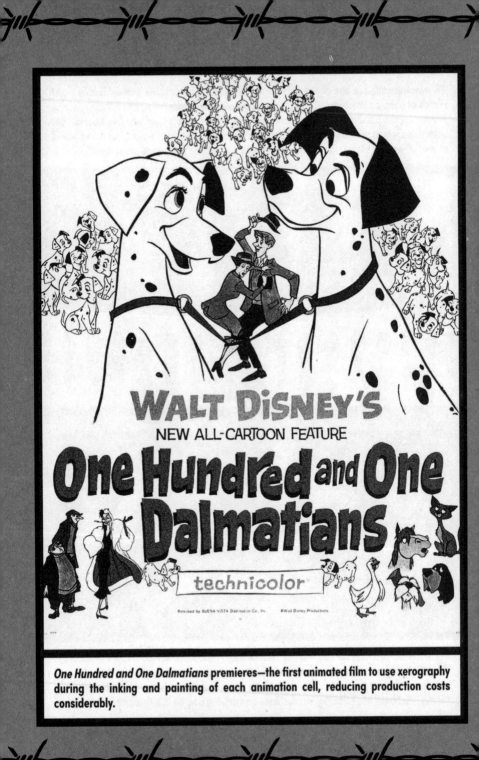

WALT DISNEY'S
NEW ALL-CARTOON FEATURE
One Hundred and One Dalmatians
technicolor

Released by BUENA VISTA Distribution Co., Inc   ©Walt Disney Productions

One Hundred and One Dalmatians premieres—the first animated film to use xerography during the inking and painting of each animation cell, reducing production costs considerably.

CHAPTER SIX

JANUARY
1961

"Careful, son, don't go against the hair growth. Not until you're more practiced at this." Drew's dad was coaching him through his first real shave before Matthias arrived for a sleepover.

Drew dunked his new razor in the sink full of water to rinse it. He'd dealt with a peach-fuzz moustache and a little scruff along his jaw since summer, but the past month had wrought a full-on invasion. Like his face had made some sort of New Year's resolution, a whole lawn of red bristles was growing on his cheeks atop his splotch of freckles. Bob had announced in the cafeteria that Drew could pass for a leprechaun if he let it grow until St. Patrick's Day. He might as well have called Drew a freak.

Then, trying to be all friendly, Bob had elbowed Drew and joked that he could use his wild red beard as great cover someday, shaving after going on a spy mission to avoid being identified. Of course, he'd followed that by asking whether Drew had learned anything worthwhile over Christmas from his "commie cousin."

"What's the matter with you?" Bob had shot back when Drew said he hadn't.

Drew had just walked away, not wanting to admit that the idea of gathering intel on Matthias was making him feel like a total creep since Matthias had brought Linda that dachshund on Christmas Eve.

Sighing, Drew began on the other side of his face.

"That's it. Slow and short."

"Dad"—Drew rinsed again—"did you ever think of joining intelligence?"

His dad laughed. "Is that your way of saying I'm stupid?"

"No, I meant . . ." Drew hesitated, thrown off a bit by his dad's joke. "Did you ever think of being CIA or an intelligence analyst?"

"No, never did," said his dad. "I prefer a unit command—straightforward job. Hold the wall for democracy. Really important, though, our intelligence officers. They're the ones who assess threat levels and let us know what we're walking into during combat."

"What about counterintelligence?"

"Don't have the patience or the poker face for that. CI requires slow-boil coaxing and watching, piecing together little clues until you see the big picture. But those guys are vital, too. They watch for signs of foreign sabotage, enemy infiltration of our ranks, and attempts to recruit and turn Americans. And they devise ways to push back."

Leaning against the tiled wall, Drew's dad crossed his arms. "Truth is, son, the Russians are constantly trying to plant spies among us. Here in Berlin, they exploit East German refugees to do it. Your mom was telling me about two East Berlin mathematicians processed through Marienfelde a year ago. After clearing them, we sent them both to Cape Canaveral—they were that good at calculating equations for space launches. But just this week, the FBI was tipped off that those guys have been sending info about our astronauts back to the Russians!"

"Seriously?" Drew gasped a little. NASA was sacred! "Why would the Germans do that after we helped them escape?"

"Blackmail. You know how hell-bent the Russians are on beating us into space—they wanted inside info. So the KGB had the GDR threaten family members that the two mathematicians left behind in the East."

Drew thought fleetingly of Cousin Marta talking about the doctor's sister who'd been imprisoned after he fled to the West, accused of helping her brother escape. Had that been a ploy to get the doctor to spy as well?

"Hell, the Russians and their Stasi flunkies are really good at that kind of insidious stuff," his dad continued, "putting the squeeze on innocent people to manipulate others. They also spread conspiracy theories, smear American leaders to undermine our elections, and generally gin up arguments among us—anything to fuel division. A house divided against itself and all. Things like that also deflect attention from what jerks like Khrushchev might be doing." He cocked his head. "Why all the questions?"

Shrugging, Drew stayed casual. "Just wondering. That's what Bob's dad does, right?"

"He works in the Berlin Brigade's intelligence office, but I couldn't divulge whether that involves any espionage, son, even if I knew. But I will say Jones definitely has a BTO streak in him. Not sure that's what intelligence really needs."

Big-time operator. The closest Drew's dad ever got to calling someone a blowhard.

"Well, you're not a bragger, Dad. So you'd be good at intel gathering."

His dad laughed. "I'm proud to be protecting Germans who want democracy. And frankly, part of that job is providing cover for intelligence guys so they can keep an eye on the Russians' ulterior motives in Europe. That's why the Soviets are always trying to pressure us out. The free sector of Berlin is the proverbial thorn in their greedy guts."

"Bob was saying I should keep my eyes open whenever I'm over in the East visiting Matthias." Drew stopped short of sharing how anxious Bob was for information to pass along to his dad.

Drew's dad reached over and turned on the hot water faucet. "You want to keep that warm, son." As the water ran and steam rose, he added, "Yeah, it's important to know our enemy, so to speak, even just details of daily life over there. But that's the job of grown-ups, son. Not for high school kids to worry over." He nodded toward the razor. "Keep going."

His answer made Drew smile in relief. And nick the heck out of his chin.

When Matthias arrived, Drew answered the door with three small squares of toilet paper stuck to his chin. His stupid shaving cuts were still bleeding.

Matthias deadpanned, "Taking it on the chin? Is that the saying?"

It took a beat for Drew to catch that Matthias was joking again. "Nah. Keeping my chin up." He motioned with his thumb.

They laughed.

"A strange language, English," Matthias said.

"Say whaaat? German is the strange one. Your words are so long! Like . . . like *Freund-sch-schafts-bejesus.* However you say it."

"*Freundschaftsbezeugung*," Matthias corrected him. "But they are specific. Clear in meaning and . . . poetic. *Freundschaftsbezeugung* means *demonstrations of friendship.* Friendship takes more than words. Action. Yes? Mere words can be . . . empty. Meant to . . . *mmm . . . zwingen?*"

"Coerce." Drew provided the English word, feeling a flicker of discomfort. He wondered what the German word would be for *I don't trust you, but my mom wants me to*

encourage you to defect by becoming your friend, and the guy
across the hall wants me to spy on you as an enemy.

Matthias kept talking, much more open than usual—enthusiastic, even. About words, of all things!

"An English word can mean so many different things." Matthias paused, thinking. "Like *current*—a water tide or a trend. Or *bark*—for a dog or a tree. Or … or … *play*—a drama like Brecht's or a game. Worse—when two different words sound the same. *Descent*—going down—and *dissent*—to disagree. It is most confusing. In conversation, how am I to know which you mean?"

"Okay, hold on." Drew held up his hand. "I just heard a whopper from my German teacher. Your way of saying, 'Let's put an end to this.' *Klappe zu Affe tot.* He said its literal meaning is—"

Matthias finished for him: "Close the lid, the monkey is dead."

"Right! What the heck?"

The boys laughed again.

"Your English is much better these days," Drew complimented his cousin.

"Your German, as well."

Drew nodded. "My German teacher's great. He's helped my comprehension a lot. He's really nice, too. He's going to coach our soccer team, actually. Baseball's my thing, but he needs some bench players as backup. It's a different season, so I can do it. I've been trying to dribble a little with the ball you gave me, but I don't think I'm doing it right. Can you show me?"

Matthias smiled, pleased. "Yes! I will school you."

As Drew trotted to his room to retrieve the ball, it occurred to him that Matthias might know the other American meaning to that phrase—to show him up—and be joking with him again. He chuckled.

In the living room, Matthias demonstrated. "Most important—control the ball." He dropped the ball to the floor and immediately trapped it under his foot before it rolled an inch. Then he pulled it backward up onto his toes and flicked it into the air, bouncing it off his head to land with precision on his knee, where he popped it up to chest height, then off the other knee. "This is the beginning. You learn possession. Touch. Then to dribble, to pass, to match your teammates' stride. But first, you must be able to handle the ball."

Matthias let the ball fall back to his upheld foot, where he balanced it, cradled atop his shoelaces. After a few seconds, he tossed it up again, circled his leg around it as it sank back to earth, caught it atop his other foot, and repeated the juggle. In a final flourish, he trapped the ball between his calves and then hop-flipped it over his back and head to catch it in his hands.

Whoa. Drew applauded.

Linda, too. "You're just like Uwe Seeler!" She'd come out of her room to watch, Heidi at her heels.

Turning, Matthias and Drew stared at her. "You are a Hamburg fan?" Matthias asked with surprise.

"I read the newspapers." She tilted her chin up, a bit defiant. "Hamburg just won the German championships, didn't they?"

"Of *West* Germany, yes."

"And Seeler scored thirteen goals during the championship series, the paper said."

"Yes." Matthias nodded, a smile growing on his face.

"Isn't that a lot?"

Matthias laughed. "Yes!"

Linda smiled back shyly. "Do you really think you can teach Drew to play like that?"

Again, Matthias laughed. "Let's see." He bounced the ball to Drew. "You try, now. Pull it back with your foot. Pop it up and catch in your hands to begin."

Drew pulled back and kicked. The ball hit him in the face.

He tried again, more gently this time. The ball puttered off under the sofa, sending Heidi yapping into a corner.

He tried more force, and the ball flew, bouncing off the keys of his mother's piano—*pling, plang, thud-thud-thud-thud.*

"Hey!" Drew's father appeared from the kitchen. "You two will get me in deep doo-doo with the missus if you hurt that piano! Go outside with that ball. You've got an hour before the sun goes down. Vamoose!"

Linda started to follow.

"Not you, cutie. I need your help, please, pulling together what Mom set up for me to cook tonight."

With a heavy sigh, Linda hung her coat back up.

Outside, Drew was hopping along, cursing, trying to walk off the pain of a throbbing toe, while Matthias shouted, "I said use the *inside* of the foot. Not the tip of your toe!"

The cousins had been passing the ball on the grassy medians of the apartment parking lot, moving farther apart each time Drew managed to boot the ball back to Matthias. Drew was now well out of Matthias's hearing unless he shouted.

That's when Bob showed up. He made a beeline for Drew. "So, whatcha got?"

Drew couldn't be sure, but he thought he caught the same sweet scent of booze in the cloudy vapor of Bob's words that he'd smelled at the Sadie Hawkins dance. "Matthias is teaching me some soccer skills," he answered.

"I mean, whatcha got for me from this guy?" Bob stepped in close.

"Leave off, okay?"

Bob frowned. "Who's gonna make me, Mac? You?"

Back to being called Mac.

They glared at each other.

"Here's the deal, Mac. If I don't feel like you're serious about looking for intel to report to me, I might need to tell *my* dad that I'm worried *your* dad is letting things slip to your buddy over there." He nodded toward Matthias. "And who knows who that card-carrying commie cousin of yours talks to . . ."

Drew felt the blood drain from his face. That kind of rumor could ruin his dad's career. Bob was as bad as the frickin' Stasi! "Are you trying to blackmail me, you

KGB knockoff, you son of a—" Drew's hand curled into a fist.

Bob stepped up to loom over Drew, toe-to-toe. "You calling me—me!—some kind of commie fink?" He drew back his hand, balled, ready to strike.

But before he could land a blow, the soccer ball came hurtling toward them and glanced off Bob's shoulder hard, knocking him back a step.

"*Entschuldigung!* Sorry!" Matthias called, waving. He jogged toward them. "You trying for soccer, too? Need schooling?"

Instantly, Bob planted his feet, ready for a brawl.

Bob was almost a head taller than Matthias and probably had twenty-five pounds on him. Drew had seen how quickly Matthias moved, how wiry he was. But he'd be no match for Bob if it came to blows. Drew started to wave Matthias off, but then he saw that a hand-to-hand fight was not Matthias's plan.

With an almost imperceptible flick, Matthias lofted the soccer ball over Bob's head. He skittered around Bob in time to pop the ball off his own forehead and over Bob again, then ran round to face Bob, stopping the ball with his chest and dropping it back to his foot. He grinned, his eyebrow shooting up in challenge. "Play?"

"You're on," Bob growled.

Matthias pushed the ball to the left, leaning like he was about to sprint in that direction, then struck it to the right with the outside of his right foot, darting around Bob again.

Bob swiveled and kicked out, hoping to steal the ball, but Matthias faked left, right, booted the ball between Bob's legs and ran to catch up to it, dribbling away.

Furious, Bob pursued him. Matthias slowed, waiting. As Bob thundered up behind him, Matthias suddenly stopped the ball so Bob overshot it. Again, he seemed to wait for Bob to steady himself. Then Matthias knocked the ball backward with his heel, waltzed it around and around in two balletic turns, lightly switching feet, flipped the ball into the air, and kneed it over Bob's head again, darting past him to dribble it away.

Bob head spun round trying to follow. He twisted and lurched, and then he fell—right on his butt.

"Damn it!" he bellowed.

Matthias trotted back, pulled Bob to his feet, and brushed him off, apologizing. *"Entschuldigung, Genosse. Nicht dein Sport, denke ich."*

Sorry, comrade. Not your sport, I guess.

Comrade. Drew had to bite his lip to keep from guffawing.

Before Bob could gather his wits, Matthias walked away toward the apartment building. Drew quickly joined him. Throwing his arm over his German cousin's shoulder, Drew said, "That—that 'play' was a high drama of *Freundschaftsbezeugung.* Thank you."

"We have bullies in the East, too," Matthias answered. "I have learned that to confuse them is best."

"That was some pot roast your mom set up for us." Drew's dad patted his stomach and pushed back slightly from the table, tipping his chair backward to stretch.

After a moment, Matthias did the same, awkwardly balancing his chair on its back legs.

Linda imitated Matthias.

"Wonder how the ladies are enjoying the performance," Drew's dad mused. Joyce and Drew's mom were with Cousin Marta and Aunt Hilde at a Berlin Philharmonic concert— part of the reason Matthias was there for the night, and all part of an Emily McMahon grand plan for family bonding. Drew had seen right through her.

"Mrs. McMahon is very excited to meet the conductor," his dad continued, talking to Matthias. "I mean, *very*. I don't know anything about classical music, but she must have all the recordings Herbert von Karajan has made with the orchestra." He gestured to the big record player console under the window. "It was very kind of your grandmother to offer to introduce them. How does she know him?"

"I am not sure. From before the war." Matthias looked uncomfortable. "She does not talk much."

Drew's dad smiled. "Still waters run deep."

Matthias frowned, not understanding.

"A woman of few words," Drew's dad explained. "She sure spoke volumes through the piano at Christmas, though."

"Yes."

"Bet she's enjoying the music. Some important guest artist is performing a Mozart piano concerto, right?"

"She did not go."

Dropping his chair legs back to the floor, Drew's dad asked in surprise, "Why not? I hope she isn't ill."

Matthias looked down at his plate, fidgeting with obvious embarrassment. "She was afraid to leave the apartment when Cousin Emily came with Joyce. She had . . ." He searched for the English word and resorted to German. "*Ein Anfall von Hysterie.* At the door."

"Oh no! We were hoping that Christmas Eve had cured her of those panic attacks."

"*Nein.* They are worse. She shrieks." Matthias turned to Drew, accusation in his expression. "It was Elvis."

Drew shook his head, confused. "Elvis?"

"The record you gave me. The Vopos saw it. In the S-Bahn, on the way home I . . . I pulled it out of my coat to look at it." He stopped and damned himself—"*Dummkopf!*"—then started fiddling with the silverware as he continued. "The Vopos were young and . . . mmm . . . *dienstbeflissen . . . leidenschaftlich.*"

Drew's dad looked to him for translation.

"Zealots."

Matthias nodded. "They are the most dangerous. They pulled us off at the station. They said I was guilty of smuggling Western filth. They started to search *Mutter.* I was very afraid. She carried your other gifts—things that are contraband. That book—that slanders the Party."

"*Animal Farm,*" Drew exhaled. Just as Joyce had predicted.

"Yes. Having that in her bag, she could be accused of treason, of bringing in capitalist propaganda."

Drew heard his dad mutter, "Jesus, Mary, and Joseph."

"But *meine Oma*," Matthias continued, astonishment replacing his embarrassment, "she . . . she stepped in front of *Mutter*. She took hold of the Vopo's coat sleeve. She asked how they could be so . . . mmm . . . *respektlos*."

"Disrespectful," Drew offered.

"Yes. Disrespectful. Of elders. That was not the German way, she said. She told them she knew they were good boys, no matter their uniforms." Matthias's voice cracked. "They stopped. Because of her. They kept Elvis. But they wished us a happy Christmas and let us go. Because of *meine Oma . . .*" He paused to let that wonderment hang in the air. "But at home, the terror returned to her."

Drew had felt his face flush hot, then ice cold as Matthias told his story. That near arrest was his fault. "Matthias, I am so sorry to have caused trouble. I . . . I wasn't thinking."

Abruptly, Matthias stood and carried his plate to the kitchen. Drew's father held up his hand to stop Drew from saying anything else. "Okay, troops," he said, using his army voice, "time to do the dishes."

>)))\k—

Linda, Drew, and their dad were listening to *Gunsmoke* on the radio when Matthias finally emerged from the bathroom. He'd been standing in the shower forever.

When Drew had complained that there'd be no hot water left for his own shower, his dad answered, "That kid can take as much of our hot water as he wants, son. Your mom told me that all she saw in their apartment was a deep old tub with a large kettle attached to its pipes and a tiny coal oven. That's how they have to heat their water. And they sure don't have a shower." He grinned. "Who knew our army-issue apartment was the lap of luxury?"

Rubbing his blond crown of hair with a towel, Matthias came down the hall to join them just as the next program, *Dr. Sixgun*, was announced:

Tonight, Dr. Ray Matson, the hero of Frenchman's Ford, roaming the Wild West with his medicine bag strapped on one hip and a pistol on the other, will need to defend a mail-order bride in distress . . .

"Is this a Western?" Matthias asked.

"Yes!" Linda answered excitedly. Then she blushed and hugged Heidi.

"It's pretty old. They don't play it in the States anymore," said Drew. "But AFN runs it every weekend. It's primo."

"That's right—saddle up for a great program, pardner." Drew's dad adopted a ridiculous Texas twang. "Dr. Sixgun is a man of justice and mercy in the outlaw West."

Matthias plunked himself down right in front of the console. "Cowboys and Indians. Neato."

Drew stared at him.

Matthias flushed. "That is the right word?"

Drew's dad grinned. "It is indeed. I think you need some All-American popcorn, Matthias. We've got that new Jiffy Pop I can cook on the stove." He stood and winked. "I'll be back in a jiff. Get it? Jiff—jiffy."

Linda and Drew both rolled their eyes. But Matthias chortled.

Later that night, lying in a sleeping bag on the floor of Drew's bedroom, Matthias said, "I like your father."

"Yeah. He's a good guy." Drew's dad had been his best self that evening—goofy, relaxed. Lying very still, Drew asked the question he'd been wondering about ever since he'd met Matthias. "What happened to your dad? Did he die in the war, like your brothers? During the bombing?"

Wrapped in the darkness, Matthias was invisible to Drew except for the lump of his silhouette. "He never came home from the Eastern Front."

So Matthias's father did fight for Hitler's army. Drew weighed that information. Maybe the guy was career military, which would mean he might not have been a member of the Nazi Party. Although it was more likely he'd *had* to join. Even if he'd been halfhearted about it, that was a heck of a family bloodline.

Matthias rolled over. "Thank you for the very nice day. *Gute Nacht. Schlaf gut.*"

"Yeah," Drew responded quietly, "you too, man." But his head was full of confusing thoughts that were sure to keep him awake for a while. A commie cousin with a Nazi father. *Swell.* But Drew had to be honest—he liked Matthias.

The distant sound of grinding metal and sharp scrape-squeaking woke Drew and Matthias at sunrise.

"*Was zum Teufel?*" Matthias shot up and crawled to the window to look out.

Drew rubbed his eyes and listened, recognizing the sound. "It's just a field drill of our armored divisions in the Grunewald."

Running along the edge of the British and American sectors, the forest was enormous—more than seven thousand acres—and the perfect place for military exercises to keep Allied troops on their toes. Hearing troop movements at dawn always unnerved Drew a bit, too. It was a harsh reminder of the deadly backdrop of their lives in Berlin.

Drew knew that Matthias might say the exercises were evidence of the Soviet claim that the Allies were warmongers, posturing and threatening the East. Of course, his dad and everyone else in the Berlin Brigade would say the practice maneuvers were to counter the regular exercises done by the Russians who surrounded Berlin and vastly outnumbered the combined American, British, and French forces. Tensing, Drew sat up, awaiting some political barb.

But Matthias turned away from the window and sniffed. Sniffed again. "Bacon!" he said with hushed excitement. He got to his feet and padded to the kitchen.

"Good morning, boys!" Drew's mom trilled, putting plates overflowing with eggs and biscuits and bacon in front of them and Drew's dad. As she did, she kissed them all—including Matthias—on the head. Matthias blanched but didn't protest.

"The concert last night was glorious, and oh—meeting the maestro," she sighed, as starstruck as any Elvis fan. "Even though Aunt Hilde didn't come, we still got to go backstage afterward. Von Karajan was as charismatic in person as he is on the podium. And oh my goodness, boys, another friend of his came backstage—Elizabeth Grummer!" She looked at them expectedly.

They gazed back at her blankly.

"The opera singer! She was nice as could be. She offered to give Joyce lessons!" Drew's mom plopped herself down across from them. "Isn't that amazing?" She looked from one to another, waiting.

Drew's dad held up his empty cup. "Um, is there any coffee this morning?"

"Oh! What am I thinking? Of course!"

As she swept to the stove to retrieve the pot, Drew's dad explained to Matthias, "Mrs. McMahon's enthusiasm and joy is why I fell for her. But sometimes I need a cup of joe to keep up." He grinned at Drew's mom as she poured. "Now, please start over, honey."

It had snowed about two inches during the night—nothing unusual for Berlin, but Drew's dad offered to drive Matthias home rather than making him wait in the slushy S-Bahn rail station. The Bonneville fishtailed a bit through the streets, but Drew knew it cut a pretty blue streak through the fresh snow.

They swung south and then due east through the American sector, coming to the border and Zimmerstraße by way of Schöneberger Straße. Down the long block, they spotted two young West German policemen pacing back and forth, mirroring two East German Vopos on the other side of the street. Matthias leaned forward from the back seat and asked, "Can you pull over, please? I wish to walk from here."

"Sure, kid."

Before last night, Drew might have sniped, "Ashamed to be seen with us?" But now, given the terrifying shakedown Matthias had described at dinner, Drew understood Matthias not wanting to call attention to his American ride.

Pulling over to parallel park, Drew's dad announced that he was going to check out the tobacco shop on the corner. A series of shacklike booths dotted the Western edge of Potsdamer Platz, selling magazines from London and Paris and American cigarettes, toothpaste, shoes, and razor blades. East Berliners hovered nearby until the Vopos rounded the corner, then rushed to purchase a few items and darted back to their houses just as the East Germans reappeared.

The boys stood beside the car, watching the four enemy guards approach each other as they patrolled, then stop and talk for a moment—friendly—before splitting up to continue walking their beats.

"That was weird," Drew murmured through the scarf he'd pulled around his face against the January cold.

"Oh, they do that." Matthias shrugged. "They grew up together. That line"—he nodded to the white streak painted down the middle of Zimmerstraße—"means little in this neighborhood. Each summer, the mayor of Kreuzberg—the borough we stand in now—hosts a festival. He invites all of us living across the street in the Russian sector to celebrate childhood with those on the Western side. A *Kinderfest*." He smiled at Drew. "There is a carousel, puppet shows, fire-works. You should come."

"I'd like that," Drew answered.

Their breathing wreathed them in cloudy vapors. It was hard for Drew to tell which exhale belonged to him, which to his cousin.

"Do not mistake me," Matthias said slowly, considering each word. "I still believe our society is more just than yours, more fair to workers." Then he added, totally straight-faced, "You fascist, petty bourgeois," before he punched Drew's shoulder and smiled wryly.

Drew laughed.

"But . . ." Matthias watched the Vopos pace. "I begin to see how . . . mmmm . . . *un*just is the way . . ." He paused.

"The way they threaten and police you?" Drew offered quietly.

Matthias nodded, turning to go home.

"Hey, Matthias?"

"Yes?"

"Thanks for your help with Bob yesterday." Drew knelt and packed snow into a tight ball. "I can't do squat with a soccer ball, but if you ever need me to return the favor, I can do this." He pointed to an empty, dilapidated house a good hundred yards away. "See that building?"

Matthias eyed it. "No way you hit that."

"Oh yeah?" Drew flexed. "Watch this."

He pulled his arm back and whipped it forward with force. The snowball lofted, spinning fast toward the building, a beautiful missile rocketing toward its target. But just before hitting the dingy brick wall, its arc curved down. The snowball dropped. And splatted on the back of a Vopo's head!

"*Scheiße!*" Matthias dropped to the ground and hid behind the Bonneville's enormous front bumper. "Get down," he hissed at Drew.

The Vopo whirled around, fumbling to yank his Russian-issue AK-47 rifle off his shoulder. "*Wir werden angegriffen!*" he shouted to tell his comrade that they were under attack.

But his patrol partner bent over, belly laughing at him, and gestured toward the West German guards, obviously assuming *they* were the culprits. The communist youth knelt and made his own snowball, vaulting it at one of his friend-enemies for a direct hit.

"*Was zum Teufel!*" The West Germans guffawed and quickly packed snowballs to hurl across the line, each landing with a terrific splatter on the Vopo's chest.

"*Du willst es nicht anders, Bruder!*" Another gleeful throw. Another hit.

And another.

People on the street tensed, ready to sprint and scatter. Worried faces appeared at the windows. But all they saw were four German teenagers bombarding one another with snowballs, slipping in the snow, and shouting playful taunts in sheer joy.

And for those few moments, Drew witnessed everyone on that corner of Berlin laugh—together.

He walked with Matthias to the corner and then watched his cousin disappear down the street before going back to the Bonneville. His dad got there at the same time. "Dad, did you see those guards throwing snowballs at each other? That was so funny. It all started when I pitched a—"

They both froze. On the windshield, carefully tucked under the wipers, was a sealed envelope addressed to Sergeant Major James McMahon, U.S. Army.

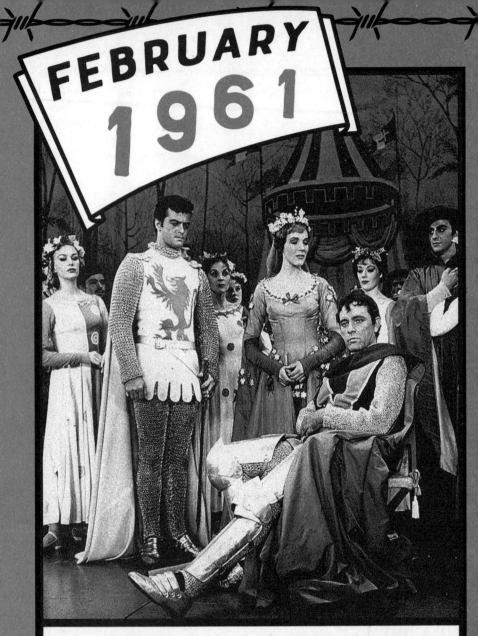

FEBRUARY 1961

The musical *Camelot*—about King Arthur, his code of chivalry, and his charming queen—becomes a metaphor for the idealistic, glamorous Kennedy administration. Fans flock to Broadway to see Julie Andrews, Richard Burton (King Arthur) and Robert Goulet (Lancelot) in the starring roles. The adaptation of T. H. White's *The Once and Future King* runs for 873 performances and wins four Tony Awards.

Bonanza bucks the typical Western convention of gunslingers and main street showdowns that America was known for across the world. The Cartwright family lives on their Ponderosa ranch, near an old mining boomtown, and settles regional disputes with the force of personality and folksy diplomacy. The show runs for fourteen seasons.

A
N
D

Economist Robert C. Weaver becomes the first African American to lead a major U.S. government agency when JFK appoints him administrator of the Housing and Home Finance Agency.

The touch-tone phone is invented, though it will take years for it to replace the rotary model.

CHAPTER SEVEN
FEBRUARY
1961

"They're still there, Mom." Drew was staring out the living room window at the Volkswagen bus parked across from the building's front entrance. It'd been there almost three weeks, ever since the night Matthias had slept over.

"Try not to notice."

"Try not to notice? It's a VW bus sitting right in front of our apartment. It's kind of hard to ignore."

Getting up from her piano, Drew's mom gazed out the window. "It's just a precaution, honey. They're going to give the surveillance another week or so more for good measure. Then things will go back to normal."

After having a team of MP bodyguards keeping watch over them round the clock, Drew's definition of *normal* would never be the same again.

"I should really make those boys some cookies," his Mom mused. "It's so cold here in February. I hope they have something hot to drink."

Drew threw his hands up in exasperation. "How can you think about snacks when the army thinks we're in enough danger to need a round-the-clock protective detail?"

"Oh, it's not that big of a deal, sweetheart." She tried to pull him into a hug.

But Drew dodged her. "Mom, I don't know anyone else who's had a mysterious envelope left on their windshield by the Stasi, or the KGB, or whoever it was."

"You'd be surprised." His mom lowered her voice, as if someone could overhear. "Mrs. Jones told me her husband has received a number of recruiting letters just like that one, left willy-nilly on their car or in their mailbox. She even found one in her grocery bags one time—at the commissary. On an American post! That's how audacious they are. Russian intelligence and the Stasi are perpetually fishing."

"Offering an officer ten thousand dollars a month to turn traitor?"

Drew's mom quickly reached out and took his arm. Her face paled. "How did you know that, honey? Were you eavesdropping on Dad and me?" She pulled him over to sit on the sofa beside her. Taking both his hands, she waited until he was looking her full in the eye before she spoke. "I'm going to talk to you right now like the man you almost are, and I need you to listen carefully to every word."

She didn't continue until Drew nodded. "Berlin is a complicated place, sweetheart. It's riddled with suspicions and the hardest of choices—like having to leave behind everything you love to escape a police state that claims to be all about helping workers but is really about exploiting them. All while the Communist Party leaders get rich and fat off their labor, just like those pigs in *Animal Farm*.

"Frankly, Stalin was as bad as Hitler in terms of purging entire groups of people. And Khrushchev may not be that much better. He was the one who ordered Russian tanks to roll into East Berlin to crush the workers' protests here a few years ago. And he's the one who is now threatening to ignore West Berlin's right to exist and to forcibly annex the city to be the capital of East Germany. He could order tanks into the city again any minute, but this time against *us*."

Drew squirmed. *Thanks for reminding me, Mom*, he thought.

She softened. "I'm sorry that life here is a perpetual standoff, honey. But we should be proud of helping Dad and the United States hold an outpost of freedom against communism and its oppression."

She squeezed Drew's hands. "Now, this is the most important part for your dad. Because the stakes here are so high, American personnel in Berlin have to be squeaky clean, above any kind of rumors or questions of loyalty. You remember that your dad did *not* open that envelope when you two found it, correct?"

Drew remembered. He couldn't believe his dad hadn't torn it open on the spot.

"He took it immediately to his CO."

"Yes."

"So the only way your dad knows the letter's contents, or that the Russians or East Germans tried to recruit him, is because his commanding officer told him. The CO even kidded that your dad could be a very rich man if he took the bribe. That's what you overheard your dad telling me."

"Yeah, Mom—so?"

"Soooooooo, if your dad *had* opened the letter himself without a superior officer present, HQ might have worried that your dad had already read the offer, been tempted by the bribe, decided to become a Soviet mole, and only then turned in the letter to his CO as cover."

Drew shook his head, following her trail of logic. "That's crazy."

"Maybe so. But even a hint of such concerns about him could mean your dad wouldn't be given sensitive assignments anymore. He might even be rotated back to the States."

Pointing toward the window, Drew's mom suddenly looked oddly paranoid. "Besides protecting us, I worry those gentlemen might be keeping a log of your dad's comings and goings . . ." She trailed off.

"What?" Drew spluttered. "You can't be serious, Mom."

She seemed transfixed, her gaze still on the window.

"Mom!"

Startling slightly, Drew's mom tried to sound breezy. "I'm sure I'm being ridiculous, honey. I've heard too many horror stories from the refugees, I suppose. Too many conspiracy theories. But"—she kissed his hand before concluding—"it is critically important to remember what I've said. And please do not let on to Linda about this. No need to frighten her."

"What about Matthias?" After their sleepover, Drew was beginning to consider Matthias a friend. His cousin was coming that afternoon to go swimming in the army's indoor pool with him and Charlie, Shirley, Joyce, Linda, and a new friend Linda had made while walking her dog. His mom had gone to all sorts of trouble to wrangle special permission for a guest—entry required an American ID. "Shouldn't he be warned, Mom? The jerk who left Dad that envelope could be someone who knows Matthias and tailed us when we took him home."

"Marta and I have already talked about the envelope so she could be on guard," his mom replied. "But she doesn't want Matthias to know. She's afraid that he is . . ." His mom pressed her lips together.

"That he is what?"

"Under pressure . . . maybe in trouble with the FDJ. They use kids against kids over there, you know." Shaking her head in sympathy, Drew's mom said, "One of the refugee families I processed last week at Marienfelde told me their son—a bit younger than you—was reported for lack of enthusiasm at the Russian's annual May Day parade. By a boy he thought was his best friend." She paused. "Can you imagine? The complaint went into his school file as *Schwäche*, official demerits. Each student has to keep a little black book of records, which parents sign weekly, so his mother saw the demerits."

Wow. Drew couldn't imagine his every move, his every

facial expression being scrutinized like that. He'd be in big trouble if they were.

"At the end of the school year, the boy was told he didn't have the proper attitude for university. He was expelled from the academic high school. The GDR assigned him instead to a trade school for masons. The boy had dreamed of becoming a violinist, but he mishandled a cement block and crushed his hand."

An involuntary shiver ripped through Drew. "Why would a kid rat on his friend like that?" he blurted.

"Fanaticism breeds that kind of betrayal, honey," his mom said sadly. "Plus, the government rewards them for it. The GDR sends teenagers up on roofs of apartments and row houses to hunt for TV antennas turned to receive signals from West Germany. When they find them, they break them off. For that, the teens earn a tracksuit like the Olympic teams wear."

"What the—" Drew spat out. "Why do Cousin Marta and Matthias stay there?"

His mom sighed. "Marta wants to finish her training to be a doctor so she can help other women in her sector, give them decent medical care. Plus, once she is a doctor, there are personal benefits—more food rations, the promise of university for Matthias. She'd lose all that if she crossed into the West. Still . . ." She paused, thinking. "As long as the border stays open between East and West Berlin so that she and Matthias can come and go, it makes sense, I suppose. But I know Marta thinks about defecting. Unfortunately, Aunt Hilde's fears and inability to leave their house is a problem. It's evidently gotten worse since Christmas."

Drew squirmed again, this time with guilt. That Elvis record the Vopos had found on Matthias on the S-Bahn—he was to blame for that. Part of the reason Drew had given Matthias the record was to remind his commie cousin that the music he loved was banned by East Germany's censors. Just as his gift of *Animal Farm* was meant to open Matthias's eyes to communism's corruption and cruelties. But Drew had never meant to get him in trouble. And Aunt Hilde's renewed agoraphobia and panic attacks were technically Drew's fault, too. He felt terrible.

"Remember that oath to the state Matthias signed?"

His mom's question pulled Drew back to her. He nodded. How could he forget?

"Right now, Matthias is a believer. Marta doesn't want to lose her last son. Her other two boys—I think they wouldn't listen to her, and ..."

"What?"

Drew's mom hesitated and then said carefully, "I'm trusting you not to repeat this, because it would hurt her standing at the hospital. My instincts were right. Marta recently confided that she tried to get her boys out before the final days of street fighting against the Russian army. But they were recruited by the Nazis for Operation Werewolf. Twelve-year-olds were convinced to fight on for the fatherland, even though it meant certain death. They were told that such a sacrifice ... was somehow noble. Boys manned the last guns. Only a handful survived. Marta's boys died in a final stand, protecting Charité Hospital as the staff inside tended the wounded."

"Cousin Marta's hospital?"

"Yes." She gazed at Drew sorrowfully. "I think . . . that's another reason she stays."

Drew swallowed, his mouth suddenly dry.

"Anyway, all this is why your befriending Matthias means so much to me, sweetheart. If he comes to trust you, perhaps it will help him see the good in the West and make him want to leave. So, for right now, the less Matthias knows about that letter, the safer it is for him. Marta suspects the teenager who lives on their home's top floor might be a Stasi informer. And Matthias is friends with him."

"That guy who shouted *Freundschaft* the day we met Aunt Hilde?" Drew choked on the irony.

"Yes. She doesn't know for sure that the boy spies for the Stasi, but she suspects." His mom stood. "Just try to have fun this afternoon, honey."

Sure. No problem with that now . . .

"I don't think he's coming," Linda said, disappointment in her voice. She shifted her dachshund in her arms and gently stroked the old dog's head. "Is he, Heidi?"

Sitting beside her on the couch, Joyce looked up at Drew—who'd been pacing, mulling over the conversation he'd had with his mom and getting more and more agitated—and said, "I think we'd better go ahead, don't you?

Matthias is an hour late. Everyone else is waiting." She and Drew were both excited that Linda had made a new friend—finally—and Joyce clearly didn't want to screw that up by making the girl wait.

"I wish Cousin Marta had a telephone," murmured Linda. "It's not like Matthias to—" She broke off as the sound of shouting exploded from Bob's apartment across the stairwell.

Joyce and Drew exchanged a knowing glance as their mother emerged from the kitchen, wiping her hands with a towel as she listened, too. "Why don't you ask Bob to join you?" she suggested quietly.

Drew wanted to say she shouldn't be so quick to invite Bob into their fold. Maybe he should tell her that Bob had threatened to spread rumors about his dad being soft on commies and letting slip sensitive information to their East Berlin cousins. Heck, if Bob were to be questioned by the MPs in that VW bus, he might tell them his accusations if he were in one of his bad moods and mad at Drew for not coughing up intel drawn from Matthias.

Drew opened his mouth but then stopped. His mom had her do-gooder Emily McMahon look; there was no arguing with that.

Sighing, he opened the door and crossed the hall. His knock cut short an overly loud command: "C'mon, boy, that's not the way! Put up your dukes and—"

Instinctively, Drew took a step back as the door flew open and Bob appeared, red-faced. "Mac. What's up?" Bob's typical bluster was laced with even more defensiveness than usual.

"We're heading to the pool. Wanna come?" Was that a flicker of relief on Bob's face?

"Who is it?" Sergeant Jones barked from inside.

"Drew," Bob shouted back.

A momentary silence. "Jim McMahon's boy? Tell *that* kid you're busy."

Bob pursed his lips. "Thanks, but no thanks, Mac. Sorry." Then he closed the door, not looking Drew in the eye.

What the heck did the sergeant mean by *that kid*? Drew leaned against the closed door and tried to eavesdrop, but the voices inside had quieted.

He crossed the landing back to his family's apartment. "No dice, Mom," Drew announced as he reentered. "We should probably go."

As he and his sisters tumbled out the building's front door, gasping at the February chill and yanking on their mittens, Drew threw a furtive look toward the van. Two guys sat in the front, all bundled up, anything but inconspicuous. Heeding his mom's order to not let on to Linda, he kept silent.

But Linda smiled and waved—at the van!

"Who . . . who are you waving at, sis?" he asked.

"The men, silly. The men watching us."

Drew and Joyce stopped in their tracks, staring at their little sister.

"They're really nice," Linda went on. "I was out walking Heidi with Patty, and Heidi bolted away from me. She can run faster than you think! One of those guys caught her for me." She smiled. "He told me never to talk to other men who might try to catch Heidi, though. And I told him I knew better than to talk to strangers—I'm not a baby. And then Patty told me about a man trying to convince the daughter of a colonel to get into a car last year at the Grunewald. The MPs nabbed him—he was an East German spy! The MPs had been watching the colonel's family because of some weird message he'd gotten from the KGB and because of how important the colonel is to the Berlin Brigade's mission." She looked up at Drew. "Guess Daddy's really important now!"

She skipped ahead. "Hurry up. Patty's waiting for us!"

Joyce looked at Drew with horror on her face.

"Yeah, I know." Drew nodded, grim. "Let's not let Linda out of our sight for a while." They hurried after her.

Drew and Charlie came to a halt just outside the one-time Nazi compound that housed an indoor practice pool Hitler had built for the 1936 Olympics. They stared up at the twenty-foot stone relief statues flanking the entrance. Charlie saluted and blew a raspberry.

Shirley swatted him. "Quit it," she teased.

"Can't help it. These guys get me every time."

The statues were of two muscular male athletes—one holding a sword, the other a discus—triple the height of real humans, totally naked, totally to scale, and totally anatomically correct.

Linda's new friend Patty elbowed her and whispered, "Ewww, that's so gross."

Linda inched away from Drew and Charlie, suddenly horribly uncomfortable to be standing next to them.

Gently, Joyce put her arm through Linda's and pulled her close. "Thank goodness Bob isn't here. Can you imagine what he'd say about those?" She nodded toward the equally impressive females nearby.

Charlie snorted. "Bob does know some fascinating stuff, though. You know how these buildings were the headquarters for the SS during World War II?"

Drew and Shirley nodded somberly. Military brats all knew about the infamous *Schutzstaffel*, Hitler's elite Aryan corps most responsible for carrying out the Nazis' horrifying "final solution" and notorious for brutal interrogations of downed Allied flyers.

"Well, before the SS, this place was a military academy with lots of statues of German soldiers. The main gate was guarded by two massive 'eternal corporals' called *Rottenführer.*"

"I've never seen those," Drew commented.

"That's because—according to Bob—the statues were so solidly embedded in the gate's columns that destroying them would've meant tearing down and rebuilding the entire entrance. So when the American Army took over the building, we just poured concrete over them to hide them. Now those pillars are full of cracks. Bob says locals claim it's because the German spirit is trying to break free and rise again."

"How does Bob hear that kind of stuff?" Drew asked. His dad's assets? Was that the right spy term?

Charlie shrugged.

"Well, I heard the ghosts that really haunt this place are the victims of the Night of the Long Knives," said Shirley. "All those government bureaucrats and journalists who were rounded up and murdered here in this courtyard because they opposed Hitler. One of my dad's men swears that at night, he hears a voice crying '*Gib Acht*.' Beware!"

They all stood in silence for a moment.

"Hey, didn't you say Matthias was coming with us today?"

Drew winced, recognizing what had prompted Charlie to mention Matthias at that particular moment. "He didn't show up," Drew said, trying to sound unperturbed. In fact, he was worried that his cousin not showing was somehow connected with the envelope and the presence of those MPs. His head was filled with new suspicions after that conversation with his mom. If Matthias was such a believer, could he have been in on the KGB or Stasi attempt to recruit his dad? Drew ground his teeth at the thought.

He started walking briskly to end the discussion and swim back into normal American teenage life, just an afternoon of hanging out with friends who had no weird walls of Cold War prejudice and paranoia standing between them. "Let's go in. I'm freezing."

Charlie dove into the pool first, popped up, and treaded water. "Come on, girls," he called. Linda and Patty were testing the water with their feet while hugging bleached-white towels around themselves. "Last one in is a rotten egg! Make it be Drew!" He rolled over and freestyled away to lead the charge.

Chuckling, Drew stalled on the starting block at his lane's edge. Charlie—who had only older brothers—somehow knew there was no way Linda and Patty would drop their towels and dive in until he swam away to give them a little privacy. Charlie's easy understanding of all sorts of people was one of the things that made him such a born leader. Like the majority of brats, Charlie was aiming for West Point and then a service career of his own. The difference was that Drew would unquestioningly follow Charlie into battle if he asked. A guy like Bob—not so much.

Charlie's strategy worked. Linda jumped in and waited for her friend to join her. Holding hands, they dunked themselves, giggling.

Launching himself off the edge to plunge deep into the cool liquid, Drew let himself glide just below the surface for a few moments. He swept the water back in strokes like a bird's wings beating. It was the closest feeling he could imagine to sliding through air, aloft. He lingered, shimmying through the watery weightlessness, until he thought his lungs would burst.

Surfacing, he coughed and sucked in air. Turning on his back, he floated, looking up at the prism of skylights and the two-story, floor-to-ceiling windows that the frigid winter air had frosted in tiny patterns like cutout paper snowflakes. The musical echo of swimmers' splash and surge, ricocheting off the glass, swirled in the air like the light steam rising off the heated water. It was an incredibly beautiful building for a pool. Drew wondered fleetingly about the Nazi athletes who had trained in it and whether Matthias's brothers had ever swum in these waters.

Then Drew rolled over and started to swim, slow, methodical, testing the flex and strength of his muscles. He would need to complete four hundred meters continuously, two lengths of the fifty-meter pool for each stroke—back, breast, butterfly, free—to earn his lifesaving badge.

He and Charlie passed each other mid-lap several times before they ended up holding on to the same wall, breathing hard, just shy of the eight laps that made up four hundred meters.

"Next week I'll make it," puffed Charlie.

"Me too. Just gotta build up to it," heaved Drew.

"You were making some pretty decent time. If we'd started at the same moment, you'd have beaten me," Charlie complimented. "What sport are you going to do in the spring?"

"Track."

"Me too!" Charlie did a back push-up to lift himself onto the pool's edge, making a puddle as his trunks drained. "You know, Bob is a pole-vaulter. And stellar in shot put. He'll be on the team, too."

Drew groaned.

Charlie laughed. "Aww, c'mon. Quality time with your nemesis!"

"You know, the weirdest thing just happened with Bob," Drew began, but he stopped short with a sudden realization. The van. His mom's fear that the MPs might be keeping a log on his dad as well as a protective eye on the family. Sergeant Jones worked in intelligence. *God almighty.* Drew caught his breath. How had he not seen it earlier? He'd just experienced a shunning. Bob's dad didn't want him to be around Jim McMahon's boy—*that* kid— until command knew for sure that Drew's dad wasn't a traitor.

"What weird thing?" Charlie asked. "You okay, man?"

"Yeah," Drew muttered. Would Charlie want to keep his distance, too, if Drew told him about the van and Sergeant Jones? "It's . . . it's nothing. Just thinking."

"Suit yourself, buddy. But you know I'm all ears if you need to think aloud." Charlie gazed across the pool to the deep end, where Joyce skip-bounced off the diving platform to soar, arms outstretched, before bowing forward to flip herself into a pointed-toe arrow, piercing the water with barely a sound.

"Wow. Where did she learn that?" Charlie murmured.

Where did Joyce learn anything, Drew thought. It was almost as if she could do everything she attempted from the get-go. "She just went to the pool in Arlington every day last summer."

Charlie sighed, long and wistful. The guy had it bad.

"Think she'd ever compete as a diver, like that East German girl who just won the gold medals?" he asked.

"Naw. She's concentrating on her music. She just started taking singing lessons with some opera diva in town. I think Joyce is already completely focused on next year and college. You know"—he made himself sound as offhand as possible to avoid embarrassing his friend—"she's dating some guy at Free University."

Charlie straightened up abruptly, like Drew had jabbed him with a stick. "Lucky fella," he said, lost in thought for a few beats. "Hey, I thought you were thinking of trying soccer."

"God, no way." Drew laughed ruefully. "I'm a total doofus with my feet."

"Isn't Matthias some soccer wunderkind? Bet he could teach you some skills."

"Oh man, you shoulda seen him—" Drew started to tell Charlie about Matthias schooling Bob, but he broke off again as he noticed Shirley sitting near the diving platforms.

Charlie grinned at him. "And you think *I'm* the pity case?" He dropped back into the water. "I'm going to swim some more laps to improve my butterfly—it stinks. Good luck, buddy." Charlie plunged forward, struggling with the double over-the-head strokes and undulation needed for the butterfly. Charlie was right about his technique. Some people might have mistaken it for an overly enthusiastic dog paddle—or a guy drowning.

As nonchalantly as he could in a crowded pool—which wasn't very, he knew—Drew breaststroked his way over to

Shirley. She was swishing her legs in the water, watching Joyce climb the five-meter platform and swan dive into the deep end, yet again with hardly a ripple. Finally bobbing beside her, Drew asked, "Aren't you coming in? The water's great."

"I will in a minute." Shirley fluttered her feet in the water some more. "Talking about those statues out front just set me to thinking."

Drew threw his arm up to hang on to the tile along the pool's rim, submerged from his chest down, feeling too wet and goose-bumpy to sit beside her. "A *Pfennig* for your thoughts," he joked, then flushed, knowing he sounded totally lame.

Turning her gaze from Joyce to him, Shirley said, "I don't want to unload on you."

"I don't mind." He shrugged, loosening his hold on the wall so he slipped and dunked himself. *So suave.* Drew resurfaced, shook his head of water, and wiped his eyes to see her brushing off the droplets he'd splattered on her.

Shirley laughed—she really was a good sport. "Okay, you asked for it. I'll give you a whole Deutsche Mark's worth." She sobered. "Those statues by the entrance—they're so . . . such idealizations of the human form."

Idealization. Shirley was the A-plus kind of smart, sure to be a National Honor Society kid next year. Drew really liked that about her, how she stretched his brain. He nodded, encouraging her to go on.

"But whose ideal is it? Certainly not mine. It's the *Aryan* ideal. It's so weird here in Berlin, how we just walk around in places where so many people were murdered, in the ruins of Nazism. Swimming in a pool Hitler built to train Third Reich athletes to dominate the Olympics and eventually the world . . ." She reflexively yanked her legs out of the tainted water and wrapped her arms around her knees.

"These people . . ." She closed her eyes and shuddered slightly. "Nearly half a million American men and women died fighting in World War II. A lot of them to stop Nazis from slaughtering Jews and other ethnic groups they considered a scourge on their lily-white, blue-eyed Aryan *ideal*. . . And here we are now, our dads protecting the freedoms of the very people who killed millions and millions of souls. And doubly ironic, there are people back home in the States waving swastikas and spewing Hitler-worthy hatred about American Blacks and Jews." Agitated, Shirley chewed on a fingernail. "You know my nana?"

Drew nodded.

"She's Jewish. The people who carved those statues— they'd have gleefully gassed her. And guess what? According to the Nazis, Nana's heritage would make me a 'quarter Jew,' which would have been enough for the SS to label me a '*mischling* of the second degree.' A human 'mongrel.' I would have been prevented from attending schools or marrying a German so I wouldn't sully the purity of his Aryan bloodline. And I might have been sent to a concentration camp, too."

Drew felt a wave of nausea at the idea. Without thinking, he put his hand on her knee protectively.

"See, I told you that you didn't want to hear what was rolling around in my head." Shirley smiled wanly. "I . . . I just don't understand how people have so much hate in them. I mean, I know intellectually that it comes from fear and ignorance. Looking for scapegoats. But . . ." She trailed off.

"It's beaten into them, I guess," Drew muttered. He repeated part of what his mom had said about Matthias and his Hitler Youth brothers: "It gets stuffed into their heads through the lies and conspiracy theories and prejudices their political leaders spit out."

Shirley looked down at him. "You're thinking of your cousin, aren't you?"

Frowning, Drew nodded.

They were silent for a few moments, and then Shirley spoke again, softly. "You know the thing about Karl Marx? What he wrote in his socialist manifesto is so . . . so . . . *idealized*, to keep using that word. But it's really humane, too. He proposed making the world better by making it more equal, by offering the same opportunities to everyone, regardless of class. But today's communists twist Marx's concept, making it about repression, censorship, retribution, and painting democracy as evil. I can see how a smart guy like Matthias might cling to the original ideals, though."

She shrugged. "You know, my nana always says if you stand in someone else's shoes for a while, you can understand their walk better. But that doesn't mean you shouldn't try to help that person pick another pair."

Drew laughed. "A wise woman." His hand was still on Shirley's knee. He smiled up at her. "I hope I get to meet her someday."

Shirley met his gaze, then looked away, suddenly shy. "Me too," she murmured. Then she stood up abruptly. "Race you to the end of the lane!" she cried, and dove over him, leaving Drew in a blinding splash and a wake of churned-up bubbles.

MARCH 1961

Vice President Lyndon Johnson chairs JFK's Committee on Equal Employment Opportunity. JFK's executive order requires—for the first time—government contractors to "take affirmative action to ensure that applicants are employed . . . without regard to their race, creed, color, or national origin."

PEACE CORPS

JFK creates the Peace Corps, a legion of recent college grads to work for two years in underdeveloped, "third-world" nations. Volunteers teach things like better farming techniques and how to engineer running water in remote villages. JFK hopes the corps will not only instill the ideal of service among young Americans but that the program's non-military, humanistic methods will also combat the spread of communism—believing that people who see a way out of poverty and make strides to self-sufficiency are less vulnerable to collectivism's false promises.

NASA's Goddard Space Flight Center opens in Greenbelt, MD, where the Army Signal Corps engineers design the first weather satellite. The innovation will allow scientists to spot developing weather fronts from space and warn Americans of impending storms.

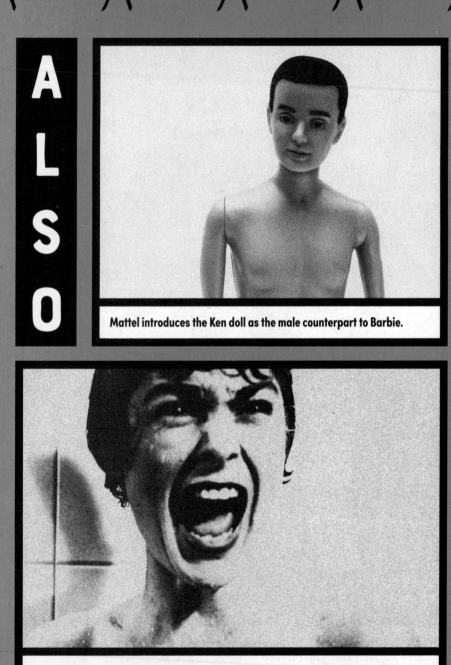

ALSO

Mattel introduces the Ken doll as the male counterpart to Barbie.

Janet Leigh wins the Golden Globe award for best supporting actress for *Psycho*.

CHAPTER EIGHT
MARCH
1961

Drew rounded a landing in his apartment building's stairwell, heading to the laundry room on the top floor. He paused to look out the big window toward the parking lot, just to make sure what he'd seen earlier that day was true. Yes! No VW bus. *Thank God*, he thought. The MP bodyguards—or the totally unfair surveillance of his dad—were finally gone after five weeks and six days. All clear.

Shifting the empty basket to his hip, Drew took in the sight of purple crocuses blooming along the sidewalks. He saluted the early-spring flowers, a sign of new beginnings. Maybe now he could stop looking over his shoulder constantly. A hymn his mom was teaching Linda to play in anticipation of Easter leapt into his mind: *Welcome, happy morning! Age to age shall say* . . . He climbed the last few steps humming its melody.

His mom was at Marienfelde for the day—again—and she'd asked him to do his own wash. She seemed to be gone more than she was at home these days. But Drew easily shook off the little flare of resentment he felt. His mom's work at Marienfelde was for the greater good, after all. That's what Shirley would say, he bet.

Drew smiled at the thought of Shirley and pushed the door open to a burst of heat scented with detergent. Leaning over to drag his dry underwear and T-shirts into the basket, he started singing aloud, "Hell today is vanquished, heav'n is won today. Lo, the dead— Jeez Louise!" Drew about jumped out of his skin.

Bob was sitting on the floor, leaning up against the back of the machines.

"What the hell are you doing down there?" Drew demanded. Mortified that he'd been caught singing—a hymn!—and doing laundry like a housewife, Drew went all swagger. "Waiting for someone? Kind of early in the day to be necking up here, isn't it? Or, wait—did you get stood up?"

Slowly, Bob turned his head to look up at him. Drew's antagonism dissolved instantly—Bob's right eye was swollen and bruised. "Good grief! What happened?"

"A mean left hook." Bob looked back down, muttering, "Really mean." Pushing himself up off the floor, he brushed himself off, his back to Drew. "Was doing a little sparring practice. Didn't lift my arm fast enough to block the blow."

He took a deep breath. "My own damn fault." Bob turned to face Drew, a fake smile on his face.

Given the scene at Bob's the previous month, Drew was pretty sure it was Sergeant Jones who'd landed the punch. Suddenly, he felt bad for Bob. Coaching your kid was one thing—most military dads did that in all manner of ways— but actually nailing your own son? That was plain wrong. But all he said aloud was, "You should put some ice on that."

"Yeah." Squinting a bit, Bob assessed Drew's expression. "It's not like this usually, Drew. This is the first time that—" He stopped. "My dad just wants me to be the best I can be."

Drew made himself smile back with military-brat non-chalance. "Don't they all?"

"Listen." Bob's voice stayed sincere—vulnerable, even. "Don't tell anyone you saw me up here, okay?"

"Sure. No problem," Drew answered.

Bob's gaze stayed fixed on him.

"Seriously, man." Drew lowered his voice. "I won't tell anyone."

Satisfied, Bob pivoted and faked a playful punch at Drew. "You ought to come up here with Shirley one night."

"W-what?"

"Aw, c'mon. I know you're sweet on her. Everybody does." He threw his arm around Drew's shoulders. "You know, a bunch of us are going to see *Spartacus* tonight at the Outpost. Charlie's even asking Betty the cheerleader, his old flame. You should come with Shirley."

"Can't. I . . . I'm going to a Brecht play with Joyce and Matthias."

Bob's eyebrows shot up. "A commie play . . . at the commie-run Berliner Ensemble theater . . . with your commie cousin? Are you—" Bob broke off and shook his head slightly as he looked Drew over carefully. Finally, he said quietly, "Another night, then."

He patted Drew on the chest and grinned, wincing a bit as his smile stretched and pushed up against his bruised eye. "I heard Shirley talking in the hall yesterday. She was telling her friends how *nice* you are. Gotta change that *nice* thing, Drew. Bo-ring. That's the kiss of death with dames. If you wanna get the girl, take my advice—they go for the bad boys. Believe me, I *know.*" He stepped back and pointed at the basket. "First off, don't let anybody else catch you doing laundry for your mom."

Bob made for the door, squaring his shoulders. As he opened it, he glanced back at Drew and winked with his good eye. "See ya, Mac."

For hours, Drew stewed over the fact that he was missing an opportunity to ask Shirley out on a sort-of date. Going to the movies as a group was a safe first move, like practice for the real thing. And he loved Kirk Douglas, the lead in *Spartacus.* It was an important film, too, a cultural event— Drew could milk that with his mom. Douglas had braved hiring a screenwriter, Dalton Trumbo, who'd been blacklisted for being some kind of communist. JFK had made a big deal about going to see the film, crossing a picket line of American Legion members who were boycotting it, holding signs accusing it of being un-American and Douglas of being a Red.

Drew paced, ready to pounce on his mom the instant she walked through the door. He was going to ask to be excused from the play. After all, Matthias had stood him up last month, and Drew really wasn't interested in some opera by Brecht.

But it wasn't until an hour before Drew and Joyce were scheduled to leave—first to meet Fritz and then Matthias—that his mom made it home, looking exhausted. As she hung up her lavender swing coat and pulled off her white gloves, she called to Drew, "I want to talk to you for a few minutes, please, honey."

She sat on the piano bench and patted it, indicating that he should sit down next to her. "Tomorrow, could you please see if there are a few things in your closet that you wouldn't mind donating to the refugees? We've been flooded with people this whole month. Twice as many have made it through as in February. The warmer spring temperatures make it easier for them to move through the forests at night by moonlight."

She reached out and brushed back Drew's hair a bit. "There was boy about your size at Marienfelde today who had nothing but the clothes on his back. Maybe you can find a sweater and a pair of pants you've outgrown?"

"Sure, Mom."

She nodded and smiled. "Thank you, sweetheart." She laid her head on his shoulder for just a moment.

Drew saw his opening. "Mom, do I really have to go tonight? Joyce has that guy Fritz to take her. I'm not interested in some opera by Brecht. And why do I have to spend my Saturday night in East Berlin? Charlie and"—he felt his face flush a little—"and the gang are going to see *Spartacus*. I'd much rather see that and be with them."

His mom stiffened and sat upright. "Won't you be glad to see Matthias?"

Would he? The last time they'd been together, back in January, he'd really enjoyed Matthias's company. He'd even started to feel like his cousin could be a friend to count on, given how he'd schooled Bob in soccer when Bob was harassing Drew. But then the envelope had happened, and he was still worried that Matthias could be involved with it somehow, wittingly or not. And then Matthias hadn't shown up to swim, giving no explanation. What had that been about?

"When you and Cousin Marta had lunch and she invited Joyce and me to go with Matthias to Brecht's *Threepenny Opera*," Drew began cautiously, "did she say why Matthias didn't come last month to go swimming?"

"No." His mom paused. "She didn't know he hadn't."

"What?" Drew jumped to his feet. "Doesn't that sound pretty suspicious to you, Mom?"

"Suspicious how?" His mom smiled. "It may have just slipped his mind. Goodness knows you've done that yourself a few times. You boys." She stood up as well, switching into her music teacher mode. "I want to hear all about the operetta when you get home, honey. Honestly, you are in for a real cultural treat. Brecht is such an influential playwright, and Weill's music has totally changed musical theater. Matthias seems quite interested in Brecht—remember how he pointed out the theater to us when we did that tour of East Berlin back in October? This will be a nice thing for him to share with you."

"But Mom . . ." Drew looked around, as if others were watching, and lowered his voice. "What about that envelope? What if someone tries to plant something on Joyce or me?"

For a moment, his mom paled. "I thought of that," she said slowly, "but the brass thinks there's nothing for us to worry about now. They didn't turn up a connection to a known KGB network. Nothing. It may be that someone in the East decided to jerk your dad's chain just for the heck of it, to see what he'd do. Or maybe someone over there needed to get the Stasi off their back and agreed to plant the envelope." She paused. "I feel better about you going tonight, knowing that boy Fritz will be coming along as Joyce's date. His father had trouble with the Stasi before they emigrated to the West—Fritz is alert to such things."

Laughing lightly, she kissed Drew's cheek. "That's how I convinced your dad to let Joyce go out with a college boy."

With that, she headed into the kitchen.

>////-

Clack-clack. Clack-clack.

The S-Bahn shook and rattled its way through Berlin to the Friedrichsstraße station. Sitting next to the window,

Drew focused on the city passing by and tried to ignore Joyce snuggling up to Fritz. His big sister had had boyfriends before—he'd seen her holding hands with them in the hallways at school or wearing some guy's oversized letterman jacket. But her past boyfriends seemed like little more than idolizing puppies.

This guy had a slight edge to him. Tall and sinewy, Fritz had a tousle of thick honey-brown curls sweeping over his forehead like those radical beatniks back home in the U.S. His jawline was sharp. And while his gray eyes snapped with a boyish sense of adventure, there was nothing wide-eyed or innocent about Fritz. The way Joyce rested her head on his shoulder—grown up, serious, intimate—was a harsh reminder that she'd be leaving for college in a few months. Drew would be losing his best war buddy.

The elevated train crossed the Spree River, dancing merrily with light that spilled into its waters from the buildings and streetlamps. But as the train passed into the ill-lit streets of the Soviet sector, the same currents turned inky dark. With a screech of wheels echoing off the station's vaulted steel-and-glass walls, they pulled into East Berlin.

"Here we are," Joyce warbled, fluttering off the wooden bench and pulling Fritz to his feet. She reached for Drew as well. Swinging their hands playfully, she started singing softly, "Oh, the shark, babe, has such teeth, dear, and it shows them, pearly white . . ."

She twirled and smiled up at Fritz, who looked completely entranced but a bit puzzled by the song. "It's the

English translation of the *Threepenny Opera*'s signature song, 'Mack the Knife,'" she explained. "Just think—a number-one hit in the United States is from an East German satire written by a communist. And tonight we get to hear the original in the playhouse where Brecht wrote it!" She turned to Drew with a dimpled grin. "It's going to be like one of Mom's cultural field trips on steroids!"

Still holding both her brother and her boyfriend by the hand, Joyce sashayed them off the train, Fritz beaming as Joyce sang, "Just a jackknife has old Macheath, babe, and he keeps it, ah, out of sight . . ."

Passersby smiled. A young man with a ducktail hair sweep snapped his fingers along with the song's swing beat. A couple in black tie and evening gown did a slow spin and dip. And, hanging his cane on his arm, a gray-haired, stooped man actually attempted a moment of soft-shoe tap.

Encouraged, Joyce kept singing, louder now, pulling Fritz and Drew around her in a circle. "When that shark bites with his teeth, babe . . ."

The whole thing was ridiculous, thought Drew, like they'd been dropped into a movie musical or something. But he had to admit it was pretty amazing to watch Joyce's effusiveness spill into the station like sunshine, lighting up weary souls in that once-grand, now-dingy place.

Amid the crowd, Drew picked out Matthias, waiting at the prearranged meeting spot. He was leaning against the wall and copping a gigantic attitude, like he'd done at the Victory Column the first day Drew had met him. Drew started to wave, but Matthias looked away, searching the station furtively, pushing his collar up around his face. Then, he pulled down the brim of his flat cap and didn't move until Joyce nearly crashed into him while doing a pirouette and singing.

"Fancy gloves, oh, wears old Macheath, babe, so there's never—*oh!*" Joyce stopped abruptly. "Matthias?"

"*Freundschaft!*" Matthias fairly shouted.

A look of anger flared across Fritz's face at the sound of the FDJ greeting.

But Joyce just reached out to pull Matthias's collar back from his face and burbled, "Friendship? Friendship, yourself!" and burst out laughing.

Lo and behold, so did Matthias.

As they settled into their posh, red-upholstered seats in the balcony—which gave the illusion of being held aloft by enormous marble muses that looked a lot like the statues at Hitler's pool for master-race swimmers—Drew couldn't help but note how bizarrely opulent the Theater am Schiffbauerdamm was. Given that it was the favorite playhouse of the GDR's communist culture bureau, anyway.

They were great seats—one of Cousin Marta's doctor friends had given her the four tickets. "Why didn't your mom use these herself?" Joyce asked Matthias.

"She knows I like Brecht more than she does. And she wants us to be friends, not just cousins." Matthias shrugged and changed the subject. "Why were you singing American words to 'Moritat von Mackie Messer'? Were you making the words up?"

Joyce looked at Matthias in surprise. "No, it's the English translation. There's an off-Broadway production of *Threepenny Opera* that's been running for years now. I think it's even broken the record held by *Oklahoma* for most performances. The song 'Mack the Knife' is a big hit. Even Frank Sinatra sings it."

Matthias looked bewildered. "But , . . this is Brecht's attack on capitalism. The exploitation of the poor. How is it playing in the United States, where the common man is put under the boot?"

"You see?" Fritz said, raising his eyebrows at Joyce. "This is the propaganda the GDR fills young East German heads with." He turned to Matthias. "*How?* It's called artistic freedom—that's how. Freedom of speech. Any kind of play can be staged in the United States, even if it's disliked by the ruling class, those"—Fritz made his voice growly—"greedy capitalists.'" He paused. "And that's how it should be here in Germany."

Joyce elbowed Fritz, who rolled his eyes but eased up. "You know who did improvise lyrics to 'Mack the Knife'?" he asked. "Ella Fitzgerald. When she sang here in Berlin in the Deutschlandhalle last year. She forgot the lyrics, so she started scatting and imitating Louis Armstrong. That's free-dom—to ad-lib, to imagine. To not be terrified of making mistakes or of being punished for not spitting back pre-scribed words. Her improv was brilliant. She was brilliant. Did you go to that concert?"

Matthias shook his head. "Who is Ella Fitzgerald?"

"Oh man." Fritz grinned. "She's only one of the greatest jazz singers alive! Okay, let me raise the Iron Curtain an inch, for *you*, anyway, *Herr Freundschaft*. I will take us all to the Plänterwald Jazz Café next month. I play piano there sometimes. In April, they will host a hot Scandinavian jazz combo that I want to hear. You will come." He patted Matthias on the back. Then he looked at Drew. "And you can bring . . ." He looked to Joyce. "What is the name of the girl you told me of?"

"Shirley," Matthias answered for Joyce. Then, looking at Drew, he deadpanned, "But this I cannot school you in."

Even Drew had to laugh at that.

After the performance, the foursome headed to Matthias's house. They'd promised Drew's mom that they'd say hello to Aunt Hilde. "What did you think of Brecht?" Matthias asked excitedly as they walked. "Did you like it?"

"It . . . the German was a little hard for me to follow," Drew equivocated, unsure of what he actually did think about the searing satire of the West. But seeing Matthias's disappointment, he added politely, "I liked it, though."

"I loooooved it!" Joyce exclaimed. "Thank you so much for taking us, Matthias. The music was amazing. So biting . . . so disturbing. Like nothing I've ever heard before."

"Yes!" Matthias lit up at her response. "Brecht *wished* to disturb. He believed theater must expose class struggle.

To make comment that can inspire society to change. To Brecht, art just to entertain was a waste of time. It is even ... mmmm ... *amoralisch*."

Amoral.

"And yet," Drew couldn't help saying, "you like Elvis."

"Elvis?" Fritz nearly shouted in surprise. "There is hope for you, then, *Herr Freundschaft!*"

But Matthias's smile froze. His gaze darted up and down the street as he hurried to unlock the massive door to his house and hustle them upstairs.

Inside, Aunt Hilde was sitting on a faded brocade settee, awaiting them. But at the sight of Fritz, she gasped and bolted toward her bedroom.

Matthias sighed and looked at the floor.

Cousin Marta was working the night shift at the hospital, so Joyce took it upon herself to coax their great-aunt out. Wrapping her arm around the frail lady's shoulders, she explained that Fritz was her sweetheart and that they wanted to tell her all about the operetta. "It was so amazing, Aunt Hilde. I am hoping to learn some of the songs the character Polly sings," Joyce explained in German.

Aunt Hilde smiled as Joyce talked. Within minutes, she, Joyce, and Fritz were in a musicians' huddle, fervently discussing the *Threepenny Opera*'s music and the enormous challenges it presented for the singers and pit orchestra.

Bored, Mathias yawned and motioned for Drew to follow him. The boys retreated to Matthias's small bedroom—a long, narrow room with one skinny window at the end. Shelves ran along the length of one wall, and a narrow cot and a clothes rack strewn with everything Matthias owned lined the other. Remembering that the GDR had forced Aunt Hilde, Cousin Marta, and Matthias to give up an entire floor of their home to another family in a state-ordered "redistribution of wealth," Drew wondered if the tiny room had originally been an oversized linen closet for his once-aristocratic Becker relatives.

Matthias pulled a string hanging from the bare bulb in the middle of the ceiling to throw gray light onto them.

"Whoa, look at all your books!" Drew breathed. Goethe, Keist, Hölderlin, Schiller. "Mom has some of these."

"My grandmother's books. She hides them here because they are now *verboten*, condemned by the Party. They are filled with characters who grow from what you call psychology—individual . . . mmmm . . . *Offenbarungen*." He paused.

"Epiphanies."

Matthias nodded. "Changed from *e-pi-phi-nies*, not social transformation. These works do not reflect the impact and nobility of a new and more humane society."

"Seriously?" Drew asked.

Matthias refused to return his gaze. Drew looked back to the shelves. "Hey!" He reached out to tip forward the paperback copy of Orwell's *Animal Farm* he'd given Matthias for Christmas. The pages had definitely been thumbed and turned. A few were even dog-eared. "Did your mother read this?" he asked quietly. Drew's mom would be thrilled if she had. "Did . . . did you?"

"I find the portrait of Boxer to be over-simple," Matthias murmured.

Carefully, Drew asked, "You mean the old plow horse?"

When Matthias didn't answer, Drew kept prodding. "The character that literally works himself to death for the new socialist state that he believes in no matter what obvious lies or cruel things the Party leaders do? Even when they send him to be killed in the glue factory because he is no longer useful?"

Frowning, Matthias simply pointed to a row of crisp new books. "This is what my school gives me. *Dmitri Saves Two German Children. How the Steel Was Tempered*, by Nikolai Ostrovsky. Anna Seghers's *The Seventh Cross*. That one is good. A thriller. About prisoners escaping a Nazi concentration camp and the torture planned by the commandant when they are recaptured."

Drew knew this was the kind of "intel" Bob wanted, but suddenly, all he really cared about was how this stuff affected his cousin. "Is it hard for you to read books like that, about what the Nazis did?"

Without the hesitation Drew expected, Matthias answered, "Yes. Very hard to read about the persecution of German communists by Hitler's fascist Reich. But they were martyrs for the cause of socialism."

"No, I mean . . . in general. As a German. Because of all the peoples Hitler ordered exterminated—the Jews, the Slavs, the disabled. Knowing that German people carried out those murders."

Matthias blinked and frowned. "Not all Germans. Here in the East, they resisted Hitler and his Nazis. The fascists were in the West. *Those* Germans were influenced by the

French and British, whose greed and sense of entitlement and nationalistic arrogance spread across our border like a plague. *Those* Germans became fascists and let Hitler come to power and then followed him."

Drew was dumbfounded. Matthias couldn't really believe that, could he? Was that how the Russians had won the unquestioning allegiance of East Germans—by convincing them they'd been victims and not participants in Nazi war crimes and the Holocaust?

A heavy silence rose up like a wall between them.

After a long moment of avoiding his astonished stare, Matthias scootched past Drew in the narrow space and went to a small desk crammed under the window. He switched on a desk lamp and reached underneath to pull out a box jammed with 45s—Little Richard, Chuck Berry, the Everly Brothers, Pat Boone, Bill Haley, the Drifters.

Again, Drew was astounded. It was a stash of Western contraband that would land Matthias in serious *scheiße* if he were caught. "Where in the world did you get all those?"

"Trading. Looking in the trash in the West." Matthias paused, then added in a hushed voice, "I know someone who goes to record stores in West Berlin to listen to demo discs. He takes them to the clerk and says they are scratched and skipping. The clerks—the foolish ones—throw the samples out. Then, later, he retrieves them from the bin. He used to trade with me." Matthias rifled through his cache to pull out "Rockin' Robin" by Bobby Day.

"Hey, I have that single, too. Although I can't seem to find it."

"It's yours," Matthias murmured.

"What? What the hell, man?"

Matthias held out the 45 and bowed his head as Drew snatched it from him. Remembering his missing toothpaste and acne medicine the night of Sadie Hawkins, Drew snapped, "Did you steal any *more* of my things?"

Matthias took a deep breath. "No other records. Just that one. I am very sorry. I was going to return it to you last month when we were to swim. But I could not come."

Rage boiled up in Drew. "What's wrong with you, man? And why didn't you come swimming that day, anyway?"

Matthias dropped down on his bed and leaned over, covering his face with his hands. "The FDJ summoned me to a tribunal. For a *Selbstkritik*. To give self-criticism."

As furious as he was, Drew was so completely taken aback by how miserable Matthias sounded that he remained quiet and let Matthias explain.

"My time with you has been . . . noticed. That is why I was afraid when I met you in the train station tonight. I was reported to the FDJ. They said my attitude was suspect and they wanted to test my sincerity." He looked up at Drew. "This, after I won the Gold Medal for Good Knowledge last year. Do you know how hard that is to achieve?" He shook his head in disbelief.

After a moment, Matthias continued, "The *Jugendfreund* questioned me. As judges. They are—were—my friends." He ran his hands through his mop of blond hair before hanging his head and looking at the floor. "They said my hair was a mess, a sign of"—he paused and made quotation marks in the air—"'an amoral, bourgeois disregard for the seriousness of learning and working-class dignity.' Having pimples"—he tugged on his collar self-consciously to hide an outbreak—"did not 'show the cleanliness expected of FDJ members.' Chewing on my fingernails"—he stuck his hands in his pockets—"suggested I am 'sly and untrustworthy.'"

He took in a deep breath and let it out slowly. "They said I endanger our righteous cause, and that I bring your imperialism and unclean thinking into our country. They were going to expel me from the FDJ unless I repented and confessed."

"Confessed to what?"

"*Kulturbarbarei.* Being corrupted by Americans. Your music. The evil virus coming from the West." He suddenly burst into unnervingly sharp, gallows-humor laughter. "Saying it aloud makes it sound . . ."

"Insane?"

Matthias nodded, a rueful smile on his face. He gazed out the window a moment and parroted, "'For the fatherland, no duty is too hard, no sacrifice too great.'"

"Do you really believe that?" Drew asked.

Matthias shrugged, still staring into the night outside. "I believe in purging unfairness from society. Ending poverty. I believe in Marx's philosophy: *from* each according to his talents, *to* each according to his needs. But this?" He looked down at his chewed-up, FDJ-condemned fingernails, thinking.

Drew struggled to figure out what to say. "You know, in the West, there is a polish you can put on your nails that tastes so bitter it will stop you from chewing on them."

"What?" Matthias looked back up, surprised. "Of course there is." After a moment, a mischievous—even mutinous—look filled his eyes. He checked his watch. Then, from under his bed, he pulled a bright orange, hand-sized transistor radio. "The signal is clearest now. Best time to tune in."

"Where'd you get that?"

"Trash bins in the West provide many treasures." Matthias wiggled his eyebrows playfully. "The antenna is broken in half. But it works by the window."

Snapping the small radio on, Matthias spun the dial, raised the truncated straw-like antenna, and propped it on the sill.

AFN, the American Forces Network, crackled into the room.

Gooooooood evening, Berlin! Here's a brand-new record that's sweeping folks off their feet all over the United States, and boy oh boy, is it a toe-tapper. Maybe your sweethearts have already written to you about it. It's sure to be another dance sensation—'Pony Time' by Chubby Checker!

Bouncy music replaced the announcer's voice as the singer famous for "The Twist" sang out his latest hit: *It's pony time! Get up!*

As Checker's backup singers pattered in quick time—*Boogety, boogety, boogety, shoo*—Matthias jumped up and started following the song's instructions. *You turn to the left when I say gee, you turn to the right when I say haw.*

At first dancing on his toes to be as quiet as possible, Matthias still gyrated with a recklessness that stunned Drew. It was more than a kid's war dance of defiance. There was a despair on his face, too, that Drew instinctively recognized—the soul-rattling anger and disappointment a teenager feels when his heroes reveal themselves to be full of baloney, or even to be villains.

His frenzy growing, Matthias started stomping. "C'mon!" he shouted, laughing wildly.

This was dangerously loud—even Drew knew that. But he got up and did a rendition of the twist to keep his cousin company, even though Drew could tell it was almost as if he wasn't in the room. Matthias was completely absorbed in his own shake, rattle, and roll of disobedience. Unhinged in the best way.

After a few moments, the door flew open, and Joyce was shushing them. "Drew! Stop! The neighbors. People in the street might hear you. You'll get Matthias in big trouble." She looked to Fritz for help. "Tell them!"

But Fritz nodded in approval of the brash musical rebellion and slipped past her to join in, whooping.

Behind Joyce stood Aunt Hilde, wide-eyed but smiling, tapping her foot in rhythm.

The song ended. *Whoo-eee. That's sure to be on its way to number one. That's Chubby Checker, folks! I'll be back with more after the break.*

Winded, Drew, Matthias, and Fritz stood panting, grinning, eyeing one another, triumphant and unapologetic, like boys who'd gotten away with a tremendous prank against a cruel headmaster. Then Matthias turned off the radio. Suddenly he looked scared. Really scared.

"Time for us to go, boys." Joyce motioned for her brother and her boyfriend to exit quickly. "Maybe nobody heard—or they don't know which house it was coming from," she reassured Drew.

As they said good night and moved toward the staircase, Drew turned back to Matthias, standing in his doorway. "I'll lend you more 45s, if you want," he said.

But Matthias shook his head vehemently, pointed down the steps, and abruptly shut the door.

Trotting up the stairs toward them was the teenager with one blue eye and one brown, whose family lived on the top floor of Matthias's home—the one who'd hailed Matthias with *Freundschaft*. The boy Cousin Marta had told Drew's mom she suspected of being a Stasi informant.

Drew felt his blood run cold. The youth was wearing a tracksuit with the German Olympic team's insignia, just like the ones Drew's mom had described the GDR giving as rewards to its teenage fanatics who destroyed TV antennas turned to the West. Could he be the "friend" who'd ratted on Matthias to the FDJ?

APRIL 1961

Worried about a Russian-backed communist regime only 100 miles off Florida, JFK greenlights a plan conceived by President Eisenhower to oust Cuba's new dictator, Fidel Castro. The CIA lands 1,500 U.S.-trained Cuban exiles at the Bay of Pigs, hoping to spark an uprising among prodemocracy islanders. The invasion is a catastrophe.

The mission's failure was caused in part by JFK withdrawing air support to avoid elevating tensions with Soviet Russia. Khrushchev brags that he had wanted JFK as president for this kind of "rookie" mistake and had purposely refused to release U.S. pilot Francis Gary Powers while Nixon was V.P.—to influence the election in JFK's favor.

The Russians beat the United States into space—again. Cosmonaut Yuri Gagarin successfully orbits the earth once. The Soviets name the mission *Vostok*, or East, to drive home their Cold War triumph. During his 108-minute flight, Gagarin whistles a song composed by Dmitri Shostakovich, "The Motherland hears, the Motherland knows, where her son flies in the sky."

A L S O

Adolf Eichmann, the architect of Hitler's murder of six million Jews, is captured in Argentina and taken to Israel to stand trial. Holocaust survivors testify for months, horrifying the world with details of concentration camps and Nazi cruelty. Eichmann claims he was merely following orders but is found guilty of crimes against humanity and executed.

ALSO

Fans give singer and film legend Judy Garland a five-minute standing ovation at her comeback concert in NYC's Carnegie Hall.

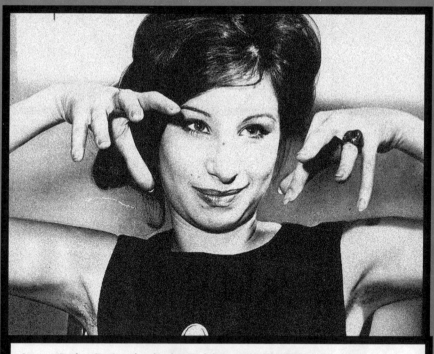

A young Barbra Streisand makes her TV debut on *The Tonight Show*.

CHAPTER NINE
APRIL
1961

Linda stopped bouncing the soccer ball Matthias had given Drew to say to Joyce, "You look soooo pretty." She'd been watching her big sister sweep mascara on her eyelashes in front of the bathroom mirror while she juggled off her knees—left, right, left. Heidi the dachshund barked as if in agreement. "You silly old dog." Linda laughed and dropped the ball to the floor. "See if you can catch me!" She took off dribbling down the hall, Heidi giving chase.

"She's getting pretty good with that thing," Drew murmured.

"*Shhhh.* Don't move. I don't want to choke you." His father was knotting Drew's tie for him as Drew held his chin up in his bedroom doorway, beside the bathroom.

His mom was also crowding the hallway, waiting with her Polaroid to capture the moment when Drew and Joyce were ready to leave for the Plänterwald Jazz Café. She'd lent Joyce a cobalt-blue dress that complemented her ginger hair and cornflower-blue eyes. His mom called it a pencil dress—it had a short turtleneck and a long straight skirt, cinched at the waist with a wide belt. "Oh, you look as sophisticated as Audrey Hepburn," his mom had cooed. That's when she'd gone for the camera, saying with a catch in her voice, "I won't be able to take pictures of you next year when you're off at college, you know."

Of course, the photo would also memorialize Drew looking about as dopey as possible. He'd managed to scrape his face shaving, so a rash was quickly spreading through his minefield of freckles. A great look for his first *real* date with Shirley.

Just as Fritz had promised in March when they'd gone to the Brecht play with Matthias, he was taking them to a "hot" jazz club. Fritz would be playing the piano as the opening act for the featured combo. Joyce was bursting with pride about that part of the evening.

Their mom posed them by the bay window. "You look handsome, honey," she tried to reassure Drew. "Smile!"

Pop! His mom counted to sixty, then opened the back of the camera and peeled the black-and-white photo off the film negative inside. Even blinded by the flash, Drew could see his cringe-worthy grimace.

"Let's go," his sister whispered, tugging on his sleeve.

"You look fine. Don't worry. Shirley is all excited about going to the café. It's going to be a great night."

Amid a barrage of *Enjoy! Be careful! Watch out for each other!*, the two exited hastily, nearly slamming the apartment door in their parents' faces to prevent them from following.

"Good grief!" Drew rolled his eyes.

"Oh, we should be glad they love us so much." Joyce laughed again. "I'm sure I'll miss their fussing next year." She'd been accepted to Vassar College and to the Royal Academy of Music in London. Drew was rooting for London; that way, he'd have more of a shot at seeing Joyce once in awhile. She took his arm, "Shall we?"

A few steps down, they were drawn up short by sounds coming from Bob's apartment. A shout. Something being overturned. The anxious tremolo of Mrs. Jones's voice.

Then, "What have I told you?" from Sergeant Jones.

"About what, Dad?" Bob's voice—loud, needling, asking for trouble.

"Are you sassing me, boy?"

A thump.

"Answer me. I'm talking to you, soldier."

Maybe it was the army's mantra of "Leave no man behind," or maybe it was the memory of Bob's bruised face in the laundry room, but Drew knew he had to do something. "Come on," he said, grabbing Joyce's hand and hurrying back up the steps to the Joneses' door. He took a deep breath and knocked.

Sudden silence. The door flew open. Sergeant Jones loomed in the entrance. Behind him, Mrs. Jones blew her nose and tried to smile. Bob leaned against the living room wall, his hands shoved in his pockets.

Sergeant Jones gave Drew a hard look. "Need something, son?"

"Here for Bob," Drew answered, speaking the truth.

"Excuse me?" Sergeant Jones barked.

Drew could see a flash of dread on Bob's face. Joyce must have seen it, too. "You haven't forgotten, have you, Bob?" She smiled sweetly. "You wouldn't stand up a girl, would you?"

Bob just gaped at her.

But Mrs. Jones picked up on the ruse. "Oh my, of course not, dear. He's been talking about this for days." She nudged Bob toward his bedroom. "Go put on that nice tweed jacket and tie I laid out for you. Hurry, now, sweetheart."

"I didn't hear about this," Sergeant Jones replied, curt, accusing.

"Oh, that's my fault, dear." Mrs. Jones's demeanor turned light and breezy. "I got all caught up cooking for the wives' club bake sale, and the fact that Bob was going out for the evening with Drew and Joyce completely slipped my mind. I'm sorry."

"At the Plänterwald Café." Drew quickly provided the destination to help Mrs. Jones play along.

"Plänterwald?" Sergeant Jones barked. "That's in the East, isn't it? Near Treptower Park, the Russians' Garden of Remembrance. That's no place for—"

Joyce interrupted, bubbling, "Bob was kind enough to offer to go along to some jazz clubs with me, so I took him up on it. You know I'm training as a singer, Sergeant Jones, so I try to go to as many live performances as possible. And we all feel *totally* safe when Bob is around."

Wow, she was smooth.

Practically pushing her son out the door when Bob reemerged in coat and tie, Mrs. Jones waved them off. "Have a wonderful night, my dears." Drew saw Bob hesitate and search his mom's face.

She gave him a slight nod and a big smile and closed the door.

Joyce tugged on Bob's arm. "C'mon." They escaped down the stairs and didn't stop to catch their breath until they reached the sidewalk.

His voice hoarse, Bob said, "I owe you, Drew." Then he bowed and kissed Joyce's hand. "My lady, I will love and serve you till the day I die." Straightening up, Bob took in a long breath of the April night air. He held out his arm, and Joyce slipped hers through it. "So, where exactly are we going? And are there dames involved?"

As Drew, Shirley, Joyce, and Bob entered the Plänterwald Café, they were engulfed in a chorus of clinking glasses and lively murmuring in English, German, French, and Russian. Drew spotted Matthias engrossed in the music in a corner, holding a table. Fritz was already playing.

"Oh no!" Joyce whimpered. "His set has started." She rushed to take her seat and then hung on every cool, lyrical phrase Fritz played on the café's upright piano. It wasn't the fast bebop or the frenzied chord progressions Drew had always associated with jazz. Fritz's music was diaphanous, even dreamy, with a haunting melancholy.

"Fritz calls this modal jazz," Joyce explained to the group without taking her eyes off him as he played. "It's influenced by a Miles Davis album titled *Kind of Blue*. Isn't it gorgeous?"

"Yes," Shirley answered, leaning forward and resting her chin in her hand. "It's exactly what I'd imagine all the shades of blue would sound like if they could sing."

"Exactly," echoed Joyce.

Both girls sighed, mesmerized, gazing toward the stage.

Drew, on the other hand, was struck by how lyrical Shirley's observations always were, marveled at the fact that she was *his* date, and couldn't stop staring at her. She was also as drop-dead gorgeous as she'd been at Sadie Hawkins. Tonight, she'd pulled her thick hair back into a ponytail and tucked a gardenia behind her ear. "Like Billie Holiday," Shirley had said when they'd picked her up at her apartment and Joyce had *ooh*ed over the flower. "She's my favorite blues singer. Nana introduced me to her songs." The slightly severe hairstyle made Shirley's large, dark eyes even more beautiful, somehow.

Shirley glanced back at Drew, catching him mid-gawk.

Matthias elbowed him and laughed as Shirley smiled shyly at Drew and then returned to watching Fritz at the piano.

Bob, of course, was ogling Joyce. Nodding toward the stage, he asked Drew, "Has your dad checked out that guy?"

"What?"

"I mean, are you sure he's on the up-and-up? Not some plant?"

Drew frowned. "He's a student at Free University. His father's a professor who fled his teaching position in East Berlin because he was targeted by Russian and East German officials."

"That doesn't mean anything. In fact, it'd be a good cover for"—he shot a glare at Matthias—"a commie spy."

"Jeez, Bob, do you have to see a commie in every corner? Relax. Enjoy the music."

"No, he is right," Matthias interjected. "It would be good cover."

Bob looked at him with surprise. "Well, whaddaya know."

Matthias shrugged, focusing on Fritz's music. "I find this new jazz very interesting. You know, your State Department drove the Russians nuts when . . ." He paused. "Nuts? Is that right?"

Drew grinned and nodded. They'd turn his cousin into an American yet.

"It drove the Russians nuts when the Americans sent Dave Brubeck to play in Poland. The pianist and his combo. The Russians agreed to the tour, yes, but I do not think they realized how the music would take hold. There are secret recordings of Brubeck's concerts on old X-ray film cut into record circles. My friend has one. You can see the ribs."

Shirley had kept her gaze fixed onstage as she listened, but Matthias's description caught her attention. "Music recorded on chest X-rays? Oh, that's so poetic. The sound of

American jazz superimposed over communist hearts—what could be more symbolic of the yearning for artistic freedom behind the Iron Curtain!"

Amazed, all the three boys could do was stare at her. But inside, Drew felt his own heart fall completely in love.

"I know about Brubeck's tour," she added. "Cultural diplomacy, my dad called it. He's serving as the military liaison for the embassy on this tour. Brubeck's band has white *and* Black musicians. The State Department hoped Brubeck's integrated quartet would improve America's image abroad, especially since the Soviets use our segregation laws to help turn East Germans against us. The practice does sort of prove all their claims about us, of hypocrisy and cruelty, of racial inequalities, doesn't it?" She turned to Matthias. "Did the tour help improve the opinion of us?"

"No," Matthias replied, ever blunt. "We still believe your capitalist society to be fascist and racist." He gestured toward the stage and added, "Except in jazz." He shrugged once more. "Sorry. It is accepted fact." He thought a moment and added, "Perhaps if you ever live like this American music . . . you will be different."

When Fritz finished his set, Joyce nearly bounced out of her seat applauding. The rest of the café clapped more tepidly, clearly waiting for the dance tunes of the featured combo. But a few French patrons approached Fritz as he sat down, flushed and a little sweaty from the spotlight, next to Joyce. *"Vous jouez comme un impressionniste."*

"Merci," he answered.

"What did they say?" asked Joyce.

"That what I played was like their Impressionism. Monet, Renoir."

"Oh, yes," she murmured, looking enraptured.

"So . . ." Fritz scootched his chair in, wedging himself between Joyce and Matthias, as the featured combo began to play. "*Was denkst du?*" he asked Matthias. "*Jazz ist hip, oder?*"

"*Ja! Es ist großartig!*" Matthias answered enthusiastically.

"Hey, you're with Americans," Bob growled. "Talk American."

Drew had noticed Bob turn sullen when several Russian and GDR officers sat down at the next table. He'd also ordered a beer that he'd drunk way too quickly. Drew understood that Bob was hurting about his dad, but did he have to deal with everything by lashing out at others? He started to tell Bob to shut up, but Fritz spoke first.

"Well, you *are* in Germany, you know," he answered, still keeping his voice low so as to not disturb the musicians. "Talk American? Let's see. Golly gee willikers . . . yippee ki yay . . . de-dee-dee, that's all, folks," he said, imitating American movie stereotypes. "Or maybe, Bob, when in Rome . . . eh? Isn't that an American saying? When in Rome, do as the Romans do?"

Bob leaned over Shirley to aim his vitriol straight at Fritz. He nearly shouted, "You ain't Romans, butthole. You're a bunch of leftover Nazis and commies and—"

Suddenly, a young GDR lieutenant and Soviet officer, who'd been enjoying the music at an adjacent table, stood up behind him. They put their hands on the back of Bob's chair and yanked him backward, spinning him around.

"*Nepriyatnyy Amerikanets,*" the Russian began, unleashing a torrent of angry words.

They all froze, having no idea what was being said, other than that the Russian and East German clearly thought Bob a rude nuisance. Only Matthias seemed to understand. He stood quickly, shaking his head and speaking haltingly in Russian. The officer frowned at what were clearly linguistic mistakes, but he listened as Matthias seemed to apologize for Bob.

Finally, satisfied with whatever Matthias was trying to say, the Russian leaned threateningly toward Bob, with a scowl that suggested he'd be keeping an eye on him, and growled, "*My sledim za toboy.*" Then he turned his attention to Shirley. "*Ty napominayeah' mne nashu favoristuyu Kirovskuyu balerinu, Natal'yu Makarovu, s takimi vot volosami.*"

The Soviet waited, expecting Matthias to translate.

Ashen, Matthias said, "You remind him of a Kirov ballerina—Natalia Makarova. Your hair like that."

Shirley forced a smile. "Thank you."

The combo struck up "Come Dance with Me." Holding a finger up in that universal signal for *listen*, the Russian extended his other hand to Shirley. "*Tantsuy so mnoy?*"

The invitation to dance with him was clear. Her expected answer, too. It felt like everyone in the club was watching, collectively holding their breath. Would an American girl—an interloper in the Russian sector—accept a dance with a Soviet officer? More ominously, what would he do if she refused?

"Wait a minute, Shirley." Drew started to rise. "You don't need to do this."

"Better not to challenge this man," Matthias whispered, catching Drew by his elbow. "He will bring Shirley back at the next song. According to the sixty-forty rule in East Berlin, the next song must be East German. Not so good to dance to. Maybe even the Lipsi. He won't know those steps."

The Russian waited through their exchange, his smile fading into a cold demand. Meanwhile, his GDR comrade pulled himself taller, his posture set to back up the Russian.

"You are in danger if they arrest us for causing a scene, aren't you?" Shirley asked Fritz in a hushed tone.

Nodding slowly, Fritz answered, his eyes fixed on the Russian. "They could claim I've caused a public disturbance as an excuse to lock me up. That would give them leverage on my father." He looked at Bob. "You too. They like to arrest children of American officers. Hold them overnight to see what they can shake out of their dads."

"Yeah, we know," Bob snapped.

"And yet," Fritz replied, "you still behave badly and attract their attention."

Shirley rose and took the Russian's hand before anyone could stop her.

He led her to the small dance floor. Drew stewed. At least the tune was an easy 4/4 swing piece so Shirley could slip and slide safely at arm's length, her full skirts swaying wide, an added buffer of fabric between her and their Cold War enemy. No other patron dared to join her and the officer on the dance floor.

The instant the drummer hit his final cymbal stroke of the song, Drew was on his feet, sprinting to take Shirley's hand.

But the Russian didn't let go of her.

"Come." Matthias shot up, pulling Joyce with him. They scurried to stand next to Drew and Shirley, as if they were about to dance as well. Awkwardly, Matthias took Joyce in his arms.

"Vy khotite vmeshat'sya?" The Russian eyed Drew with a smirk, a little amused.

"He is asking if you wish to cut in," Matthias explained to Drew while nodding at the Russian politely. "Bow and say *da, spasibo.*"

Forcing himself to bow stiffly, Drew parroted, "Yes, thank you."

The Russian officer placed Shirley's hand in Drew's, and she immediately cuddled up close to him. Drew winced, feeling Shirley tremble.

Ignoring Drew entirely now, the Russian spoke to Shirley. *"Spasibo za prekrasnyy tanets, mademoiselle."* He went back to his drink as the band began an odd-sounding song: part waltz, part rhumba, with a dash of polka rhythm thrown in.

"What the heck is this?" Drew muttered.

Matthias burst out laughing. "It is the Lipsi. As I predicted. The GDR's answer to Elvis. No wiggle-hip. If nothing else, we Germans are predictable in our rules. Try to follow me." Holding Joyce like he would for a waltz, Matthias led her in small circles, moving his feet in what looked like a cha-cha step in slow motion. Joyce followed his pivots, laughing at the jumble of moves.

A few East Berliners joined them, expertly twirling to the odd 6/4 melody.

Knowing he looked totally ridiculous, Drew gave up trying to mimic Matthias's complicated moves. He opted instead for the basic fox-trot his mom had taught him— walk, walk, sidestep, twirl. He and Shirley weren't on the beat of the odd music—they weren't even in step with each other—but he was holding her in his arms.

They stayed close together on the dance floor for an hour, switching partners among the six of them, until only Fritz and Joyce were left, gazing into each other's eyes as they swayed to a slow ballad. Shirley, Drew, Bob, and Matthias clustered at their table, winded, recovering from a fast-paced rendition of "When the Saints Go Marching In"—a Louis Armstrong favorite.

"Hey, how did you know that whatchacallit, that lip dance?" Bob asked Matthias over the music. "And what that Russkie was saying?"

"The Lipsi. It is taught at FDJ meetings," Matthias explained. "And we learn Russian in school." He seemed to brace for yet another confrontation.

But Bob just nodded. "Well, it sure saved our butts. My butt. Thanks, man." Leaning back in his chair, Bob looked around the room. "Think that *Fräulein* would be interested in a dance?" He tipped his head toward a young blond in a dark sweater and capri pants, left alone at her table as all her friends, paired up, took to the floor. "She looks like she's going stag, like me."

"I don't know if that's such a great idea," Drew began, but Bob was already on his feet. He sauntered over and chatted with the girl for a few moments before doing a thumbs-up at Drew and sitting down next to her.

"Maybe it'll be okay," Shirley said. "He can be charming when he wants to be." She leaned her head on Drew's shoulder. "Like you."

At that, Drew completely forgot about Bob. He could have been carried off by a platoon of Vopos, and Drew wouldn't have noticed.

Matthias kept watch, though. For almost twenty minutes, through three different songs, Bob appeared to be talking cordially, respectfully, with the girl. Then her friends returned to the table. And within moments, everything changed.

"Time to go!" Matthias stood abruptly and quickly threaded his way through the dancing bodies to get to Bob.

Drew pulled Shirley to her feet and darted over to Joyce and Fritz. "Trouble," he said. "C'mon!"

They flanked Bob just as one of the young men leaned into him, swearing in German, calling him an imperialist pig, among other coarser slurs.

This could get ugly fast.

Yet again, Matthias took control. "The S-Bahn closes soon," he announced, yanking Bob to his feet. "You and your American friends must go home now." He nodded at the table and rolled his eyes, as if he agreed it was time for these infuriating Americans to get lost. *"Auf Wiedersehen, Freunde."* Then he hustled Bob toward the door as quickly as possible, Drew helping to shove him along from behind. A fanfare of jazz escaped with them as they burst through the café's doors and tumbled into the street.

"What the hell?" Bob exclaimed. "I was actually being nice that time. Honest."

"East Germans have been told for years that you Americans and NATO are going to invade us any day," said Matthias. "The surprise attack your JFK just ordered on Cuba—the incident they call the Bay of Pigs—confirms our fears. The Russians have filled our newspapers and radio with it. They make fun of your defeat, and at the same time, they say you are coming here next."

"But," Bob protested, "Russia started it by backing Castro and setting up another communist puppet regime, but this one just a hundred miles off our mainland!"

"It does not matter." Matthias shrugged. "Khrushchev uses your Cuba invasion as proof that you want to destroy worker states. Also, talking to that girl, you . . . you hit a nerve?" He looked to Drew once again for affirmation of his word choice.

Drew nodded to confirm that was an American saying.

"Since World War II, many German women have chosen American men over our countrymen. To date. To marry. To defect to the West."

"But I was just *talking* to her!" Bob said, shaking his head. "I wasn't trying to snake her. I was trying to make up for being a jackass before. Doing what they train us army brats to do—make nice with the locals!" He straightened to attention and saluted, saluted, saluted, like a windup toy soldier. "I am a young ambassador of goodwill." He looked at Drew. "Remember the pamphlet they gave you when you got to Berlin?"

Drew couldn't help but laugh. "Yeah, man." He straightened and mimicked Bob's salute. "Ambassadors all!"

Joyce and Shirley joined in, reciting, "'Well-mannered children can be a tremendous help in showing foreign men and woman American ideals and democracy's way of life.'"

"Oh, oh! What about this one?" Drew added. "'Do not be arrogant or rude, but help teach democracy to Germans who question it with informal discussions and patient explanations.'"

The foursome laughed, but Fritz and Matthias remained totally baffled.

Bob clapped Matthias on the back. "It's an army brat thing. Take it from me—for once, I was just being a nice guy." He looked to Drew. "I told you, being a nice guy gets you nowhere."

The café door swung open again, and one of the blond *Fräulein*'s friends planted his feet at the threshold and crossed his arms to glare at them, seeming to aim most of his stare-down at Matthias.

"I must go," Matthias muttered. "Thank you." He shook Fritz's hand. "I liked the jazz." With that, he turned and evaporated into the shadows of the barely lit streets of East Berlin without saying goodbye.

Drew sighed. "Just when I start to really trust that guy, he does something that makes me wonder . . ." He trailed off, looking back and forth between the guy in the café doorway and his retreating cousin. But this time, his suspiciousness turned into concern for Matthias. Could those Germans they'd just encountered be Stasi or FDJ fanatics? How much surveillance was Matthias really under? Come to think of it, Matthias had never said what the outcome of that horrifying tribunal had been before he'd gone into his wild war dance to Chubby Checker. And there hadn't been a chance that night at the Plänterwald for the cousins to really talk.

Bob had watched Matthias disappear, too. "I think he's A-OK, actually." He studied Drew for a moment, uncharacteristically hesitant. "I think . . . there's something I should tell you. I think you've pinned something on Matthias that wasn't—"

"Later," Fritz interrupted. The rest of the blond girl's gang had just exploded out the door, pushing up their sleeves. "We need to go. Now!"

"*Scheiße!*" Drew grabbed Shirley's hand, and they sprinted after Fritz and Joyce, who laughed uproariously in a strange mixture of defiance, adrenaline, and exuberance.

"Move! Move! Move!" Bob shouted, bringing up the rear.

It took two long, scary blocks before the Germans gave up their chase. But Drew, Shirley, Joyce, Fritz, and Bob didn't stop running until they reached the nearest S-Bahn.

Then—after they hurled themselves onto a train and its doors slammed shut and he fell into a seat with her—Shirley kissed him.

In their rush to the station, there had been no time for Drew to ask Bob what he'd meant about Matthias. But the one question he really cared about at that moment had been answered.

MAY 1961

East Berlin's annual May Day parade celebrates worker solidarity with a show of combined GDR and Soviet military might with troops, missiles, tanks, and youth groups. Spectators wave flags, present flowers to soldiers, and are rewarded with free sausage.

Harper Lee wins the Pulitzer Prize for *To Kill a Mockingbird*, her coming-of-age story about a young girl awakening to the terrible fact of racism.

A L S O

Three weeks after Russia's successful orbit, Alan Shepard becomes the first American in space. Euphoric, JFK announces his call for Americans to go to the moon before the decade is over. "Now is the time for a great new American enterprise . . . whatever mankind must undertake, free men must fully share."

In an effort to end segregation on public transport and in waiting rooms, civil rights activists ride "freedom buses" through the South. Black and white, they cross several states, stopping to eat together in nonviolent protest at "whites only" lunch counters. They are often met with police dogs, barricades, and angry mobs.

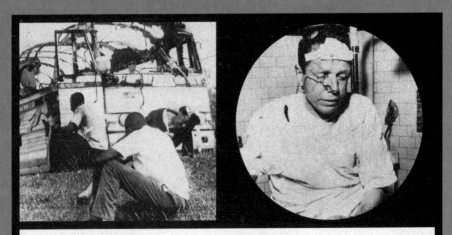

In Alabama, the **KKK** and its supporters attack Freedom Riders with iron pipes and clubs and firebomb their bus. In Mississippi, the riders are the ones to be arrested for civil disobedience and accused of inciting riot. They sing an improvised call-and-response as they are pushed into jail cells: *"Buses are a-comin', oh, yes . . . Better get you ready, oh, yes."*

CHAPTER TEN
MAY
1961

"Listen, son." Sergeant McMahon reached across the front seat and put his hand on Drew's shoulder as he opened the car door. "Be careful on this trip, okay? Tomorrow is May Day, so we're in for a lot of chest-beating from our commie neighbors." He thumped his own chest. "*Da!* International Workers Day. Parades! Tanks! Missiles! Our handsome comrade soldiers marching and singing. *Da!* Is good!"

"I know, Dad," Drew answered with a laugh. He watched Charlie get out of his family's car and trot toward the school bus waiting to drive them to the station. Their track team was headed for the military duty train that would take them through the Soviet occupation zone that encircled Berlin to a meet in Frankfurt. "I better go. Don't worry—we'll be in West Germany by the time all that baloney starts."

"Sure. But for six hours, your train moves through commie territory before you reach our American zone. And tonight, on the eve of May Day, every Russian and GDR soldier along the rail line will be jazzed to show his superiors that he's the most patriotic communist. Being stacked on top of each other in a locked-down train for that many hours is asking a lot of self-control from you guys—I get it. But"—his dad held up a finger—"tonight's not the night for goofing off. Got it?"

Drew nodded.

His dad patted his shoulder. "Good luck in Frankfurt, son. I know you'll come back with lots of blue ribbons."

"Yes, sir!" Drew pulled the door handle but stopped halfway out of the car. "Hey, Dad?"

"Yeah?"

"A couple of the guys have to be really careful about their paperwork, because the Russians know who their dads are. I heard one kid got pulled off the train last year because he's a junior and his dad's name was on a list of CIA operatives to nab." Drew swallowed, anxious. "I know it's been four months now, but that envelope left on the Bonneville . . ."

Waving his hand, Drew's dad answered quickly, "Don't give that damn envelope another thought. The higher-ups are convinced it was a fishing expedition. Or a one-off—a quick way to discredit a good American patriot." He pointed his thumb at himself. "Like yours truly. The Stasi and KGB do that all the time, just to spread doubt about an American officer's integrity. They want to fuel suspicion within the brigade, to weaken our trust in one another, which ulti-mately weakens the unit. They've wrecked a couple of guys' reputations just by leaving little love notes like that one. The SOBs."

He patted Drew's shoulder. "It's easy for them to target Americans who have some connection in the East. Maybe someone tipped off the KGB or Stasi to the fact we're related to Matthias, Marta, and Hilde. In any case, the Russkies and their GDR flunkies went after the wrong fish with me."

"But, Dad, the guys in the van—"

"Wasted their time—even though I'm grateful that they looked after my family until we knew everything was all clear. They didn't detect any kind of follow-up to that enve-lope." His dad nodded toward the parking lot. "Looks like everyone's getting on the bus. Better hurry, son."

"Okay. If you say so."

"I do." Sergeant McMahon gave Drew the reassuring smile he always used to signal that a subject was closed.

Nodding dutifully, Drew got out and darted across the parking lot. His dad's comment that someone might have tipped off the secret police that they had cousins in East Berlin had landed like a grenade in his mind, rekindling his old paranoia about *how* that envelope had ended up on their Bonneville. The people most likely to have reported that his family had East Berlin cousins were FDJ believers, like Matthias's antenna-breaking neighbor or one of the supposed "*Freunde*" on that tribunal. Or . . . maybe some-one who'd been reprimanded, accused of not being enough of a believer, someone desperate to prove he or she was a good and loyal socialist . . . like . . . like Matthias? Drew felt sick as that particular distrust resurfaced.

The only thing that was crystal clear was the fact that Drew's dad had dodged a bullet that could have killed his military career.

"Nice of you to join us, McMahon," Coach said as Drew bounded up the bus steps.

"Sorry, sir," Drew murmured.

As the bus drove the short distance to the Army Rail Traffic Office, the coach walked down the aisle, collecting passports and flag orders. "Okay, boys, hand them over." He took a quick look at each student's official paperwork.

The flag orders were specific to the trip, issued in English, Russian, and German, detailing each student's purpose for traveling and reflecting all the stops the train would make through the night. Any typo or flaw in the translation between the three languages could get a kid yanked off the train at Soviet Russian checkpoints. The train itself might be sovereign U.S. territory, but the track it traveled and the steam engine that pulled it through the Russian zone belonged to the East Germans.

After shuffling through the documents, the coach stuffed them into a big envelope to hand to the train's commander when they boarded. "Listen, guys—tonight, the train will be jammed with family dependents and officers. That means six guys per sleeping compartment. Every berth in the train's three sleeper cars is assigned. I can't spread you out this trip. Sorry."

The boys groaned. When all six bunks were pulled down from the walls, the compartment was left with a middle aisle the width of maybe one and a half skinny bodies and the length of a bed. With quarters that tight, it would be a tall order for six guys to stay out of each other's way *and* out of trouble.

"Hey, now," Charlie called out. "Blackjack is better with more players, anyway—if anyone is up to the challenge of playing me."

Bob snickered. "You're on."

It didn't take more than fifteen minutes before Drew felt like a sardine in a can. Especially since he'd ended up in a compartment with Bob and his gang—Gary, Larry, and Steve. Thank goodness Charlie was in with them.

"Pheeeeew-weee! Man, put your shoes back on!" Bob griped to the group.

"You mean these?" Larry picked up Gary's putrid sneakers and tossed them to Steve, who tried to chuck them at Charlie, but the shoes ended up bouncing off Bob.

"Hey! Cool it, pops!" Bob gave Steve a playful shove, which knocked him into Larry, who fell onto Gary, which somehow took all four of them down into a wrestling heap in the tiny aisle between the pull-down bunks.

In a tangle, they arose, Bob's butt sliding along the compartment's window. His backside squashed against the glass, Bob pushed the other boys away from him. "Hey, any-one up for mooning the commies?" he crowed.

Steve had Gary in a headlock, rubbing his skull to mess up his hair, when the head MP appeared, passenger checklist in hand. "Anyone who sticks their bare buns up against that window will find them cooked," he growled. "Understood?"

"Yes, Sergeant," Bob replied. "Sorry, Sergeant. Just mess-ing around. You know how it is."

"Yes, we do," said the train commander, who'd sidled up behind the MP and now stood in the doorway as well. The lieutenant warned, "Gentlemen, I've been in charge of your teams during these crossings for a couple of months now. I've seen all your tricks. I expect you to straighten up and fly right—you're representing the United States of America."

"Yes, sir," the six murmured.

"Pull the shade down, now. We're about to depart," he instructed. "Remember, no looking out the window—that's our deal with the Russians as we pass through their zone." He rapped his knuckle against the instructions posted on the cabin's wall. "No photos, and no conversation with Soviet and GDR guards during the trip. Got it?"

"Yes, sir."

"I'm counting on you, boys."

"Yes, sir."

"Try to get some sleep. You want to be well rested for your meet tomorrow. Show those boys in Frankfurt what you're made of."

As soon as the officer moved away to the next compart-ment, Bob snorted. "What a Boy Scout."

Charlie and Drew exchanged an eye roll. The lieutenant was young, obviously a little green and still idealistic. Nothing like their seasoned veteran fathers. Even so, the guy was in command, and Drew respected that.

Drew considered Bob a moment. Hopefully, the Bob who'd gone with them to the jazz café—the Bob who could be cordial and honest, even diplomatic—would win out over the version that itched to make trouble. If not, they were all in for a long night.

At that very moment, Larry farted loudly. Bob answered with a trumpet blast of his own.

Drew sighed. A long night, for sure.

Thirty minutes later, the train lurched into Potsdam—the edge of the American sector. It ground to a halt, belching steam, straddling the line between the city's free zones and forty-two thousand square miles of communist-controlled country.

Tweeeeeeeet. Tweeeeeeeet. KA-THUNK. Clang, clang, clang.

Engine change.

The boys quieted as the American locomotive that had been pulling their train detached and chugged away onto a side rail, its warning whistles and bells screaming, its engineer shouting out the window.

After a few minutes came an answering *clang-clang-clang. BUMP. Hissssssssssssssssss.* Their train shuddered as an East German engine backed into it and locked on, spitting steam.

Drew had taken the duty train several times. But his stomach still flip-flopped at the sound of the train coupling. He and his teammates would be traveling for hours through communist territory, pulled by a *communist* engine, policed and surrounded by *communist* officials. Add to that surreal situation the strict orders not to look out the windows or to talk to anyone, and any guy who said he wasn't weirded out by it all was lying.

German voices trickled down the narrow corridor as the East German crew boarded and the conductor asked his West German counterpart for the train's passenger list. The lieutenant and his English-Russian translator stepped off the train, stood on the platform right next to Drew's car, and spoke to the Soviet station chief and his interpreter. Their tone was oddly cordial.

Knowing they'd be sitting for a while as their documents were verified and the Soviet officer signed off with the lieutenant, the boys just couldn't help themselves. One after another, they peeped around the shade. Russian soldiers with rifles held at the ready walked up and down the length of the train, peering underneath the carriage, checking the wheels, as if the Americans had tucked contraband into the train's crevices.

"Dammit," Bob muttered as he lingered at the window, his face half hidden by the shade. "When's the lieutenant going to head into the station house? I have cigarettes to trade with the Russkies for their red star insignias."

"Don't you have a bunch of those already, Bob?" Charlie asked.

"Yeah, but the more the better. I can get a lot for those things back home."

From his top bunk, Bob leaned over and grabbed the window handle, pulling it open a few inches. "Psssst," he hissed at a Russian soldier below.

"*U vas yest' Amerikanskiye sigarety?*" a voice answered from below.

"Bob, don't be a dope," Drew whispered. "The lieutenant is right there—you'll get caught!"

"Doing all right, boys?" Their coach suddenly stood at their door.

Bob rolled back into his bunk with a low whistle, ridiculously conspicuous.

"*Sigarety?*" The voice came from below.

Sighing, the coach walked to the window and shut it. "Jones, I need you for the shot put. How about you just behave tonight—or do you need to bunk with me?"

"Oh, no, sir." Bob shook his head. "Sorry, sir."

"Twinkies!" *Thump.* "Hey, give it back!" *Thump-thump-thump.*

The muffled sounds of a food squabble from next door interrupted the coach. Clearly only half believing Bob, he left to quiet the boys in the adjacent cabin.

"Saved by the Twinkie!" Charlie joked. He pulled out his pack of cards. "Ready, fellas?"

"You're on," Drew answered. He happened to be very good at blackjack.

Twenty hands of blackjack later, the train finally began to move. Drew had won fourteen of the rounds so far, three times by splitting matching cards into two hands and once after daring to take five hits and still coming up under twenty-one. He'd already racked up fifty-two pennies from bets—enough for ten bottles of Coke.

As the train's wheels squealed and an acrid smell of sulfur drifted through the compartments from the cheaper-grade coal the East Germans used, Drew leaned back and put his hands behind his head. With calculated smugness and an arched eyebrow, he announced, "I'll stick." He had two cards, a queen on top, faceup.

"Man, he's got to have twenty-one," Steve whined, throwing down his cards.

One after another, the other boys tossed their cards at Charlie, who was dealing.

Only Bob held on and eyed Drew. "You bluffing, Mac?"

"Drew."

Bob laughed. "You bluffing . . . Drew?"

He shrugged, smiling.

"Okay, okay." Bob nodded. "I respect your moxie." He thought for a minute, then asked for a hit. "What the heck."

Charlie snapped down a ten. Busted. Bob turned over his cards, showing that he'd had nineteen before. The chance of Bob getting a two or an ace—the only cards that would have kept him in the game—had been ridiculously low.

Drew flipped over his hidden card. A three!

"What?!" Bob exploded. "You only had thirteen?" He stood up. Drew braced himself for some kind of insult or cockfight, but Bob saluted him. "Great bluff. I'm taking you with me, McMahon, when I have to stand post on a wall and stare down the enemy eye-to-eye."

As Drew pocketed his coins, Bob brushed something off his knee. "What the heck?" he muttered. He swatted at his shoulder, like a hornet was after him. Then he touched his cheek and wiped away a massive spitball.

Charlie got hit next. Then Gary, Larry, and Steve, who started punching each other, thinking one of them was the culprit.

Hearing faint snickers, Drew leaned over his middle bunk, scanning the wall beneath it, where the sound had come from. *Thwack!* He got hit in the forehead with a gooey spitball.

"Guys, guys!" He kept his voice low and pointed to the wall. What he saw had taken a lot of doing. Somehow, the boys next door had removed their light switch, which had left the one in Drew's cabin dangling. There were plenty of gaps around the wiring for straws to poke through, mini rocket launchers of spittle.

As he stared, four small reeds poked through—*thwack, thwack, thwack, thwack.*

The straws withdrew.

"Let's get 'em!" Steve, Larry, and Gary were about to dash out the door to pummel their neighbors, but Bob and Charlie blocked them.

"We need a plan first!" Charlie whispered, laughing.

"Yeah, yeah." Bob scanned their jammed compartment and spotted a few liters of German sparkling lemonade. "Sorry, boys, I'm commandeering these." He grabbed them and loosened the tops. "Molotov cocktails of pop." His grin was devilish. "Stiiiiii-cky!"

Drew dropped down from his bunk. "Hang on," he whispered. "Wait for the next shot."

Within seconds, out popped two straws.

"Follow my lead!" Drew took a deep breath and put his lips around a straw, blowing hard.

Arrrrggggg!

They could hear coughing through the wall. Drew had blasted the spitball right back into the assailant's mouth.

Charlie puckered around the other straw and blew. More coughing and laughing through the wall.

"ATTAAAACK!" Bob shouted. He and his minions charged out their door and into the next cabin.

Thump-b-sssssss. Thump-b-sssssss. Howls of laughter.

The lemon soda missiles exploded against the window and showered the compartment.

"Awwww, man! You guys are in for it!"

Bob, Larry, Gary, and Steve burst back into their compartment. Slamming the door shut behind them, they held it closed as the boys next door pounded and kicked, still guffawing.

"HEY!"

Sudden silence in the hall.

Bob waved everyone back into their bunks, retreat on the double.

The MP sergeant pulled their door open. He planted his feet and tapped his billy club against his hand. Behind him hovered the East German conductor, cursing about spoiled, ill-mannered Americans. Bringing up the rear were the lieutenant and their coach, both red-faced.

The MP sergeant didn't wait for orders from the lieutenant. "Know how we cool down men who get too rowdy in some of Berlin's finest establishments?" he asked.

"No, sergeant," Drew, Charlie, Bob, Gary, Larry, and Steve answered simultaneously.

"A few hours in the clink." The sergeant yanked their door closed again and locked it from the outside.

"Man, I gotta pee," Gary whimpered. "Anyone got an empty pop bottle?"

Precisely an hour later, the sergeant unlocked the door, telling them to go to the can and then bunk down for the night. "Quietly," he warned.

It was close to one a.m. Looking exhausted and sheepish, probably having been officially reprimanded by someone, their coach monitored the team as they brushed their teeth three at a time in the car's one bathroom. "For pity's sake, go to sleep now," he said as the boys climbed into their berths and he switched off the light.

Drew pulled up his scratchy army blanket and rolled over to face the wall. Lulled by the sway and *clack-clack, clack-clack* of the train on the track, he fell asleep pretty quickly.

"What the hell?" Bob's voice jarred Drew awake. Outside, searchlights swept along the shade. Bob was sitting up on the opposite bunk, lifting the curtain enough to peer out.

"What is it?" Drew whispered, not wanting to wake everyone else. He checked his wristwatch: 3:10. Close, but too soon for the East-West border. He knew the duty train made absolutely no station stops where Americans might mix and talk with citizens in the communist zone. It was a straight shot from Potsdam to Marienborn. There, the train manifest would be checked and approved again by the Russians to make sure they accounted for every American who'd boarded at the start of the trip, as if each one was a dangerous drop of poison that needed to be contained. At that point, the East German engine would detach, and a West German locomotive would latch on and pull them over the line into the free zone and on to Frankfurt.

"Looks like we're moving to a side rail."

"They do that, right?" Drew rubbed his eyes sleepily. "To let East German trains pass? I think they only have a single rail."

"Yeah, but that's a lot of activity out there," Bob answered.

Their train jerked to a stop.

Sitting up, Drew looked out the window himself. Bob was right—there were a lot of Soviet soldiers milling around for a side rail and small station. But maybe it wasn't *that* unusual. After all, the Russians maintained a huge occupation force of four hundred thousand men in East Germany. With that many soldiers on hand, they were sure to be distributed in big, purposefully intimidating clusters.

The oncoming eastbound train swooshed by noisily, rattling theirs and briefly lighting up the station's one sign. Magdeburg. Drew yawned and lay back down. "Another hour, and we'll be at the Soviet checkpoint," he mumbled, already starting to drift back off.

Bob remained on watch at the window.

Drew forced himself to stay awake long enough that he'd feel their train lurch forward, moving West again, moving toward American safety.

Five minutes. Ten. Nothing.

He sat back up and peeped around the shade, counting. One, two, three . . . fourteen Russian soldiers huddled together, keeping watch over their train.

Shouts and train whistles. A long, long exhaling *hisssssssssss*, and the train's engine went silent. Totally dead. Bob and Drew could see their East German conductor and engineer walking across the track, waving at the soldiers in friendly greeting, before disappearing into the small station.

"What are they doing?" Bob muttered.

Fifteen more minutes.

The railway men didn't reemerge. The Soviet soldiers didn't disperse. In fact, a few more joined them.

Bob and Drew eyed one another nervously. "Wish your cousin were here."

"Why?" Drew asked, surprised.

"He talked Russkie at the jazz club. Maybe he could find out from these guys what's going on."

"Yeah, maybe." Drew frowned a little, wondering if he would be able to trust Matthias's translation in a situation like this. Then he shook his head to dispel the question. He was way too paranoid, and he was being a jerk. Matthias had saved their butts at that club.

"Come on," Bob said, tipping his head toward the door. They dropped to the floor and slid the door open quietly, poking their heads out to look down the hall. All the compartments had at least one person doing the same.

"Anyone know what's happening?" Bob asked, to shrugs and head-shaking.

The exit leading to the next car slid open. The sergeant hustled down the corridor, followed by younger MPs holding rifles and the lieutenant, who kept repeating, "Everyone back into your cabins, please," as he passed.

"Holy hell," muttered Bob.

Darting back inside, Drew and Bob glued themselves to their window. The MPs stepped off the train, positioning themselves in front of the three sleeping cars' doors while the lieutenant and his translator talked with a Russian officer. This conversation was not cordial, not at all. The Soviet even seemed to laugh sneeringly as he walked away, leaving the lieutenant steaming.

It took the young officer several moments to collect himself before he climbed back onto the train, planting himself rigidly at the end of Drew's car. By this point, pretty much everyone was awake and crowding the cabin doors.

"In honor of their May Day celebrations," the lieutenant announced, "the Russians are stopping rail travel until the conclusion of the parades this morning so that all their workers can attend."

"What?" was the collective reaction.

"What about our track meet?"

"What about our flight out of Frankfurt?"

"What about my niece's wedding?" came shouts from the handful of other military family passengers on board.

The lieutenant held up his hand. "I plan to radio Berlin Command and ask that they intercede. I'll keep you informed. Right now, please go back to bed." He marched through the car, back to the radio operator, the sergeant pausing at each cabin door until its passengers retreated inside. No one argued with him.

Remarkably, Larry, Steve, and Gary were still snoring. Only Charlie hopped out of his bunk to join Drew and Bob at the window. Now that there were three of them, the boys crowded together on the floor so they could pull the shade up just a little to watch. Only their eyes and noses showed.

A few of the Russian soldiers paced closer and closer to the train—maybe hoping for American cigarette trades.

"Your cousin going to march in these bull-hockey May Day parades today?" Bob asked.

"Yeeaaah," Drew answered cautiously. "It's not like he has a choice. My mom told me that a refugee boy she was helping at Marienfelde was booted from his academic school for not being enthusiastic enough at a parade, and Mathias told me—" Drew stopped himself, realizing he might open Matthias up to trouble if he told Bob about the tribunal his cousin had been hauled in front of.

"Told you what?" Bob turned away from the window to face Drew.

"Nothing," he mumbled.

Bob studied Drew. "Why does Matthias stay in East Berlin?"

"Beats me." Drew knew all the reasons from his mom, but sharing them with Bob just didn't feel right.

Bob continued to stare at him.

Jeez, he'd be a good interrogator, Drew thought, squirming a bit under Bob's silent gaze. He tried joking. "Learn that glare from your dad?"

Bob blanched. "No. Learned other things—not that." He nodded to himself and to Drew. "*You* know." He didn't break his gaze, but Drew saw the unspoken gratitude in it. After a pause, Bob began again, "Drew, there's . . . there's something I should tell you."

"What?"

Taking a deep breath, Bob whispered, "That van outside your apartment . . ."

"So you did know about that."

"Drew," Charlie interrupted gently, "everyone knew about that van full of MPs and why they were probably there—either to protect you from something, or investigating your dad for CIC."

The army's Criminal Investigation Command. *Jesus, Mary, and Joseph.* Drew's mind reeled. So his family *had* basically been on probation with the entire post. "Okay, so?" he asked defensively. "What about it?"

"Look," Bob started again, "I . . . I owe you, Drew. And . . . and I can't believe I'm saying it, but I kinda like that commie cousin of yours. I . . . I know that a suspicious envelope was left on your dad's windshield . . . and . . . I bet you think Matthias was involved somehow."

Drew just scowled, holding his breath.

"He wasn't. It was me."

"What?" Drew exploded.

Larry, Gary, and Steve stirred, rolled over, and mercifully snorted back to sleep.

"I . . . I didn't leave the thing," Bob hurried to explain. "But . . . but I told my dad that Matthias was spending a lot of time at your apartment . . . and . . . I think Dad got one of the intelligence office's assets to follow you and leave the note . . . to see . . ." Bob sucked in another deep breath. "To see what your dad might do."

"Son of a—!" Drew grabbed Bob's shirt to shake him.

"Yeah, he is," Bob murmured, not fighting back.

"Have you got any idea how—we were—" Drew spluttered. "My dad—*your dad could have ruined him!*"

"Your dad didn't take the bait. So in the long run—"

Drew shook Bob even harder. "Of course he didn't! But this is probably in his file now—that test of his loyalty!" He pulled his fist back to punch Bob, not caring that Bob flinched.

"Drew, stop!" Charlie blocked the blow. He held Drew's fist and pulled him off Bob. "Guys, you need to see something." He pointed out the window. "Look! There's a kid out there. I think he's going to try to climb up under our train—to defect."

Still too furious at Bob to listen to anything else, Drew fought to shrug Charlie off. "Let go of me!"

"Drew, seriously, look!" Charlie urged, holding fast. "Look!" He pushed Drew toward the window so he couldn't help but see.

Bob followed.

In the shadows of the station was a teenager watching the pack of Russians. As the soldiers joked and laughed, the youth darted to hide behind a coal bin closer to the tracks.

"Yeah, yeah, I see him," said Bob. "Come on, kid," he whispered.

"Oh god, they've seen him." Charlie pressed his face against the pane. Two guards who'd been chatting nearer the bin were starting to stalk the German teen, who was focusing so hard on the train that he didn't notice he was being tracked from behind. "Dammit," Charlie breathed. "They're going to get him."

"No way," Bob muttered. "Not on my watch." He yanked up the shade and threw open the window. "Hey!" he bellowed. "Who wants some American cigarettes? Trade for your red star." He reached under his pillow to grab his pack of cigarettes and clambered up onto his bunk to hang halfway out the window.

"Bob! Don't!" Drew and Charlie gasped.

"*Amerikanskiye sigarety?*"

"*Da!* Good!" Bob glanced over to where they'd spotted the German youth, then back at Charlie and Drew, holding their gaze for a long beat before taking a deep breath and leaning way too far out of the window, his feet flailing off the bunk.

"Bob!" Drew and Charlie lunged to grab his legs, but Bob fell out of the train headfirst, onto a Russian soldier.

All the soldier's comrades rushed toward him to help nab the AWOL American.

The German teenager got away.

Bob was hauled into the station in his bare feet and pajamas, the lieutenant and MP sergeant running to catch up.

JUNE 1961

JFK travels to Vienna for a two-day summit with Khrushchev, stopping in Paris on the way. He himself will say the only real diplomatic success of the trip was garnered by the First Lady. Jackie totally charmed France's President Charles de Gaulle with her fluent French and deep knowledge of his nation's art and culture.

"I'LL BURY YOU."

JFK had planned an informal discussion of a nuclear test ban with Khrushchev, thinking he could use his eloquent charisma to impress and negotiate with the Soviet leader. However, the combative 67-year-old Russian—to quote JFK—"beat the hell out of me." Bragging he had sufficient weapons to destroy all American military bases, Khrushchev demands the U.S. and NATO stop challenging Russia's position in Berlin. If not, "we must respond," threatens Khrushchev. "It is up to the U.S. to decide whether there will be war or peace."

Saying he'd "never met a man like this," JFK triples the military draft, calls up the reserves, asks for an additional $3.25 billion in defense spending, and urges Americans to stock their basements as shelters with water, food, and first-aid kits. Khrushchev resumes aboveground nuclear tests.

In a dramatic escape, Rudolf Nureyev, the Kirov Ballet's most famous male principal, defects. Buoyed by the success of his space program, Khrushchev has allowed the ballet to take its very first foreign tour to also prove to the world what he believes to be Russian cultural superiority. Nureyev breaks free from Russian KGB officers to leap over a security barrier at the Paris airport, shouting: "I want to be free." French police whisk him away, pursued by furious Russians. Nureyev is granted asylum in the West.

In a devastating Cold War double-cross, a Berlin-based British MI-6 agent is revealed by a Polish defector to be a Russian mole. While George Blake was supposedly recruiting East Berliners to work for the Western Allies, he was actually reporting to the KGB. Besides exposing several Allied intelligence operations, Blake betrayed the identities of many U.S. and British assets in East Germany—civilians the GDR's Stasi arrest or assassinate.

CHAPTER ELEVEN
JUNE
1961

A month later, Drew and his friends were still talking about the night Bob dove out the train window into the Russian zone—and the fallout from it.

"Will Bob make it to the end-of-year picnic next week?" Shirley asked as she, Drew, and Charlie walked home from school.

Drew shook his head. "His family's been transferred stateside. Just like they always told us would happen to our dads if we did something stupid and got in trouble here. Mrs. Jones told Mom they're shipping out tonight, in fact. The transport van pulled up this morning as I left."

"The whole thing must have been so traumatizing for Bob," she murmured. "You sure the Soviets didn't hurt him?"

"They didn't," Charlie answered. "Not with a train full of Americans watching. The Russkies are smarter than that."

"It was actually a good thing for Bob that the train was stopped for the GDR's May Day shenanigans," Drew added. "That way, the lieutenant could stay with him until his dad and someone from our embassy could get there. We were stuck on the side rail for twelve hours. The train didn't budge until three o'clock that afternoon, after all the International Workers parades were over."

"Hell of a poker game, though." Charlie elbowed Drew as he looked around him to Shirley. "Your boy won close to twenty bucks! He's a bit of a card shark."

Smiling, she threaded her arm through Drew's. "I know. He told me that's how he bought me such a beautiful corsage for prom."

The trio walked on in silence for a few moments, thinking.

Quietly, Shirley asked, "And you're sure the East German kid got away?"

Drew nodded, looking to Charlie for confirmation. "We think so. We didn't see the guy being dragged into the station house. Everyone's focus seemed to be entirely on Bob. He created a helluva diversion. I swear every Russian at the station jumped on Bob in order to prove how committed a Red he is." Just like his dad had warned.

"It's not that I don't believe Bob is capable of something that heroic, but . . ." Shirley paused. "Do you think he knew what would happen?"

"Oh yeah," breathed Drew and Charlie together. It was the way Bob had looked back at them right before shimmying out the window—like a warrior going over a wall into enemy territory who knew he wasn't coming back.

"It's such a shame we can't celebrate what Bob did for that German boy, though, don't you think?" murmured Shirley.

"Yeah, it is," the boys agreed, again simultaneously.

"But when Charlie and I explained to the lieutenant why Bob went out that window, he was crystal clear that it wasn't to be broadcast," Drew said.

"It's because of another incident," Charlie explained. "There was an East German who did manage to climb through a duty train window when it was pulled to the side to let an East German train pass. But a Russian soldier saw him and sounded the alarm. That brought on a helluva standoff between our MPs and the guards. Our guys refused to hand over the East German—our duty train is sovereign American territory. The guy was seeking asylum." Charlie paused. "Can you imagine? A half-dozen MPs standing post at the train doors against a whole garrison of Russian and GDR soldiers in the middle of the Soviet occupation zone? That took some guts."

"Did . . . did we take the man to freedom?" Shirley asked, barely above a whisper.

Grimly, Charlie shook his head. "No. After hours of trying to negotiate with the Russian high command to let us keep the guy, HQ ceded the battle and ordered the train commander to turn the German back over to the Stasi. My dad said we had to—it was too much of a powder keg. Refusing to give the guy up could have been the spark that ignited World War III."

"Oh," Shirley gasped. "That's . . . awful."

Drew nodded. "Yeah. They had no choice, I guess. But lord knows what happened to that poor guy."

Sighing, the trio stopped, standing at the street corner that sent them in separate directions to their apartments.

"So," Charlie concluded, "if the Russians knew about another potential defector—the kid we saw—trying to hop on our train, that could have been reason enough for them to shut down American passage through the occupied zone. They could've said the duty train presents a lure and provocation for—" He broke off, looking to Drew. "What's the right GDR term for escape, the one that means treason?"

"Republikflucht."

"Right. So *we* can know what Bob did, but the official report on the incident has to say that a military kid was screwing around, trying to swap cigarettes for Russian insignia pins."

"That's technically why Bob was suspended," Drew added.

"Life here is . . . is so . . ." Shirley trailed off.

"Strange?" Charlie offered.

"Harsh," she answered.

Drew kissed her forehead.

Blessing him with a sad smile, she murmured, "I should go. Mom's waiting to take us shopping at the PX so I can get a new bathing suit for Wannsee Lake tomorrow." She brightened a little at the thought of their outing. "Till then."

They watched her until she made it to her building, and then Charlie said, "That's a lovely lady, Drew. You're a lucky dog." He punched Drew's shoulder and turned toward his apartment. "See ya tomorrow."

As he headed home, Drew spotted Joyce walking with her arm around Linda's shoulders. He hadn't been able to find his sisters in the halls after school, and he trotted to catch up. "Hey! I was looking for you two! Where were you?"

Linda looked up at Drew, her eyes red from crying.

"What happened?" he asked, looking to Joyce.

"Twelve-year-old girls," she muttered angrily. "They were passing notes in class, and one of the ninnies dropped hers."

"It was Patty," Linda wailed. "She dropped it right in front of my desk. My teacher thought I'd written it, so she opened it in front of the whole class to reprimand me." Linda took a deep breath. "It . . . it was a really mean drawing of me, with my hair all frizzled in red pen, holding a stuffed animal." Embarrassed tears slipped down her face. "I should never have played vet with her and my teddy bears."

"Why the heck would Patty do something like that?" Drew asked, angry and surprised both.

"Some girls just get mean and cliquey the instant they discover lipstick," Joyce said. "You don't know, because you have Linda and me as sisters, and we aren't like that." She hugged Linda. "Right, soldier?"

"Right," she murmured.

"Listen, cutie, forget Patty. Drew and I are going to Wannsee Lake with the gang tomorrow. Come with us."

"Yeah! Be with the cool guys," Drew joined in. "That's where you belong!"

Linda wiped her eyes. "Is . . . is Matthias coming, too?"

Joyce smiled and nodded.

"Ooooookay," Linda said slowly.

Joyce and Drew flanked her, and arm in arm, they started home as Linda asked, "May I bring your soccer ball, Drew?"

"Of course! You're getting good with that thing. Matthias can show you some moves."

Linda blushed and looked down, kicking at pebbles as they walked. "Thanks for finding me and pulling me out of the girls' room," she murmured to Joyce.

"That's what sisters are for," Joyce said quietly, gently tugging Linda's strawberry-blond ponytail. There was a little catch in her voice as she said it.

It gave Drew a pang, too. He hoped he'd know how to be a good brother to Linda without Joyce showing him the way when she went to London for college. Truth be told, Drew wasn't sure how he'd do with Joyce gone, either. Their unit was breaking apart, their leader promoted out of the ranks.

Later that afternoon, Drew opened the front door to find Bob standing there. They hadn't really talked since the train; Bob had been in the penalty box all month. "Take a walk with me?" he asked.

The boys made it all the way to the swing sets behind the school before Bob started talking. "Berlin Command is sending Dad back to the Pentagon."

"Jeez, I'm sorry, Bob." Drew meant it. His own dad would hate being behind a desk again, no matter how close it put him to the military brass. And if Drew were the cause of that transfer, he wasn't so sure how his nice-guy dad would react.

"No, it's okay," Bob murmured, sitting down on a swing, absentmindedly swaying back and forth. "It could have been a lot worse of a reprimand. And Berlin brought out the worst in him. The worst in me." He thought for a moment. "Listen, Drew. I didn't get to finish my apology before . . . before I did a Humpty Dumpty out the window. But I'm really sorry about that envelope. I had no idea that telling Dad about Matthias hanging with you so much would give him the idea to—"

"Try to screw over my dad?" Drew interrupted.

"Yeeaah," Bob said slowly. He didn't try to shrug off Drew's damning interpretation of Sergeant Jones's actions.

"What if my dad hadn't said anything about that envelope and had just torn it up and thrown it in the trash?" Drew felt his freckles nearly scorch his face in renewed indignation about the whole thing.

"Honestly? I don't know," Bob answered. "But I mean it, Drew. I didn't have any idea my dad would concoct that kind of setup. He didn't tell me until after the van was sitting outside your apartment. Then, once the MPs were gone, he said what a good guy your dad was. So in the end, maybe it was a good thing for your dad. But I . . . I hope you believe me." He put his hand out for a shake. "Are we jake?"

Grudgingly, Drew took it. "I guess. Out of respect for what you did on the train, if for no other reason. That was . . . outstanding."

"Thanks, Drew." Bob started his slow swing again. "Of all the things I've done to try to get my dad's attention, that window thing—which I did without thinking, and what should have gotten me in a heap of trouble—seems to have finally gotten through to him." Bob stopped swinging abruptly. "He actually said he was proud of me."

"Yeah?"

Bob nodded. "He got all protective when he got to the station and saw a bunch of armed Russkies surrounding his kid." Bob grinned. "And when we got back home, I explained *why* I did it—that for once I wasn't just goofing off. That we'd spotted the German kid trying to escape, and that he was about to get caught." Bob shrugged. "I don't know, but I think it's going to be better with Dad now. I hope so, anyway."

"How is your mom taking it?"

"Oh, she's relieved. She's never liked it here." Bob stood and started walking back to their apartment building. "She's actually been packing a Smith and Wesson in her purse this whole time, in case the Russkies decided to invade our sector in some surprise attack. We'd put up a good fight, of course. But c'mon, we're outnumbered ten to one. It'd take a miracle for us to hold the fort. She's really afraid of being an American woman here if Berlin fell, after what happened to German women at the end of World War II when the Red Army captured the city. It just wasn't safe in the streets for a long time. A lot of moms go home because they can't handle that fear." He paused and heaved a sigh. "Thinking about that guy being so desperate to get on our train . . . it's really not all that safe now, either. Is it? Especially given how Khrushchev just wiped the floor with your guy last week in Vienna."

Drew ignored the criticism of JFK—he knew Bob was a big Nixon fan, and Kennedy had kind of blown it at that summit. "But that kid *wasn't* caught and hauled off by the Stasi, thanks to you, Bob. That's something."

"Yeah." Bob stuck out his lower lip, considering. "I guess. But being free would have been better."

After several heavy beats of silence, Bob punched Drew on the shoulder—friendly, the way he had the day they'd first met. "Gotta go. We leave in an hour. Thanks for everything, man. Keep in touch, okay? Really. See you at West Point, maybe."

"Not if I see you first," Drew joked.

Giving Drew a playful salute, Bob jogged away.

━᚜ιιƙ━

Drew was still mulling over his conversation with Bob the next morning as he, Shirley, and Charlie sat on towels at Wannsee Lake. They were watching the growing throng of sunbathing West Berliners settle on the grassy banks.

It was the first really warm summer day, and Berliners were out in force. A man and woman plunked themselves down right in front of their group and quickly stripped down to their bathing suits.

Blushing, Shirley looked down at the grass and plucked a few blades. The guy's bathing suit was European-style tiny and about as revealing as the statues at the Olympic pool.

Drew put his arm protectively around her.

"It could be worse," Charlie gently teased Shirley. "There's a nude beach on the bank over there." He pointed across the wide lake, crowded with sailboats.

"Are you kidding?" Drew asked.

"Nope." Charlie shook his head. "We went there by mistake last year. Old guys. Lots of flab and wrinkles and"—he laughed—"*you-know-what* on full display. Au naturel."

"Ewww." Shirley managed a nervous giggle.

"Hey, guys! Sorry we're late." Joyce dropped her bag and towel and started pulling off her blue-and-white-striped culottes and matching blouse. "Where's Linda?"

"Over there with Matthias and Heidi." Drew pointed toward the tree line, where Matthias was dribbling his soccer ball in circles, chased by Linda and a happily barking Heidi.

"She's okay?"

"I think so," Drew answered.

Shirley looked up at Joyce, shading her eyes against the sun. Drew had told her and Charlie about Patty's drawing. "Aren't you glad you're not that age anymore?"

"Heck, yes," Joyce answered emphatically.

"I can't believe anyone could be mean to Linda. She's total sweetness." Charlie shook his head.

"Do you think Patty dropped the note on purpose?" Shirley asked.

"Yeah," Joyce responded just as vehemently.

"Girls do that kind of stuff?" Charlie asked with surprise.

"Oh, honey." Joyce smiled. "This is why we like you so much, Charlie."

Shirley and Drew shared an *awwww* look at the way Charlie sat up tall at Joyce's compliment. But his pleased look evaporated instantly as Fritz appeared.

"*Bist du bereit?*" he asked Joyce.

She nodded happily. "Fritz rented a Sunfish to show me how to sail. Anybody want to join us? It just holds two people, but we can take turns."

"*Ja, ja.* Come with us," said Fritz as he dropped his pants to his ankles and stepped out of them.

Shirley started pulling at the grass again—fistfuls of it.

"Ah, thanks, but we'll stay here," Drew answered for her. "Why don't you go with them, Charlie?"

Charlie was desperately fighting off a laugh. "Nah, I'm happy here. Have fun."

"Suit yourselves!" Joyce said merrily as she took Fritz's hand and practically skipped to the water's edge with her basically naked boyfriend in his handkerchief-sized bathing suit.

"Goodbye, Berlin, *auf Wiedersehen* . . ." Charlie began singing.

" . . . so *wunderbar,* so *wunderschön* . . ." Drew joined in the popular song.

"*Auf Wie-der-sehen* . . ." Shirley rounded out the trio's amusement as they all waved a joking goodbye to Fritz's retreating butt.

Shirley ended their laughter abruptly. "Speaking of goodbyes . . ." she said. Then she hesitated.

"What?" Drew nudged her. "A *Pfennig* for your thoughts." He repeated the awkward phrase he'd used during their pool outing back in the winter. "Remember?" he asked.

"Yes." She smiled shyly. "Of course." Still she paused.

Drew waited.

When Shirley spoke again, Drew could tell it wasn't what she had originally planned to say. He'd seen the slight shift of expression on her beautiful face, like a sailboat on the lake gracefully changing tack to catch the wind. "So . . . Bob's gone? *Auf Wiedersehen?*"

"Yeah. Totally cleared out."

"Is he okay?" Charlie asked. "Do you know how . . . what did his dad say about everything?"

Charlie clearly knew some of what Drew did about the troubled relationship between Bob and his dad. But Bob had earned Drew's discretion, even with someone as trustworthy as Charlie. "Things seemed to be okay" was all Drew said. "Saying goodbye to Berlin is going to be good for that family, I think."

Taking another deep breath, Shirley repeated, "Speaking of goodbyes . . ." This time, she rushed to say what was on her mind. "Dad told us last night that the State Department has been really impressed with his work here." She paused, pressing her lips together to suppress their trembling.

Drew felt his heart flip-flop. He'd heard the beginning of this type of conversation before.

"He's been offered the chance to attend the War College in DC, and . . ."

Charlie stood. "I'm going to get us a few root beers," he said, and hurried away.

Shirley took Drew's hand. "We're not leaving until July."

Drew wanted to howl in anger. *Why?* Why did military families have to move around so much all the damn time?

But Shirley's eyes were begging him to help her deal with what this meant for them. He sucked in his breath and managed to croak, "Then we'll just have to make the most of June, I guess. Summer love and all."

The smile Shirley gave him was as good as a kiss.

Good thing, too, since just as Drew leaned over to give her a real one, a soccer ball bounced up against them.

"Sorry!" Linda called as she darted toward their encampment, followed by Heidi.

The little dog bounded into Shirley's lap as Matthias threw himself down beside Drew. "She has skills, your little sister."

Flushed from running, Linda beamed. "Matthias says he'll coach me over the summer so I can get good enough to play for school."

"She would make an excellent midfielder." He tapped his forehead. "Very smart. She would distribute the ball well."

"I'm afraid there isn't a girls' soccer team," Shirley said gently. "No girls' athletics, just cheerleading."

Linda frowned. "Well . . . maybe I'll start one. Matthias can teach me how to do that." She gathered her dachshund into her arms. "Heidi can be our mascot."

Damn, thought Drew. He glanced over at Matthias and murmured gratefully, "Thanks."

Matthias smiled back. "*Kein Problem*. I have decided I like having cousins."

>)))k-

"Cupcakes!" They'd all regathered for lunch, and Charlie was digging through the picnic basket Drew's mom had packed before she'd left for Marienfelde for the day. "Oh, wow," he breathed as he bit into one. "Marble cake. Your mom's the best."

"Yes, she is," said Joyce.

Cross-legged, eating her cupcake as she pulled back the paper, Linda mumbled, "I just wish she'd come to the lake with us. Ever since we got to Berlin, she seems busy all the time."

Joyce reached over, napkin in hand. "You've got icing on your nose, kiddo." Then she gave Linda a hug. "Mom's never not been there when you needed her, right?"

Linda shrugged. "I guess."

"The camp only gets busier and busier. They need her, too. Frankly, I don't know how she does it all," Joyce continued.

"She made these cupcakes from scratch this morning. At 0630, when I was just crawling out of bed."

"But why did she have to go help refugees today? It's Saturday!"

"*Torschlusspanik.*"

They all turned to look at Matthias.

"*Torschlusspanik,*" he repeated.

"Closing-door panic," Fritz translated. "Since the failed U.S.-Soviet summit, the GDR is more confident and is tightening the noose. They announced they will soon issue fewer passes for East Germans who live outside Berlin to visit their families here in the city. Being granted the right to visit Berlin is how most refugees slip into the city's American sector and then into Marienfelde to ask for asylum. So any East German who has considered fleeing to the West is hurrying to try it now, fearing that the escape hatch is closing."

"Your President Kennedy did this," Matthias added with some anger. "He made a mistake thinking Chairman Khrushchev was just a peasant, not smart like him. Our newspapers in East Berlin say Khrushchev humiliated Kennedy. Now Khrushchev thinks he can push Americans out of Berlin and take the free zone into Russian control." He turned to Drew. "I thought you said your President Kennedy was clever."

"He is!" protested Drew.

"But he's made things worse. Now Khrushchev is more bold. As Fritz says, he makes things harder for East Germans who wish to defect, yes. But also for Berliners who believe in the equality and justice of socialism and return dutifully to the Eastern sector every night. Like me. Like *Mutter*. We have proven our loyalty and deserve open borders," said Matthias. "The rumor is that Khrushchev has sent the Russian chief of secret police to East Berlin to oversee the crackdown. I may have to carry a *Kennkarte*—an identity card that will only allow me to be in a district the SED chooses. Like the Russians do in the Soviet Union. If this happens, I will not be able to visit you."

"W-what?" Linda whimpered.

Matthias frowned. "I would not like this, either." He rubbed his forehead like his head was suddenly pounding. "Because of the panic, the Stasi, the FDJ, the Russians—they watch us more. They search for *Republikflüchter* and anyone they think helps them." He looked to Drew. "On high alert, yes?"

"Yes, that's the right phrase."

"The *Republikflüchter* endanger us all."

"But the urge to live free is so strong, my friend," Fritz said, patting Matthias's back. "Think on it." Then he turned to Linda. "German-speaking people like your mom, who can translate, are of great importance to the refugees at Marienfelde. You should be proud of her."

Linda sighed. "I suppose." She stood. "Come on, Heidi. Let's go for a walk."

Joyce and Drew watched their little sister pick her way through the sunbathers towards the tree line where she'd been dribbling the soccer ball with Matthias.

"It's going to be hard for her to trust new friends after Patty," Joyce said sadly. She touched Drew's arm. "You'll keep a good eye on her after I'm gone? Promise?"

Drew nodded. "Hopefully, there'll be some nice kids coming in as their dads get new orders." He choked a little on the words and glanced toward Shirley. Her eyes glistened with held-back tears.

They went back to their cupcakes silently until Joyce found some cheerful small talk to chat about. "I'm so happy *West Side Story* is coming to the Titania Palace Theater before I leave for London. I've been learning 'One Hand, One Heart.' It's so hard to hit those high notes delicately and on pitch. I can hardly wait to hear how this Maria performs it."

"Well, I can't wait to see Natalie Wood in the movie version that's coming out later this year," said Shirley. "She was so good in *Rebel Without a Cause*."

"But can she sing?" asked Joyce.

"She must be able to," Shirley insisted. "Fun fact: did you know her parents fled Russia?"

Charlie shook his head, but all Drew could think about was how much Shirley's beauty reminded him of Natalie Wood.

"Her real name is Natalia Nikolaevna Zakharenko."

"Really? Bet the Russians are steamed that she's such a big star in the West now," said Charlie.

"Yes," Fritz gloated. "Just as they fume about Nureyev— Russia's best dancer leaping over chairs at the airport to escape KGB agents. Crowds of people watching Nureyev cry out that he wanted freedom—*ha!* That threw some mud on Khrushchev!"

Matthias had been gazing into the distance, not seeming to pay much attention to their conversation. He stopped it short when he quietly warned, "It is best not to poke at a bear unless you truly mean to fight it. That is the question, is it not? What can Americans do if the Russian bear rises up against West Berlin? What are you willing to do? That is what brings *Torschlusspanik.*"

He turned to look at Drew and Joyce, letting a beat pass before asking, "May I have a cupcake, please?"

Drew cringed inside, watching Matthias linger over each bite as if memorizing the taste of the cupcake, while his mind reeled at his cousin's rhetorical question. What would Drew's father have to do if Khrushchev ordered a takeover of West Berlin? What should Americans risk for German freedom? For Germans like Matthias? The words Shirley had quoted from her nana—to not just stand by, to get involved, that the worst sin was indifference—came to him.

Staring off in the direction Linda had gone while he munched, Matthias seemed unaware that Drew was watching him. So Drew took careful measure. He'd known his cousin almost a year now, and Matthias still looked as pale and scrawny as when they'd met. He wasn't that much taller than Linda, which made it hard to believe he and Drew were the same age. Drew thought about the constant bread and meat shortages reported in East Berlin. Apparently, a guy could grow only so much on cabbage and onions and the state-run People's Own Enterprise goulash.

Last August, Drew had been appalled—and a little disgusted, if he was honest about it—when he'd spotted Matthias pocketing food at their welcome party. This morning, Drew made a mental note to send whatever cupcakes were left home with Matthias.

"*Wer ist der Mann?*" Matthias muttered.

"What man?" Drew followed Matthias's gaze to the tree line, where Linda had been tossing a stick for Heidi to retrieve. The old dachshund had given up and was lying in the shade, chomping on the twig a few yards away from her.

A man was approaching Heidi. Amid the sunbathers, he stood out, since he was fully clothed, but he was clad in typical-enough summer attire—a bright madras short-sleeved shirt and linen pants. He walked with a bit of a limp, but that was not uncommon among men in their forties in Berlin—lingering war wounds. Probably just a dog lover.

When the man leaned over to pat Heidi, Matthias sat up tall, straining to see. When he scooped up Heidi, Matthias stood.

A dog lover—just like the MPs had warned Linda against! Just like the guy in the Grunewald who'd tried to nab a colonel's daughter! Drew catapulted to his feet and bolted. Matthias was right behind him.

As Linda trotted toward the man to retrieve her dog, they rushed up so quickly that she nearly tripped, she was so startled. The man almost dropped Heidi. "*Was ist los?*" Matthias shouted at him. The dachshund yapped and squirmed.

Instinctively, Drew planted himself between Linda and the man. "Hey, sis." He tried to sound calm. "What's going on?"

"N-n-nothing," she stammered.

Matthias wrested Heidi out of the stranger's arms.

"*Was ist los mit dir, junger Freund?*" the man asked Matthias gruffly. He was pasty-faced, his bald head smooth and shiny. His eyes blinked, big and froglike, behind wire-rimmed glasses.

Matthias held his ground. "*Sie beißt,*" he proclaimed. Heidi was really barking at the stranger now.

"No, she doesn't bite at all," Linda protested, gathering the old dog up in her arms.

Drew had never seen Heidi growl like that before. The dachshund's reaction fueled his own distrust of the man. He followed Matthias's lead. "Oh yes, she does bite, sis," he insisted. "Ripped a big ol' hole in the *Bundespost* guy's pants last week."

"What?" Linda looked up at Drew, shocked. "Mom didn't tell me that."

Drew put his arm around his little sister, bade farewell to the man with as much politeness as he could muster, and turned Linda back toward the rest of their group—all of whom were now standing, looking alarmed. Matthias followed.

Making his eyes wide, Drew looked straight at Joyce. "I was just telling Linda that Heidi bit the German postman the other day," he said over Linda's head.

Joyce took his cue. "That's right. I think Heidi just doesn't like men she doesn't know. So in the future, kiddo, to keep the silly old girl happy, don't be talking to strangers, okay?"

Keeping up his pretense of nonchalance, Drew clapped his cousin on the back and announced, "After that race, I need an RC. Come on, Matthias—I've still got a little dough left over from taking Charlie to the cleaners in blackjack. My treat."

"Cleaners?" Matthias looked baffled.

Charlie started to follow, but Drew waved him off, sensing the conversation he was about to have with Matthias needed to be private. "I'll bring one back for you, Charlie."

"Did you recognize that guy?" Drew asked when they were out of earshot.

"No," Matthias answered.

"Me neither," Drew said. Worrying that maybe he'd overreacted, Drew hesitated to tell Matthias about the MPs' warning. "I just . . . I didn't like the looks of him."

"Me neither," Matthias echoed. "*Torschlusspanik* has me on . . . high alert." He gave Drew a chagrined smile of apology. "I am most likely wrong about the man. But we must all be careful of strangers who could be *Spitzel*—the Stasi spies I told you of. Linda especially." He put his hand on Drew's arm. "The Stasi are everywhere in Berlin, even your sector. They want information about *Republikflüchter* so they can harm family left behind to make an example. To scare others from the thought of leaving."

"But that doesn't have anything to do with us," said Drew. "My dad doesn't work with the refugees."

"No. But your mother does. To them, she is more dangerous than a soldier like your father. As a translator, she helps the West woo away our most talented citizens, a drain that destroys our country. The Party calls it *Menschenhandel*— Western abduction, capitalist man trade."

"That's a crazy way to look at people choosing to flee oppression," Drew insisted.

Matthias shrugged. "To the Party, it is all an American conspiracy. They teach us that you are the devil. You tempt good socialists away." He studied Drew for a moment. "But . . ." He looked pointedly at Drew, then at his backside, and deadpanned, "I see no tail or horns on you today."

"Ha-ha," Drew pretended to laugh. "I left my pitchfork behind at my apartment."

Matthias stopped walking to make sure Drew was really listening to him. "Working at Marienfelde, your mother knows the names of refugees who go through the camp. She may also know where you Americans relocate them in West Germany—that's the kind of detail the Stasi would love to learn. But to get that information out of her would only be possible if she were scared. What better way to coerce your mother than by holding—"

"Linda," Drew whispered.

Matthias nodded. "But I am on"—he made quotation marks—"'high alert.' I see things that are not there sometimes. Shadows. What is your saying about shadows?"

"Being afraid of your own shadow."

"Ah." Matthias considered that a moment. "Yes. Hard to know what is real and what is only my imagination."

Drew certainly knew that feeling. Berlin bred it.

JULY 1961

Khrushchev's escalating threats to forcibly annex West Berlin sparks a *Torschlusspanik*, "closing-door panic." East Germans scramble to escape while they still can, flooding Marienfelde in staggering numbers—30,415 in July alone. After harrowing escapes—hiding from neighbors, dodging patrols, bluffing their way through checkpoints—many collapse emotionally once they reach the camp's safety.

Stasi agents infiltrate the camp as well, posing as workers or asylum seekers. These spies hope to gather personal info on refugees to use in coercing them into becoming Russian assets once they are settled in their new lives in the West. Many refugees hide their faces—terrified a Stasi agent might recognize or photograph them.

To keep pace with the humanitarian crisis and surge in refugees to the camp, the American Berlin Brigade provides 2,500 field rations each day.

The camp rushes to find refugees housing and jobs so they can be relocated quickly. Pan Am, Air France, and British European Airways (BEA) airlift 1,000 refugees a day from Tempelhof Airport to safety in West Germany.

A GDR refugee, Marlene Schmidt, wins the Miss Universe pageant, representing West Germany. Schmidt was an electrical engineer, well employed and favored in East Germany's socialist state, and had planned to make her life there. She fled only after being threatened with jail for not turning in her own sister and mother for wanting to escape. After Schmidt is crowned, the GDR denounces her as a greedy, corrupt traitor, prostituted by an amoral West.

Despite the growing crisis between East and West Berlin, annual cultural events go on in West Germany as symbols of artistic freedom. American opera singer Grace Bumbry becomes the first person of color to sing at the legendary Bayreuth Festival, long associated with Hitler's favorite composer, Richard Wagner. The 24-year-old gives such a moving performance as Venus in *Tannhauser*, she wins over conservative operagoers shocked by her casting and receives 42 curtain calls.

CHAPTER TWELVE
JULY
1961

"It's so nice of you to come today," Drew's mom said, smiling over at him as they drove to Marienfelde. "Are you sure you really want to spend a beautiful July Saturday at the camp? You don't mind missing *Volksfest* this weekend?"

Drew made himself smile back at her. "It's okay. I did my time manning the popcorn booth last weekend. We've already raised enough money to buy new couches for the teen club. And besides . . ." He broke off. Drew had been with Shirley at the post's German-American festival the previous weekend. Now she was gone, sailing back to the States. It would be too empty at the carnival without her.

Reading his mind, his mom said, "I'm so sorry about Shirley's family being transferred, honey. She is a lovely girl.

You'll stay special friends, though. You can write, and . . . and who knows—maybe you'll go to the same college."

Drew ground his teeth. He knew his mom meant well, but being pen pals with a girl he loved wasn't exactly what a guy wanted.

His mom stayed silent for a few moments and then tried light and breezy chitchat instead. "It seems like the *Volksfest* has been a good idea. I'm so glad the CO is taking a cue from Jackie Kennedy—winning people over with cultural events."

Drew managed a laugh. "You sure a carnival with a Wild West theme is a *cultural* event?" he teased her. Drew had felt like an idiot wearing a cowboy hat and toy six-shooters. Shirley, of course, had somehow remained sophisticated and beautiful even done up in a red gingham dress and enormous pioneer sunbonnet.

For a bittersweet moment, he flashed back to the mini Ferris wheel stopping with them in the top bench, dangling, treating them to a two-minute sweeping view of the city. "Here's looking at you, kid," he'd said, pointing to the Brandenburg Gate in the distance and imitating Humphrey Bogart in *Casablanca*. "We'll always have Berlin."

Clearing his throat to keep from tearing up, Drew joked halfheartedly, "Matthias gave me heck about those dumb plastic pistols I was packing. He kept asking me to spin them the way John Wayne does and calling me 'pardner.'"

"Did Matthias enjoy the carnival?"

The image of Matthias shouting, "Yee-haw!" every time

he bashed his bumper car into Drew's did cheer him up a bit. "Yeah, he did enjoy it."

"You and Matthias seem to be getting close. Real friends."

"Yeah." Drew nodded. He fell silent again and stared blankly out the window.

"Well," his mom said, "I'm really grateful to have your company today, and I'm proud of you for coming. The camp has become such an all-hands-on-deck emergency. We can feed and house three thousand refugees at a time during the week it takes us to verify their stories, check their health, and find suitable resettlement situations for them in West Germany. But every morning, we open the doors to a thousand more people, desperate to get in. We're overwhelmed. So anything you do today will be an enormous help."

"Glad to help, Mom. It's . . . it's what Shirley would do."

"Awww, honey," his mom murmured. She reached over and took his hand. "This is the hard part of our life in the army—the constant uprooting, and the sudden good-byes with people we've come to love. But it's also the good part—the fact that we meet so many people with so many perspectives and experiences widens our minds to things we may not have thought of ourselves. Makes our hearts bigger, even if they ache when we part. I know Shirley has touched you in so many ways—maybe even changed you a little for the better, sweetheart—and in that way, she will always be part of you.

"Oh gosh," Drew's mom interrupted herself as the radio broadcast switched from music to the news. "Sounds like they're playing the president's remarks from the Oval Office last night." She turned up the radio. "I wish we had a TV."

JFK's polished Bostonian voice filled the car: *Seven weeks ago tonight I returned from Europe to report on my meeting with Premier Khrushchev . . . His grim warnings about the future of the world . . . his subsequent speeches and threats . . . and the increase in the Soviet military budget . . . these actions will require sacrifice on the part of many of our citizens . . . The immediate threat to free men is in West Berlin . . .*

Drew and his mom exchanged a troubled look.

Kennedy continued: *For West Berlin—lying exposed one hundred and ten miles inside East Germany, surrounded by Soviet troops and close to Soviet supply lines—has many roles. It is more than a symbol . . . more than a link with the Free World . . . an escape hatch for refugees. West Berlin is all of that. But above all, it has now become—as never before— the great testing place of Western courage and will, a focal point where our solemn commitments stretching back over the years since 1945, and Soviet ambitions now meet in basic confrontation . . .*

Drew's mom extended her right hand protectively, pulling him to her side of the bench seat, under her arm.

I hear it said that West Berlin is militarily untenable . . . Any dangerous spot is tenable if men—brave men—will make it so. We do not want to fight—but we have fought before. And others in earlier times have made the same dangerous mistake of assuming that the West was too selfish and too soft and too divided to resist invasions of freedom in other lands.

Those who threaten to unleash the forces of war on a dispute over West Berlin should recall the words of the ancient philosopher: "A man who causes fear cannot be free from fear."

Drew and his mom reached the southernmost corner of the American sector of Berlin as JFK ended his address with a plea. *Now, in the thermonuclear age, any misjudgment on either side about the intentions of the other could rain more devastation in several hours than has been wrought in all the wars of human history. Therefore, I, as president and commander in chief . . . need your goodwill, and your support—and above all, your prayers.*

The weight of the danger, the apocalyptic consequences of any mistake JFK, his nation, or any American in Berlin might make settled as heavy as the city's rubble mountains on Drew. Turning off the radio, Drew's mom spoke in a grave voice. "Honey, the eastern perimeter of the camp borders the Russian zone, so please don't meander out that way when you take a break today. We're all very careful to avoid creating any kind of confrontation at the line."

"Wow—that close?"

She nodded. "It couldn't be helped. This is where there was available land. But that proximity—the refugees seeing Russians on patrol as they wait for asylum with us—really rattles them. So be prepared for some to be pretty fearful on top of being hungry and exhausted."

They rounded a corner.

"Oh my goodness!" Drew's mom caught her breath. "I've never seen the line stretch this far this early in the morning."

"Guess they heard Kennedy's speech, too," Drew murmured. He slid back to his side of the front seat and took in the morass of people who'd managed to escape a police state that had to keep its citizens by force.

Snaking toward them was a restless, thrumming line of hundreds of people, clumped together in family units. Elderly Germans sat slumped on bundles of whatever they'd been able to smuggle across the border and carry away from the homes they'd never see again. Mothers held up umbrellas against the already-hot July sun to shield children, who napped on coats on the pavement. Babies cried in strollers. Fathers paced. Young adults talked animatedly, testing out American slang that before would have brought them trouble. Others hungrily read West Berlin papers they'd purchased from newsboys working the sidewalk.

Drew's mom parked, and she and Drew hustled through the camp's entrance, where a massive sign read: THE FREE WORLD WELCOMES YOU.

"Entschuldigen Sie, bitte." His mom excused them as she guided Drew through throngs of people to the main reception building. She headed for the door reserved for the five hundred American, British, French, and German workers who manned Marienfelde's medical clinic, mess halls, screening offices, and apartment complexes.

"Bitte . . ." An older lady reached out and caught his mom's sleeve, tugging fretfully on it. *"Hast du meinen Man gesehen?"*

The elderly refugee was so distraught, Drew's mom hesitated, gently answering that no, she hadn't seen the lady's husband.

"*Wir fuhren getrennt mit der S-Bahn . . .*" The woman explained that the couple had traveled in separate train cars once they reached East Berlin, promising that if one was stopped and detained, the other would continue on to freedom. Tears streaked the lady's furrowed face. *Please*, she begged. Her husband's health was poor. Could Drew and his mom help her look for him? He had to be somewhere inside.

Seeing a sympathetic American, other refugees surged forward, a tidal wave of anxiety, imploring Drew's mom to help them, too.

"*Es tut mir so Leid, gnädige Frau*," his mom apologized, plucking the woman's hands from her sleeve. She held them together, as if in prayer, and explained that she couldn't help right that instant, but that she would once the lady had been processed inside. She pulled away, waving *no, no* to the dozen or so people clamoring after her.

"*Bitte*," the woman wailed as Drew and his mom rushed through the door, slamming it behind them.

"That poor lady," Drew's mom murmured as she stopped to collect herself, taking some deep breaths. "I suspect her husband was caught." Suddenly, she looked weary.

"Are you okay, Mom? Is it always like this?"

"It is lately." She took one last deep breath, drawing herself up tall. "Come on, honey, let's see how they'd like to use you today."

She took Drew down a hallway. It was already packed tight with refugees parked elbow-to-elbow against the wall, holding official questionnaires, awaiting their first intake interviews. Drew's skin crawled when he saw a sign written in bold lettering. He translated the German to himself:

BE CAREFUL:
DURING CONVERSATION (DANGER OF SNOOPING);
WITH INVITATIONS (DANGER OF ABDUCTION);
IN CORRESPONDING WITH THE EAST ZONE
(DANGER OF THEIR ARREST).
HEED THE SECTOR BOUNDARY.

Drew had to force his eyes away from the sign's distressing message to meet his mom's superior, who greeted Drew with, "So, this is your famous son?"

"Famous?" Drew asked as he shook hands.

"She's very proud of you, young man."

"Of course I am!" Drew's mom beamed. Then she introduced them. "Honey, this Mr. Klein. He—"

"No names, no names, my dear," Mr. Klein cautioned her, only half joking. He waited through a loud intercom announcement: *"Two hundred twenty-two, two hundred twenty-three..."*

"You see," he said to Drew, pointing to the loudspeaker, "we don't use the refugees' names. Just numbers that we assign each day. The walls have ears, you know. Stasi spies everywhere." He gestured to the waiting refugees. "They're looking to find out where we relocate these people so later, they can kidnap them and drag them back into the arms of the KGB. That's why we ask each refugee so many questions—why they left, how they crossed over to us, where they came from. To make sure they are indeed who they claim to be. Your mother has become quite a heroine among our debriefers."

"Oh no, nothing like that," she demurred.

"She's too modest. Just last week, she sensed a young man's statements didn't add up. She kept questioning him—and he turned out to be a member of the Stasi elite guard." Mr. Klein lowered his voice so much that Drew had trouble hearing him. "Once she got that out of him, he claimed he wanted to defect. So we told the kid to prove his good intentions by going back to East Berlin and returning with something of value to us."

Drew's mom looked down and fidgeted with her purse.

"Because he'd been granted a few days' leave for R and R in West Berlin—that's how he was able to get to Marienfelde—we asked him to go back to his regiment and use the ruse of telling the guards at the gate that he just needed some fresh laundry. He returned with the latest Soviet gas mask, thanks to your mom."

"It seemed a terrible risk for that boy to take, all for the sake of a Russian gas mask. It's not as if we didn't know they had them."

"In intelligence, my dear, any bit of information might prove important."

"But you've processed him through to the West now, haven't you?" she asked.

Mr. Klein smiled. "Your mother believed he wanted to defect," he said to Drew. "She has a big heart." Then, without answering her question, he walked down the hall to his office, wading through refugees.

✂

Drew was assigned to the cafeteria, where a mass of people had already queued up, holding large tin bowls, awaiting their breakfast.

How many runaways were already crammed inside the camp?

"You will give each person two sausages," the head cook explained as he dumped peeled onions and potatoes into vats of soup bubbling on the stoves. The man had a long, razor-thin, horizontal scar across his cheek—a healed dueling cut, most likely, a telltale sign that the man had attended an elite German military academy before World War II. *I wonder what this guy's story is*, Drew thought as he took his place behind the steaming pots of hotdog-sized sausages.

About fifty people into Drew's shift, a thin boy around his age approached him. As the teen held up his bowl, Drew speared a pair of sausages and dropped them next to the generous hunks of bread and butter already on the plate.

"Bitte, darf ich noch eine Wurst haben?" The teenager asked for an extra sausage. His stomach growled so loudly, it sounded like a snare drum. Even over the clank of forks, Drew could hear its anguished rumble.

"I . . ." Drew hesitated, not knowing if he was allowed to give the boy extra. He felt dozens of eyes on him as the line stalled.

"*Bitte*," the youth repeated. At first he wouldn't look up at Drew. But when the boy finally did, Drew winced at the starvation and embarrassment in the young German's hazel eyes.

"I'm sorry, son." An American officer stepped up beside Drew and explained that they had just enough to feed the number of people they'd counted that morning. If Drew gave the boy a third sausage, someone else down the line would be shorted. The officer spoke in English, so Drew had to translate. He felt his freckles fry with shame at the memory of the enormous pancake breakfast he'd left unfinished that morning.

The German teen just frowned, biting his lower lip.

"*Es tut mir Leid.*" Drew murmured how sorry he was. He and the boy stood frozen in mutual mortification.

Everyone around them in the cafeteria seemed to hang suspended in time as well.

Then a little girl stepped out of line and approached the teen. "*Du kannst eine von mir haben.*" She offered to share her sausage with the boy, claiming she couldn't eat two.

Grateful beyond words to the child, Drew added a third to the boy's bowl and then fished out the biggest, fattest single sausage from the bunch for the girl. As she moved away, Drew heard her stomach roil in concert with the boy's.

"Sweet Jesus," murmured the officer. "*And the children*

shall lead us." He cleared his throat awkwardly and patted Drew on the back. "Carry on, soldier."

After his breakfast shift was done an hour later, Drew went out to the wide courtyard encircled by the apartment buildings where refugees were housed four to a room. Sitting on the steps, he watched children racing, mothers hanging out fresh laundry to dry, and a young woman giggling about the Coca-Cola she'd just purchased at the snack bar—her very first. She held her hand to her nose and warned her friend not to take too big of a sip—*Es kitzelt in der Nase!*—because of the fizz.

An older man and woman, arm in arm, asked timidly if they might sit next to Drew. They were farmers, most likely, given their rough hands and homemade clothing. He smiled and welcomed them: "*Willkommen in Berlin.*" Drew started to ask from where they'd traveled, but the pair seemed so wide-eyed and jittery that he let them enjoy the sunshine in silence instead.

As he took in the scene, Drew overheard refugees sharing their stories, the safety of the camp making some talkative, despite the signs warning against divulging specifics of their lives.

A muscular man in his late twenties had left after pushing himself to exceed the state-mandated quota at his mill, only to be told that he wouldn't be given the promised raise for doing so unless he served an additional eighteen months in the *Nationale Volksarmee*. He'd already done his time in the army, he said gruffly.

A woman approached a young father sitting on a nearby bench, surrounded by his five children, the youngest three fretful and clinging to him, the smallest whimpering and tugging at his diaper. "The child needs changing—may I help?" the woman asked gently. But the man just looked up at her, unresponsive. Saying she would be right back with him, the woman simply picked up the toddler and cradled him, humming reassuringly.

As she passed Drew to head inside, an older woman asked what was wrong with the father.

"He just lost his wife," she replied softly. "Miscarriage. Hemorrhage."

The older woman tut-tutted in sympathy. "Did he not get her to a hospital?"

"He did. But he was a *Grenzgänger*. The East Berlin doctors called him a criminal, a parasite for working in the West. They refused to admit her, saying that since he earned his money in the West, he was not entitled to free medical care in the East. She bled to death in his arms in the street."

Drew stared at the bereaved husband and his herd of motherless children. How could someone be that inhumane because of politics? Drew stood to search for his mom. She'd know how to help this family.

But the older gentleman sitting beside him finally spoke. Apologies for disturbing the young master, he said in a painfully nervous voice, but had Drew heard about Americans trying to poison refugees with radiation?

Drew turned to him, astonished. "What?"

"Ach, nein!" the woman breathed. *"Er is ein Amerikaner!"* She struggled to stand, her old, overworked knees popping, and looked like she might shriek.

With considerable coaxing, Drew got the frightened pair to divulge that another refugee had told them they'd be taken to a clinic and shot with radiation, an American conspiracy to kill off Germans too old to work.

Jeez Louise, the irony, he thought. Drew explained that the camp was just taking X-rays to check the refugees' lungs for tuberculosis so they could treat anyone who had it. The couple didn't believe him and scurried away across the courtyard, passing a man in a straw fedora and seersucker suit, holding a clipboard.

Drew started to shout at the couple to ask that guy—he looked official. But his words stuck in this throat, an unease tugging at him. There was something weirdly familiar about the fellow. Drew crossed the courtyard to get a better look.

Moving to another group of refugees, the man noticeably limped. When he took off his hat to wipe sweat from his forehead, his noggin so bald it practically reflected the sun like a mirror, Drew stopped dead in his tracks. It was the man who'd picked up Linda's dog at Wannsee Lake.

Holy moly. Drew fought the urge to sprint to his mom. What exactly would he say? It could be a total coincidence that the man was at the lake the same day they were. He seemed to be a Marienfelde employee, so the guy should be on the level. Shouldn't he? Maybe Drew was just seeing shadows, like Matthias had said. Overreacting. Overimagining.

On too high of an alert. Still, Drew stood behind the snack truck, like he was just catching some shade, to observe what the official did next.

The man approached a group of young mothers who were folding diapers and watching their toddlers play in a sandbox. As he talked with them, the official marked off a few things on his clipboard, then moved on to a group of men playing cards. Finally, he came to a klatch of college-aged boys sharing a newspaper and debating. The man singled out one youth, who reluctantly stood and followed him to some distance away.

Drew tracked the pair, stopping to peer around the corner of a building and watch them. The teenager looked unhappy. His lean, angular figure slouched, like a kid sulking over being pulled out of class by the principal. As the man lectured him, the teen vehemently shook his head. Their disagreement escalated. The man put his hand on the boy's shoulder. The boy knocked it off. The man grabbed the teen's collar. The youth contorted and broke free, loping away, straight toward Drew.

Quickly turning, Drew leaned against the cinder-block wall, stuck his hands in his pockets, and kicked at the ground as if he just happened to be there, pouting about a crisis of his own as the youth rushed past him. At the same moment, the teen glanced back over his shoulder to make sure the man wasn't following him—and that's when Drew saw the boy's enormous eyes. One blue, one brown!

It was the teenager who shared Matthias's home! The FDJ believer who'd shouted *Freundschaft* and made Matthias so skittish. The kid rewarded by the Stasi for *something* with a GDR Olympic tracksuit. Probably the Judas who'd turned him over to the tribunal. What the heck was he doing at Marienfelde?

Then a more ominous question surged through Drew: How did this kid know the man from Wannsee Lake who'd gotten too close to Linda? Were they in cahoots somehow? Did the fact the bald official had singled out Matthias's neighbor from the other refugee youth suggest he was the guy's Stasi handler? *Good God.* Had the teen sent the man looking for them at the lake? For Linda?

Drew spun around and saw that the man was already scuttling away. He let the guy go, bolting after the youth instead. If that boy had somehow endangered Linda . . . Drew was filled with wrath he didn't know he was capable of feeling.

The German teen slowed to a walk on his way to rejoin the clutch of boys he'd left behind. He seemed completely unaware of Drew sprinting up behind him.

"Hey! *You!*" Drew launched himself, wrapping his arm around the teen's neck, hurtling them both to the ground in an explosion of kicks and grunts.

"Runter von mir!" The youth was bigger and stronger and punched Drew hard in the gut. He rolled Drew off of him and sprang to his feet, poised to flee. But Drew managed to kick out, buckling the German's knees and knocking him back down to the ground. Drew pounced, and they wrestled, flailing, cursing.

People around them scattered, crying out, "*Ein Kampf! Ruf die Wachen! Hilfe! Hilfe!*"

For a triumphant moment, Drew had the German pinned and started shouting himself. "This guy's a *Spitzel*! Get the MPs! Get my mother, Emily McMahon!"

The refugees around him panicked even more when he shouted the word *Spitzel*. The youth shoved himself up, hurling Drew off to land flat on his back, the wind knocked out of him. The teenager would have gotten away but for Drew blindly grabbing his leg and hanging on, coughing and gagging as the teen kicked dirt in his face.

"That's enough!" With an easy grab and jerk, two MPs separated the teens and dragged them both into the camp's main building. Drew spotted his mom running up the hall, tailed by her superior. He had never in his life been more relieved to see her.

"Mom! There's another guy, a man with a clipboard! He was talking to Linda at the lake. He—"

"All right, all right." Mr. Klein quieted Drew before telling the MPs to bring the boys to his office. He slammed the door shut behind them as the MPs shoved them into seats.

"You watch the way you manhandle my son," Drew's mother reprimanded the police with startling authority.

They sheepishly *Yes, ma'am*'ed her.

"What's the story, Drew?" Mr. Klein asked.

"Go ahead, honey," his mom reassured him.

The story cascaded out of him—of the teen living in Matthias's house; of him wearing one of the Olympic tracksuits the GDR gave loyal youth fanatics for breaking TV antennas; of Matthias being pulled in front of an FDJ tribunal. "Probably because of this jerk," Drew concluded, pointing at the teenager beside him. Then he told his mom and Mr. Klein about Linda's weird encounter with the man at Wannsee. "When I saw the man from the lake talking with this guy here at Marienfelde"—he gestured around him—"I knew something wasn't right."

His mom's face was ashen.

"Describe the man," Mr. Klein said.

"Bald, limps, glasses, big buggy eyes, seersucker suit." Drew looked imploringly at his mother. "Something's fishy about that guy, Mom."

Mr. Klein picked up the phone and called the security detail. Then everyone turned to the German teen.

"*Bitte*," he snuffled, starting to cry. "I will tell all I know. Please—may I stay in the West?"

⇥⫰⫱⇤

After an hour, Drew's mom had all the information she needed from Matthias's runaway neighbor. She came back to the office where Drew had been waiting, bursting with questions of his own.

"I'll tell you what I can, honey." She sat down and took Drew's hands in hers. "The man from Wannsee Lake is likely a Stasi mole," she explained. "He could move only so fast with his limp, so the MPs apprehended him. They're interrogating him now." She squeezed his hand. "Mr. Klein says you will be famous among us for real now."

As for the German youth, Drew's mom shared that he'd quickly confessed that he'd been forced to spy on his neighbors. Caught coming back from the West with a dozen 45s he'd fished out of trash bins, he'd been given the choice to spy or "reeducate" at a work camp for juvenile criminals. He chose espionage. But, sick with guilt, he'd made his escape to Marienfelde, hoping to disappear in the West. He'd sworn to Drew's mom that he hadn't met the man with the clipboard before that day.

"And you believe that, Mom?" Drew was skeptical.

"I do, honey. I've done thousands of these interviews now. The poor boy seemed so relieved to finally be telling someone the truth."

"Did you say he'd gotten 45s out of trash cans?"

"Yes. Evidently, he'd convince record stores along the Kurfürstendamm to throw out demos by claiming they were scratched and skipping. Then he'd retrieve them later. An enterprising fellow," she said with a small laugh. "Guess rock 'n' roll is cause for rebellion everywhere."

Drew caught his breath—this boy who'd likely turned Matthias in to the FDJ must have been the same one-time close friend his cousin had talked about trading records with! "What will happen to him?" Drew asked.

"This time, I got my way," his mom answered proudly. "I was able to reach his aunt, who lives in Cologne. He's leaving on one of our planes tonight to live with her."

Drew frowned. "You think that's adequate consequence for all the sh— I mean all the stuff he's done? Matthias was pretty ripped up by that tribunal, Mom."

She nodded, thoughtful. "Sometimes, honey, our job here in the West is to show mercy. That's what allows people to change."

"That's asking a lot, Mom. This guy was a creeper, a regular Benedict Arnold—to Matthias, anyway."

"Yes, it is asking a lot, honey."

Drew crossed his arms. "Can I talk to the guy before you ship him off?"

His mom studied Drew for a moment, then lifted her finger in a motherly way. "No fisticuffs." She hugged him, then took him to the room where the teen sat waiting, red-eyed from crying.

"So, a-hole," Drew began.

"Drew," his mom gently reprimanded him.

"Is there anything you want me to tell Matthias?"

The teen blanched at Matthias's name. After a moment, he looked eagerly at Drew and said, "Yes. Tell him to look under the floorboards beneath my cot. My records are there—I would like him to have them. But tell him he must be careful not to let my father see him. My father would turn him in if he knew about the 45s. Matthias should go in through the fire escape. Like we used to do when . . ." He cleared his throat and whispered, "When we were friends."

The boy sat in silence for another long moment until a wry smile grew on his face. "Please tell Matthias this joke: At dawn Khrushchev wakes up. 'Good morning, sun!' he shouts. The sun snaps to attention and replies, 'Good morning, Herr Chairman.' Then, at noon, Khrushchev shouts again, 'Good day, sun!' and the sun answers dutifully. But that evening, when the sun begins to set, it does not answer when he shouts 'Good night.' Khrushchev takes off his shoe and pounds the table. 'How dare you not answer! I will arrest you!' Finally, the sun answers, 'Tough luck, Herr Chairman. I'm in the West now!'"

The teen laughed. "Tell Matthias—tell him to follow the sun."

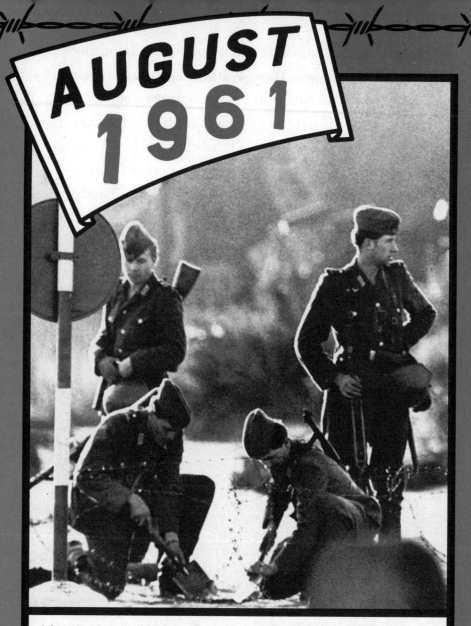

AUGUST 1961

A few minutes past midnight on August 13, the GDR unleashes its insidious Operation Rose, a Russian-backed secret plan to wall off East Berlin. Soldiers and paramilitary factory workers will unfurl 27 miles of barbed wire before dawn. To maximize the surprise and minimize Berliners' ability to resist, the operation is timed for a summer holiday weekend. Enjoying an annual children's festival and fireworks, Berliners don't notice GDR military trucks and armed vehicles stealthily gathering around the city.

A total of 38,400 GDR soldiers, paramilitary police, transportation policemen, factory militia, and Stasi secret police are mobilized and begin unloading 330 tons of coiled barbed wire—ordered, of all places, from Britain. That fencing and hundreds of protective gloves had been stockpiled for weeks in East Berlin warehouses. At 1 a.m., the GDR cuts all streetlights, plunging the city's Eastern sector into darkness. At 1:30, all trains and subways are stopped, and all but 13 of the city's 81 pedestrian crossing points are closed. Streetcar tracks are cut and rolled up as barricades, paving stones pulled up and piled high. Sewer manholes are guarded. The workers hurry to fence off the 193 streets that straddle the border between East and West Berlin, stringing barbed wire straight down the middle of many. At 2 a.m., Russian tanks and infantry surround the city with orders to move in to crush any uprising. Also backed with their own armored cars and water cannon, GDR soldiers line up at the Brandenburg Gate with orders to shoot to prevent a mob trying to push through—from either side.

Once the waist-high barbed wire snakes from one end of the city to the other, GDR militiamen begin jackhammering holes for premade concrete posts to secure it—right as dawn breaks and Berliners wake. Stunned crowds gather on both sides of the barrier.

Some onlookers convince themselves the barrier is temporary. Other East Berliners realize they are trapped with only hours, at best, to escape through holes in the flesh-tearing fence before it is entirely sealed. They grab whatever they can and run. Other families are instantly cordoned off from one another and can only pass emergency food, notes, and money over the wire. For many it will be the last time they physically touch.

Some East Berliners are able to scramble out windows of buildings flush to the border as GDR police storm front doors to shut them down. Others risk plunging from breathtaking heights into nets held far below by West Berlin firefighters.

It takes only 12 hours for the GDR to cut Berlin in half. While paramilitary factory workers secure the barbed wire to posts, young Vopos stand against their peers with bayonets out to stop any youths, even friends, who might rush the wall. Over that holiday weekend, 3,400 East Germans manage to flee to freedom—most before midnight Saturday. But few who face off with GDR troops or police, trying to convince them to stand aside, make it across the line.

CHAPTER THIRTEEN

AUGUST
1961

Three weeks after his day at Marienfelde, on a radiant, seventy-five-degree August afternoon, Drew stood once again with Matthias on Zimmerstraße, where months ago he'd witnessed Vopos playfully throwing snowballs at their Western counterparts across the demarcation line between the American and Russian sectors. Now he was watching little children, who were technically supposed to be enemies, scampering about together. They shrieked with glee, darting between carnival games and food tents on both sides of the street under a swag of colorful streamers stretching like a bridge across the boulevard.

It was the annual neighborhood *Kinderfest*—the borough's celebration of *all* the city's children, democratic and communist. And after a week of solid rain, Berliners,

East and West, were out in force to enjoy the sunshine and camaraderie.

"Whoa! Who is *that*?" Drew asked as he noticed a robust man with moustache-sized eyebrows, wearing an enormous white Stetson hat as he glad-handed the crowd. Each person the boisterous middle-aged man greeted—especially young children and older women—seemed to bloom like a flower kissed by the sunshine.

"Willy Kressmann," Matthias answered with obvious admiration. "He's the mastermind behind this *Kinderfest*. The mayor of Kreuzberg borough. We call him Texas Willy. He got that hat when he visited the States two years ago. He was made an honorary citizen of your San Antonio."

"Texas? Isn't that about as American fascist bourgeoisie capitalist pig as you can get, *mein Freund*?" Drew teased. "What's he doing in East Berlin?"

Matthias laughed at the ribbing. "Remember, we do not stand in East Berlin now. This side of the street is in the American sector, the Kreuzberg borough. Over there"—Matthias pointed across Zimmerstraße—"begins the Russian sector. It is the Mitte borough.

"All Berliners, East and West, love Texas Willy," Matthias continued. "He is the only mayor in the Western sectors who meets with East Berlin mayors. Before World War II, he was a socialist himself. He had to escape Hitler and went through Scandinavia to England. After the war, he returned, committed to your Western ways. But he has sympathy for socialists. He lets artists from the East show their work in his town hall. And he hosts this children's festival every year to remind us we are all Germans, no matter what sector we live in. He gives the fest the motto: 'We are all one.'"

Matthias nodded in approval as Kressmann scooped up a little girl, who was hiccup-sobbing because she didn't have money to purchase a ticket for the carousel. Wading through the throng, he made his way to a merry-go-round, a splash of color and joy put up for the fair amid Potsdamer Platz's weeds and gray rubble. The mayor plopped the child down on a brightly painted horse and whispered into the ear of the operator, who started up the carousel without protesting the free rider.

Satisfied, Kressmann crossed his arms and watched the horses going up and down and the children clapping their hands in time to the oompah-pah music. He lingered in the shade of a large wooden sign erected right beside the official sector marker, facing its hand-painted message toward the Russian East: DO AWAY WITH THE BORDER! GET RID OF THE CONTROLS!

Surveying the crowd, Kressmann spotted the boys. "Matthias!" the big man boomed as he strode over and gathered Drew's cousin into a crushing embrace. "How is your grandmother? Next week is her birthday, yes? I will bring my trio to serenade her. Perhaps this year she will dance with me."

Matthias shrugged. "I hope she will. But . . . but you know how she is."

"But who can resist this?" Kressmann spread his arms wide, grinning. Then he abruptly turned his attention to Drew. "Who is this?" he asked.

"My American cousin."

"Ah!" Kressmann's cigar-thick eyebrows shot up. "Military? State Department? Or Pan Am?"

"My dad is in the army," Drew answered.

Kressmann took Drew's collar in both of his meaty hands—not threateningly, but in a nose-to-nose manner befitting a political boss. "You Americans must send aid to the East Berliners. They starve. Send economic aid, and they will rise up."

"I am not sure the Russians would let us do that," Drew answered, a bit flummoxed.

"Ha! They do not like our *Kinderfest*, either!" Kressmann gestured to the frolicking children. "But we do it anyway. Tell your people." He patted Drew's chest, letting go of his shirt. "And you," he said, turning back to Matthias, "do you have more trouble?"

Matthias turned as red as Drew, minus the freckles. "No, Herr Burgermeister."

"*Gut*." He ruffled Matthias's blond mop and then strutted away, bellowing, "Come, children, time for Mr. Punch to heal the princess with his magic flower! Come!" Knee-deep in giggling followers, Kressmann led the children toward a makeshift puppet theater.

Beaming with hero worship, Matthias watched Kressmann herd the children.

"Trouble?" Drew asked with concern.

"Mayor Kressmann knew of my . . . the tribunal," Matthias answered quietly, carefully.

"Can Kressmann help with that kind of thing?"

"Not the way you hope," Matthias said. "He has no official power in the East. He has no influence with the FDJ or the Stasi. They would love to hurt him. But people who live in this neighborhood listen to him. He is so popular with them, many call the borough Kressmannsdorf instead of Kreuzberg." He looked around and pulled Drew over to sit on a bench under a young linden tree. "He knows my accuser. The . . . the boy . . . who lives upstairs."

Drew squirmed inside, itching to tell his cousin that teenager would never rat on him again, that Matthias was safe from him, at least. But he stifled himself, warned by his mom not to discuss Matthias's neighbor with him, not to reveal the boy's decision to defect at Marienfelde. "Safer for Matthias," she had told Drew, "if he is questioned by the Stasi once they figure out the boy is gone. And certainly safer for the boy, so that he can start his life in Cologne anonymously."

"The father of my"—Drew could see that Matthias was about to say *friend*—"neighbor plays cards, drinks too much. He would send my . . . neighbor to the pub to get siphons of beer. Late at night, sometimes in his pajamas. When Mayor Kressmann saw that one evening, he marched home with my neighbor and says to his father"—Matthias puffed himself large and waggled his finger in imitation—"'If you send your son to the beer hall again at night, you will get serious trouble from me!'" Matthias smiled and shook his head with amazement. "So when Kressmann heard of my . . . my trouble, he went to my neighbor. To . . . mmm . . . *züchtigen.*"

"Chastise?" Drew offered.

"Yes." Matthias nodded. "Chastise. So he would not denounce me to the FDJ again. I have not been called for another *Selbstkritik*." He paused for a moment. "And I have not seen my neighbor."

Drew stewed. Someday, he had to tell Matthias—if for no other reason, so his cousin would know that his one-time friend seemed genuinely sorry. And that there was a cache of 45s awaiting him, if he wanted them. He wondered fleetingly if Kressmann had helped the teenager across the line to Marienfelde.

They sat silently, watching the puppet show from a distance. When it was over, Matthias pointed to the windows along the American side of Zimmerstraße. "Look! Watch this." Residents were leaning over the sills, baskets in hand, waiting.

When Kressmann raised his arms and shouted, "Now!" the West Berliners threw handfuls of candy to the children, who squealed with laughter as they scurried to retrieve the wrapped milk chocolates. The jovial mayor marched up and down the street, making sure each child—particularly those from the Russian sector—had at least one treat. He even walked over to the GDR Vopo border guards and handed them some of the chocolate to enjoy.

"If only Kressmann could talk with Khrushchev," Matthias mused.

That night, leaning up against the wide brick chimney of Matthias's once-grand old building, Drew marveled at what he could see from their rooftop perch. The temple-like Brandenburg Gate flooded with spotlights so its winged Victoria and her horse-drawn chariot seemed to command the entire city; the shadowy skeleton of the bomb-gutted Reichstag next to it; a long carpet of cool green darkness over the 630 acres of the Tiergarten; a river of light that had to be the Kurfürstendamm in the distance.

Drew was spending the night with Matthias so he could watch fireworks that would be the colorful finale to Kressmann's festival. They'd be launched from the nearby Kreuzberg Park, jammed with people who'd picnicked there all day to save their spots for the pyrotechnics. Way across the city's vast expanse, Drew's parents would be watching, too, out with other military couples, enjoying live music on the Berlin Hilton's top-floor terrace. All the husbands had taken the weekend off duty so they could dance with their wives and enjoy the Kreuzberg fireworks from that great vantage point.

For one evening, anyway, Berlin was "all one," united by Kressmann's *Kinderfest*.

As he gazed out, Drew was certain he could hear waltz music dancing through the air. He cocked his head.

"It comes from the Esplanade," Matthias explained. "A few blocks away. A hotel beloved by Hitler's fascists, destroyed by bombs. They have turned what is left into a dance hall. You capitalists come in beaded ball gowns and black tie to fox-trot, just like Goebbels and Himmler once did."

Drew gave Matthias a hard look. *Really?*

Seeing it, Matthias suddenly laughed at himself. "Sorry. I often open my window to hear," he admitted. "Some nights they play jazz." He punched Drew playfully on the shoulder. "You see? You corrupt me—*Kulturbarbarei.*" He held his finger to his lips. "*Shhhhhh.* Don't tell anyone."

Drew chuckled, drawing his legs up and resting his chin on his knees. He took in all the sounds that mingled with the music wafting up from the Esplanade: an old cart horse whinnying for its dinner; someone playing an accordion; stray cats yowling; the *thump-thump-thump* of the lightweight, plastic East German Trabant cars passing over cobblestones.

"I am sorry that Linda was not with us today," said Matthias, drawing his own knees up and wrapping his arms around them. "She would have liked the exhibition of German Shepherds at the park."

"Joyce wanted to have a sisters-only day with her before she leaves for London. She took Linda to *West Side Story.*"

"You will miss Joyce?"

"Yes. A lot."

"I will, too." Mathias said quietly. After a moment, he added, "I would have liked siblings."

Drew hesitated to say anything, knowing how Matthias's brothers had died during the final battle of the war. He wondered if Cousin Marta had ever told her son the truth about that.

Pop-pop-pop . . . sssssssssss—BANG!

The first flares of silvery sparks spun up into the night

sky to explode into an enormous fan of sizzling red star-bursts, showering tiny cinders down on them—they were that close to the pyrotechnics' launch site.

"But cousins are almost as good," Matthias whispered.

Even over the thundering sound of the fireworks all around them, Drew heard him.

In the middle of the night, a tremor—like what he'd always imagined a small earthquake might feel like—shook Drew awake. He rolled over and sat up on the pallet laid out on the floor of Matthias's narrow bedroom. The moonlight sifting through the window was enough for him to read his wristwatch—two thirty a.m.

Squeeek-squeeek. A high-pitched squealing echoed off the walls of the buildings lining the street. Drew rubbed his eyes, stretched, and then crawled toward Matthias's desk to peer out the window above it.

A seemingly endless line of tarp-covered trucks rumbled along the road below.

Roadwork in the middle of the night on a Sunday? Weird. Drew lay back down, pulling his pillow over his head to muffle the sound.

Buzzzzzzzzzzzz-buzz-buzzzzzzzzzzzzz. The doorbell rang insistently. *Buzz-buzz-buzzzzzzzzzzzzzzzzzzzzzzzzzzz.*

This time, Matthias bolted upright along with Drew. They could hear Cousin Marta running to answer the door, bare feet against wooden floorboards. Urgent voices.

"That sounds like my dad." Frowning, Drew looked up at Matthias.

The boys scrambled to their feet just as Matthias's bedroom door flew open.

"Mein Schatz." Cousin Marta, clad in frayed silk pajamas, rushed to Matthias and took his hand.

My treasure. Drew had never before heard her call his cousin by that German endearment.

Behind her in the doorway was Drew's dad. In uniform. In the middle of the night. A sidearm was strapped at his hip.

"Dad—what's going on?"

"Grab your gear and come out into the living room, Drew," Sergeant McMahon insisted. "Hurry."

Nervously stuffing his belongings into his backpack, Drew followed Matthias into the parlor. Matthias reached to turn on a lamp, but Drew's dad stopped him, saying, "Better not let the Vopos know we're awake."

"Vopos?" Drew and Matthias cried out together.

"Son." Drew's dad took him by the shoulders. "The Russians are closing Berlin's border. Our southern outpost alerted headquarters that they were seeing massive columns of Russian tanks and infantry moving in to ring the city. I left to come get you as soon as I heard and had a hell of a time getting through. There are thousands of Vopos and militia— even firemen armed with machine guns—guarding workers who are rolling out concertina wire along the sector line. Truckloads of it. They're moving fast. I've got to get you out."

Drew's father turned to Matthias. "Come with us. I doubt you'll be able to leave once this barrier is up."

Matthias took a step back. "No!" he almost shouted. "It cannot be true."

"*Mein Schatz*," his mother began, her voice quavering.

Snnnnnnap!

They all startled as the radio suddenly began to blare, loud with triumphant march music, Prussian drums and cymbals crashing. Aunt Hilde had silently slipped into the room. Her white hair cascaded to her waist, and she clutched a cream-colored shawl around her throat with one hand while the other rested on the enormous 1940s radio console. Standing like that, she looked to Drew like one of those ghostly Valkyrie warrior spirits that warned of death during a battle. He shuddered.

A proclamation from the Warsaw Pact to our brothers and comrades, the *Deutschlandsender* announcer brayed and Drew translated to himself. *Our brave Volksarmee soldiers are at this moment securing our sector border. They do this to protect all East Germans from the warmongers in the West, who scheme against us. East Berliners will no longer be subjected to the degradation and deterioration of capitalism. By morning, you will be safe from NATO and its fascists. Remain calm. Rejoice. Soon, red flags will flutter across all of Germany.*

Aunt Hilde turned off the radio, trembling. "*Die Ivans, Sie kommen*," she murmured. Then she hung her head and began to sway, moaning quietly.

Tenderly, Cousin Marta took Matthias's face in her hands. "You must go. This will be nothing but a prison now. Go with Drew."

Matthias shook his head vehemently.

Drew joined in her plea. "C'mon, Matthias. Come with Dad and me. I . . . I know you believed in the socialist utopia—the ideal of complete equality. I respect that, man. But your workers break their backs for a state that abuses them. It's just . . . just like *Animal Farm*. You don't want to live in a place where your best friend would rat on you to the Party because of your taste in music . . . do you?"

Matthias stared at Drew, hesitating.

"*Liebling*," Cousin Marta whispered. "*Bitte.* I want you to grow up to be whatever *you* wish to be. To speak what you believe. To not live in fear. You must go."

"Not without you."

"I cannot go," his mother murmured, anguished.

"Why?" Matthias stepped back. "Because of her?" He pointed at his grandmother.

Cousin Marta reached for her son, pulling him to her, her lips against his blond head as she spoke urgently. "I cannot. You know what they would do to your grandmother if I left her. They have no tolerance for people who suffer as she does."

"I won't go, then. We can go later, together. After . . ." He lowered his voice to a whisper. "After she's gone."

"*Mein Schatz*, please. I did not make your brothers leave when there was still a chance for them. And they died. Trapped. Please. Leaving with Drew and his father is likely your only hope."

"They are still letting Allied army vehicles through," Drew's dad confirmed. "But I was stopped at every corner.

Threatened a couple of times, which took some nerve. They've never dared to do that with an American officer before. We may have to make a run for it through a gap in the barbed wire before it's secured. But we need to hurry. I think they're going to have the whole border locked down by dawn."

Matthias wrenched himself away from his mother. "Not without you, *Mutti*!" he cried. "Why do you always choose her over me?" He looked toward his grandmother and crumpled to the floor in tears.

"Matthias!" Cousin Marta gasped, and knelt beside her son. "Listen to me. Listen. You live because of her. And only because of her. I should have told you before. But . . . I . . . I wanted to spare you. Spare myself from remembering." She took a deep breath. "When the Russians took Berlin . . . they searched every house. Looking for German women."

Matthias's head shot up to look at his mother.

She stroked his hair. "I was eight months pregnant with you. We were starved during the bombing, and I was very weak. The Russian campaign to . . . that kind of violence . . . would have killed you and me both, before you could even be born. Your grandmother . . . she saved me. She saved you. She—" Cousin Marta choked out the words. "She took their attacks for me."

Cousin Marta glanced toward Aunt Hilde, who rocked, gripping her shawl around her frail frame as if it would make her invisible.

Awash in tears, Cousin Marta lowered her voice to an agonized whisper as she continued, "Once it was over, *Mutti* became . . . like this. But you—you live. You live because of her courage." She shook her head, as if to dispel images too horrible to recall. "*Mutti* stood in front of me and—" Her voice caught in a half sob. "That is how fierce she once was. How precious to her you were—how precious the promise of your life was. How precious it is now."

Matthias stared at his mother, paralyzed, as the horror of what she had revealed sank in.

In the hush, Drew's dad added carefully, "I don't know that I could get your mom through with us tonight anyway, Matthias. They're checking everyone too carefully. The Vopos will definitely be looking to stop any doctors or nurses trying to get over the line. But I promise I'll work to find a way to bring your mother over—maybe through the State Department. Maybe Mrs. McMahon's Marienfelde contacts can help. But tonight, you need to come with Drew and me. Now. Right now."

"Please listen to Dad, Matthias," Drew implored. "C'mon."

Matthias shook his head hard, covering his ears.

"Please, *mein Schatz*." Cousin Marta gathered Matthias tightly into her arms again, laying her cheek on his hair, closing her eyes and breathing in deeply, clearly memorizing the feel of her child close to her. Then, with a wrenching shudder, she pulled back. "You must go!" she cried. "Get out of the Russian sector. Now. For me."

"Für mich auch."

Jolted by the subdued, delicate voice, everyone froze.

Aunt Hilde leaned over, taking Matthias's hand. She gently kissed it and held it to her heart—just as Drew's mom had done to help the frail woman recognize that she was her niece. Aunt Hilde fixed her gaze on Matthias and nodded. *For me, too*, she repeated as she helped Matthias to his feet. *Live.*

Drew's own soul hurt as he watched Matthias throw his arms around his grandmother in a heartbreaking embrace. Then his mother.

Then and only then did Matthias follow Drew and Sergeant McMahon, grabbing his jacket and shoes at the door—taking nothing else that could identify him—and plummeting down the pitch-black staircase to the seething street below.

They plunged out into a darkness roiling with alarm. All the streetlights had been cut, compounding Drew's sense of disorientation as a storm surge of invisible, angry German voices rolled up the side street:

"What are you doing?"

"Stand back!"

"Please, my family is over there."

Drew's dad put a protective hand on each boy's shoulder. "Stick close to me," he said. "I had to hide the car in a plot of rubble close to Potsdamer Platz. We have to go along Zimmerstraße for a block or so. Do not say a word. Understand? You especially, Matthias. Just do as I say, and follow my lead if we get stopped."

Sticking close to the wall, dodging the frightened Berliners who were now pouring out of their front doors in their robes and slippers, the trio joined the human flood rushing along the street that just hours before had been a carnival for children.

A single *Volksarmee* spotlight illuminated pairs of young East German soldiers moving down the middle of the street. Between them, they held the spokes of massive wheels of barbed wire that, when unfurled, created a thickly coiled, flesh-tearing barrier. As they spread the thorny web, *Kampfgruppe* factory militiamen were prying up cobblestones with pickaxes to make holes for posts to anchor the wire.

A truck with loudspeakers cruised the street, blaring its warning:

The border is now officially closed. Citizens of East Berlin are no longer permitted to enter any part of West Berlin. These measures are for your own good. The American influence on the German people will stop at our gates. Disperse. Return to your homes . . .

Shielding the workers was an intimidating flank of *Grenzpolizisten,* tommy guns across their chests, at the ready. But some intrepid Berliners still tried to push their way through them and cross the street to freedom before the barbed wire trap was completely strung. A resolute old woman brought her heavy purse down on the helmet of a soldier so hard that his knees buckled. She started to dart past him, despair making her nimble, but was seized and hauled away to a waiting police van. A boy Drew and Matthias's age explained that he was expected for the christening of his sister's baby that day. When the Vopo answered, "Too bad," the teenager called him a *Rindvieh*, a dumb ox. The officer slapped the boy's face and then shoved him with the butt of his rifle toward the same van.

"Damn it," Drew's father cursed. "If only I had my unit with me to help these people."

They hurried on until they reached a jumbled hill of broken bricks and glass, a collapsed, once-graceful house, cordoned off from the avenue by its ornate wrought-iron fence. Tucked behind a heap of rubble, cloaked in shadows, was an American Army jeep.

Thank God. Drew had worried all the way down Zimmerstraße that the jeep wouldn't be there, hotwired by a desperate Berliner.

"Get in, boys."

Drew vaulted into the trunk, motioning for Matthias to get in the one passenger seat. His dad revved the engine with a backfire and a roar.

A line of trucks jammed to overflowing with wooden sawhorse barriers rumbled past them.

"Better not turn on the headlights yet," muttered Drew's dad as he blindly steered the jeep, jostling wildly over debris and through the vaulted art deco arch.

"Stop!" Matthias hissed, hunching down in his seat.

Coming toward them was a bobbling cloud of lights—a group of people glowing like a bunch of fireflies as they approached, singing:

The Party, the Party, she is always right!

"FDJ! Turn off the engine," Matthias whispered, sliding off the seat into a crouch.

The fireflies turned out to be a parade of girls in blue blouses and black skirts, carrying flashlights and sprays of summer flowers they planned to give to the GDR "defenders," the "heroic tank men" now occupying Potsdamer Platz. Following close behind the girls were several men, bright red brassards on their sleeves, carrying billy clubs like malevolent shepherds.

Drew finally exhaled when they were out of earshot. "Who the hell are those guys?"

"Proven Party believers," Matthias answered. "Those armbands mean they've been given police powers." He slowly clambered back into his seat and added grimly, "I knew every one of those faces. If they see me . . ."

"Yeeaaaaah." Drew's father rubbed his face. He looked to the back of the jeep. "Switch places, boys."

When Matthias was crouched in the small open-bay trunk, Drew's dad gave him a comforting smile. "Good thing you're small, kid," he told him. "See the part of that bed that tucks up under our seats?"

Matthias nodded.

"Can you cram yourself in there?"

Matthias folded himself up like a praying mantis and disappeared.

"Put your backpack in front of him, son," he told Drew. "You can breathe okay, Matthias?"

"Yes," his muffled voice answered.

"Whatever you do, whatever you hear, do *not* come out until I tell you. Understand?"

"Yes."

"Okay, men. Let's move out."

On Stresemannstraße, heading north, Drew's dad turned on his low beams. "If we're stopped, stick to the truth, son. You were visiting your cousin to see the fire-works for the *Kinderfest*, and I've come to bring you home. You've got your dog tags on you, right?"

"Yes, sir."

"Good man. Just remember: the best bluff is an earnest one when you're dealing with the enemy. Okay?"

"Yes, sir."

Drew's dad drove on, keeping to the posted speed limit, exuding battle readiness and a soldier's calm. "Given how fast they got that wire up near Matthias's place, we're going to have to try to get through the Brandenburg Gate. The Allies stand strong just on the other side of it. I think that's our best chance."

Remembering how the young guard at the Brandenburg Gate had shaken down Cousin Marta over a tube of lipstick, Drew didn't exactly feel confident in his dad's plan. But with all the barbed wire and troops, what else could they do?

They reached the edge of the bombed-out Potsdamer Platz that was typically a deserted expanse of broken pavement and weeds. It was studded with tanks. "Damn those Russian bastards," Drew's dad grunted. "Those are Soviet T-34s." He slowed.

Drew gasped. "What are you doing, Dad?" Didn't it make sense to get past enemy tanks as quickly as possible?

"I'm slowing so we can report back numbers. See if you can count those, son." He kept his pace.

". . . Twenty-seven, twenty-eight . . ." Drew corkscrewed in his seat a bit as they drove out of range. "Thirty. I see thirty, Dad."

"Hell's bells." Sergeant McMahon white-knuckled the steering wheel in response. "Keep your eyes open for any more Russian equipment, okay? I need to report the presence of that many tanks. Our boys are going to be facing a hell of a standoff, if that's what it comes to."

"Yes, sir." Drew sucked in a breath to steel himself. Then he coughed. "What's that smell?"

His dad sniffed. "Tear gas." He pulled out a handkerchief and handed it to Drew. Cover your face, son." Without turning his head he added, "Matthias, cover your nose and eyes." He stopped the jeep to give the noxious cloud time to dissipate, his hands over his face.

In front of them, a band of East Berlin youth were throwing paper bags over smoking tear gas canisters and hurling them back at the Vopos who'd shot them into the angry mob. Gagging on their own smoke, a few younger Vopos dropped their guns and staggered, blinded—right into the Western sector. They were suddenly free, if they wanted to be.

"Look at that," breathed Drew's dad as one young Vopo turned and ran into the arms of some West Berlin police. "Score one for liberty."

As the vapors dissolved, an older officer who'd been yelling curses at his discombobulated troops spotted their American jeep.

"Damn." Drew's dad shifted the gears and jammed his foot down on the accelerator. "Hang on, boys!"

"*Halt!*" the German shouted. "*Sofort!*"

Drew's dad shifted gears, gunning the jeep to its top speed.

"*Scheiße, Scheiße, Scheiße,*" muttered Drew as he grabbed his seat and braced his feet against the open door, almost bouncing out of the jeep as it lurched forward. He could hear Matthias rattling around in his hiding spot, whacking against metal like crackers in a canister.

KA-PING! Something glanced off the windshield rim.

"Get down, Drew!"

KA-PING!

"They're shooting at us, Dad!"

"Hang on, son. If they really wanted to hit us, I'd be shot through by now."

KA-PING!

"Dad!"

KA-PING!

"*Waffenstillstand! Waffenstillstand!*" A voice behind them shouted to cease fire.

But they only had a few seconds of reprieve. Suddenly, their jeep was surrounded by four GDR motorcycle police.

"*Zur Seite fahren!*" The commanding rider shouted for Drew's dad to pull over—*Schnell!*

The Brandenburg Gate—their portal to safety—was in view. But there was no way to reach it through the biker swarm.

"Son," Drew's dad said as he slowed to a stop, waiting for the German officer to approach, "I need your pitcher's steel nerves now. Bottom of the ninth, tied game. You're going to strike this guy out. Got it?" He smiled.

Drew nodded.

The German kicked down his motorcycle stand and

strode toward Drew's dad, his hobnailed boots *click-click-*ing on the pavement. He pulled off his helmet, revealing gray hair and rays of wrinkles spraying out from his eyes, telltale signs of years spent wearing goggles in sun and wind while riding a military cycle. *"Die Grenze ist geschlossen. Was machen Sie auf dieser Seite?"*

"I'm sorry, bud, I don't speak German."

"A pity," the German answered easily, "since you are in Germany. I said, the border is now closed. What are you doing on this side?"

"According to the Four Power Agreement, I have every right to be here," Drew's dad responded politely enough.

"For right now." The German bowed slightly. "That is to be renegotiated, I am told."

Sergeant McMahon remained silent.

Pushing out his lower lip, the German considered Drew for a moment. "Sightseeing?" He sauntered, *click-click-click*, around the front of the jeep to face Drew. "Or a stowaway? Like a Robert Louis Stevenson novel, perhaps? One of my favorite authors when I was a boy. But do not tell our comrades that, eh?" He winked and leaned an arm on the windshield, all fake friendly, clearly suspicious that Drew was an East German teen on the run and hoping to trick him into exposing himself.

Drew's dad undid the safety button of his holster. "Get any closer to my kid, and you're going to lose some teeth."

The German smirked. "A Wild Bill Hickok, eh?" He turned back to Drew, no longer friendly. *"Kannst du sprechen?"*

"Yes, sir, I speak," Drew answered quickly. "My father came to get me because I spent the night with my cousin, watching the fireworks from the *Kinderfest*." He pulled his dog tags from his shirt. "Do you need to see my ID?"

The German's eyes traveled from Drew to the back of the Jeep. "A cousin?"

"Yes, sir." Drew felt a warning tremor of anxiety shoot through him. He shouldn't have mentioned a cousin; it was easy to see what the German thought might be hidden in the back—a teenage runaway. Drew resisted the powerful temptation to catch his dad's eye. He had to throw a strike—now.

He started prattling. "My cousin ... my cousin is ..." Then Drew saw a way. Stick to the truth, just as his dad had said, but maybe make the pitch a bit of a curve ball to throw the German off. "My cousin is more like an aunt, really. She is a nurse at Charité Hospital. Very devoted. Very good. They're training her to be a doctor ..."

Click-click-click. The German started toward the back of the jeep as Drew talked.

Drew's mind raced. *Please, get away from the back of the jeep*. He saw his dad wrap his fingers around his pistol. Drew glanced at the other motorcycle police, at attention, waiting to take aim themselves.

Click-click-click.

Drew rushed on. "I had a terrific time at the *Kinderfest*. That Mr. Punch puppet—very funny. And that chocolate people threw out their windows. That stuff was delicious ..." What the heck else could he say? "I . . . I met Mayor Kressmann."

Click. The German stopped. "Texas Willy?"

"Yes!" Drew faked a laugh. "He was really nice. He told me about starting the *Kinderfest* for East Berlin kids as well as West. I thought I might write an article about it for the school newspaper. It's kinda . . . kinda like the UN, isn't it? I mean, in terms of bringing all children together."

How much longer could he blabber? "I . . . I forgot what the mayor says about the festival. It has a swell slogan. What was it?"

"*Wir sind alle eins*," the German answered.

"That's it! We are all one." Drew nodded vehemently, like one of those new World Series bobblehead toys. "German kids—all one. That's beautiful."

Click-click-click. The German sauntered back to Drew, again leaning on the windshield, appraising him. *"Kinder, die nach Kindern Ausschau halten. Eh?"*

Kids looking out for kids. Drew met the German's eyes. Chilly gray, inscrutable. Was it a trap? A code? Had he spotted Matthias back there?

A long beat passed. The German waited. *An earnest bluff*, Drew's dad had said.

Drew made himself keep his gaze steady. "Yes, sir," Drew answered, "that's a great theme for a festival. We are all one. Yessirree."

The German smiled, thoughtful.

Drew held his breath.

His dad eased his gun halfway out of its holster.

Click-click-click. The German sauntered back to Drew's dad.

Another long, terrifying pause. Then, matter-of-factly, like a traffic cop, the German said, "There are two holes through your jeep's back end. Some stones must have kicked up and nicked it at the speed you were going. The GDR regrets the damage. As you can see"—he gestured to the jackhammering troops—"we are working to improve our roads."

Drew's father smiled. "Right. Stones. Happens all the time."

The German nodded. "Go to the alcove farthest to the right at the gate. We are letting Allied personnel through there." He stepped back and waved them on. *"Auf Wiedersehen."*

They hurtled away.

"Bullet holes? In the back—"

"Hang on, son. We can't look until we get into our sector."

"But—" Drew's protest caught in his throat as their jeep reached a wall of East Germans blocking the Brandenburg Gate. Right behind them were tanks and armored trucks.

"Get down on the floor out of sight, son. They should wave us through if they think it's just an American officer. "

Drew slid down, now starting to tremble all over, a delayed reaction to his standoff with the motorcycle officer.

"What do I always say about taking a wall?" Drew's dad answered himself: "March straight and fast to it."

Drew started to complete his dad's motto—"He who hesitates is lost"—but he stopped, hearing all around him grief-stricken pleas to be let through the closing border and shouts of refusal.

"Here we go, son," his dad muttered. Then, to someone Drew couldn't see, Sergeant McMahon shouted a friendly, *"Guten Tag!"*

The jeep kept its speed. Out the open door, Drew saw startled and frightened young Vopos start to raise their rifles, then lower them to nab two Berliners who had tried to dart past them, following the charge of the American jeep.

"Almost there, son. There is an army of Allied MPs waiting for us with open arms."

They charged across the brief expanse of open pavement that served as a buffer between the sectors and screeched to a halt behind a protective phalanx of Allied vehicles and soldiers.

Safe! But what about Matthias?

Scrambling over the seat, Drew jerked away his backpack. There lay his cousin, balled up, face hidden. "Matthias! Are you okay?"

Slowly, Matthias raised his head. "Yee-haw," he murmured.

Drew's dad hauled him out and brushed him off, looking for injuries. "Praise God," he breathed, putting his hand on Matthias's shoulder. "Stay here with Drew for a minute. I need to report what we saw. Then we'll take you home, Matthias. I should warn you that Mrs. McMahon is looking forward to fixing you a big pancake breakfast. So best be hungry, son."

Matthias nodded.

As his dad walked toward other American officers, Drew felt a tsunami of relief. He punched Matthias in an exultant can-you-believe-we-got-through-that way. "Man, I was afraid I totally blew it when—" But he stopped short, seeing the tears flowing unchecked down Matthias's face. His teal-colored eyes—the unique characteristic that echoed from Aunt Hilde to Cousin Marta to Drew's own mom—were flooded with pain. Gently, Drew put his arm around his cousin's shoulders.

The two stood that way in silence, watching the chaos around them.

A huge crowd of West Berliners bunched together, shouting damnations toward the east at the GDR soldiers who sat in water-cannon trucks, awaiting orders to flatten the protestors if the mob got too angry or came too close to the line. A fast-growing river of American and British soldiers and military vehicles rushed to create a dam against the enemy tanks visible through the Brandenburg Gate's marble columns. Drew knew his dad's unit had been drilled for a hundred different scenarios of Russian aggression. But standing by helplessly, outnumbered ten to one, as a million people were caged? Had anyone anticipated this?

Drew kept his arm draped protectively over Matthias as his cousin wept, watching his people build a wall to divide themselves—a wall separating him from his mother and grandmother, perhaps forever.

"I'm so sorry, man," Drew whispered. He could only imagine the hell going on in his cousin's heart and mind.

He'd had to say so many goodbyes as a military brat, but nothing like this.

Matthias sighed, his exhale shaky, and murmured, more to himself than Drew, "*Wie kann ich von meiner Familie getrennt leben?*"

How can I live cut off from my family?

"For your mother," Drew answered him. "And for your grandmother. Because they begged you to. That's how."

After a minute, without taking his eyes off the East, Matthias asked Drew halfheartedly, "Pancakes. *Was ist das?*"

"Oh, they're great. Like crepes, sort of. I think you'll like them."

Grieving, Matthias looked at him doubtfully.

Drew shrugged in apology. "Mom means well. Trying to feed people is what she does when she knows they're hurting." He paused. "I know we're lucky to have the option of a big breakfast."

Nodding, Matthias turned his gaze back to the growing crowd, the growing barrier.

"You know," Drew said slowly, "your mom said something else—that she wants you to not live in fear. To be where you can speak what you believe. Maybe . . ." He had no idea if saying this would be any help, but Drew tried it anyway. "Maybe you can take what you had hoped for in your new just society—before the Communist Party corrupted the hell out of it—and talk about it in the West. Maybe . . . And lord knows we can use the help with soccer." He patted Matthias's shoulder and said gently, "You can *school* us."

A small, bittersweet smile grew on Matthias's tear-streaked face as he recognized his own joke.

Drew smiled back. "Linda sure will be glad to see you, and . . . I . . . I know there is no way we can fill in for your mother, but maybe . . . for those brothers you never got to know . . . maybe—"

"Cousins are *almost* as good," Matthias whispered, repeating what he'd said during the fireworks. "Maybe?"

Drew nodded. "C'mon."

Then, he turned them west, together.

EPILOGUE

Within days of cordoning off East Berlin with barbed wire, the GDR reinforces the barrier with concrete cinder blocks. They also brick up windows from which their fellow citizens and neighbors had jumped to freedom.

As the wall is fortified, family and friends struggle to find ways to speak to one another and reassure those trapped in East Berlin.

A L S O

West Berliners climb onto whatever they can to see over the wall and wave to loved ones. Within moments of these young women clambering up the light pole, Vopos launch tear gas grenades over the barricade to drive them away.

Eventually, the GDR adds a deadly "no-man's land," a 100-meter strip studded with landmines and steel "hedgehogs," monitored by attack dogs and armed border guards.

East Germans continue to try daring escapes. Eighteen-year-old Peter Fechter and a friend hide in a carpenter's workshop near the wall, watching patrols pass. When the guards walk in the opposite direction, the two youth go out a window and sprint across the "death strip." They hope to scramble over the wall where it is only six and a half feet high. His friend vaults over, but Fechter is shot while scaling the bricks. He falls back onto East Berlin soil, where he lies for an hour, with no medical help from the watching East German guards.

West Berlin police throw him bandages, but Fechter cannot move to reach them. He bleeds to death. Hundreds of West Berliners shout "Murderers!" as East Germans finally retrieve the dead teenager. Fechter was the twenty-seventh known victim to die at the wall.

AUTHOR'S NOTE

There are many people in the world who really don't understand what is the great issue between the free world and the communist world. Let them come to Berlin . . . Freedom has many difficulties and democracy is not perfect, but we have never had to put a wall up to keep our people in, to prevent them from leaving us.

—JOHN F. KENNEDY

The Berlin Wall went up when I was a toddler. It came down one jubilant, hopeful November night in 1989 as I rocked my own baby daughter, watching the TV in awe as Germans—East and West—tore the cinder blocks apart with their bare hands, hammers, and crowbars.

For twenty-eight years, that menacing concrete barrier, with its barbed wire, searing searchlights, and armed guards, loomed over the world stage—a chilling reminder of the Cold War standoff and a sickening symbol of the cruel walls people can build between themselves out of political zealotry. And yet, East Germans continued daring escapes to freedom in the West, using hot air balloons, zip lines, and tunnels. One hundred forty people are known to have died at the Wall, shot down during the attempt. Hundreds of unknown others were lost in collapsed tunnels, drowned while trying to swim canals, or caught beforehand, snared by the Stasi—perhaps reported to the GDR's secret police by neighbors, friends, or even family—and thrown into prison for "reeducation."

Such a cautionary tale needs to be remembered for its human struggle, for its people yearning to be free, and for its lessons. And so this book.

Walls is in a format I discovered worked well to distill complicated political eras when I wrote *Suspect Red*. That novel looks at McCarthyism, at what happened when political leaders' rhetoric, innuendos, and hate labels pushed Americans to turn on one another. Spanning a momentous year, each chapter covers a month's time, opening with news headlines, photos, and quotes from those four weeks, while the narrative focused on the trickle-down impact of polarized national dialogue on two teenagers—from opposite sides of the Red Scare debate—and their friendship.

With *Walls*, the post–World War II division of Germany and the treacherous overnight raising of the Berlin Wall handed me another incredibly dramatic moment in history. The question of what it would take for an East Berlin youth— raised and inculcated in communist dogma, bombarded with anti-America propaganda—to trust a Westerner, and vice versa, felt like a meaningful and poignant question to explore. The topic also gave me the chance to *show* the life-or-death reasons for NATO's formation, the harshness of daily life in a communist puppet state controlled by secret police, as well as to spotlight the courage of American military children—those "dependents" who follow their parents into dangerous postings and are uprooted constantly in service to our country.

My boys, Drew and Matthias, are fictional, but they are inspired by memoirs and interviews. For instance, Matthias's grilling in front of a FDJ youth tribunal and his agonized *Selbstkritik* (self-criticism); the coming-of-age *Jugendweihe* and its life-altering ramifications; the practice of shouting *Freundschaft* in greeting; and the pledge he signs to take up arms against NATO were all pulled from firsthand accounts and primary documents. The GDR did indeed reward fervent communist teens for spying on neighbors by giving them Olympic tracksuits, while severely punishing other East German teens for "lack of enthusiasm" at parades or lectures. (One teen was sent to a labor camp after goofing off during a classmate's recitation of Stalin's biography.) I often had to put my head down and shed a few tears when reading the heart-wrenching stories reported out of the Marienfelde refugee camp.

"Texas Willy" Kressmann and his *Kinderfest* are fact. He was mayor of the Kreuzberg district for almost twelve years, known for thumbing his nose at East Berlin authorities while somehow charming them, for championing youth and reprimanding neglectful parents, and for grand gestures like taking all of his wedding flowers to a nearby hospital for its patients to enjoy.

Drew's experiences and outlook—the constant danger of KGB and Stasi overtures and harassment of Allied personnel and their families; the unnerving aura of being surrounded by espionage and four hundred thousand Russian troops; plus the Berlin post's "little America" milieu and the eerie anxiety of traveling through the Russian zone on a duty train—are all drawn from army publications and accounts of "military brats" stationed in the divided city. The landscape they grew up in was rife with symbolism: a moonscape of rubble from World War II bombing was left in the Russia-controlled Eastern sector for decades, while West Berlin was quickly rebuilt. The Allies even created seven mini "mountains" by piling up debris. The highest, "the Hill" (which Drew mentions going to with other brats to watch for a glimpse of a new American satellite), is 260 feet tall and entombs a Nazi military college. When the building wouldn't yield to dynamite, the American Occupying Forces decided to bury it with the wreckage Hitler had wrought as part of their post–World War II de-Nazification. But things like the statues at Hitler's training pool remained, a haunting reminder of the Third Reich's idealization of the "master race."

The only slight creative license I took had to do with the standoff between American MPs and Soviet troops over an East German who'd managed to stow away on a duty train. I moved it ahead in time a few months to allow Charlie to give context to the enormous courage of Bob's actions in chapter ten. (If you're interested in a film dramatization of that historic event, watch *Stop Train 349*.)

The "Berlin Brats" who so graciously shared their experiences with me also talked of how well integrated military posts were in the early '60s. But the sad fact was that back home, the United States roiled with racial violence, like what met the Freedom Riders in May 1961, or with pervasive systemic prejudice similar to what my fictitious American GI must confront in chapter four. The civil rights movement was gathering momentum under the leadership of Martin Luther King Jr. and other nonviolent activists, following the success of the Montgomery bus boycott, which had pushed the Supreme Court to integrate public transportation. But still to come were the 1963 March on Washington and MLK's stirring "I Have a Dream" speech in front of the Lincoln Memorial; the 1964 Mississippi Summer Project to register Black voters, organized by CORE (of which Shirley's nana was a member) and the Student Nonviolent Coordinating Committee (SNCC); and the 1965 Selma-to-Montgomery march. These peaceful protesters were met with brutal police arrests, attacks by the KKK, beatings from bystanders, and even murder.

At first hesitant to send in federal forces to protect the nonviolent demonstrators, the Kennedy administration started listening to the demands of civil rights leaders. But it was LBJ who signed into law the Civil Rights Act of 1964 and the Voting Rights Act of 1965. It wasn't until 1967 that the Supreme Court ruled, in *Loving v. Virginia*, that state laws prohibiting interracial marriage were unconstitutional. In a terrible irony, Soviet Russia—which imprisoned and oppressed millions, invaded and annexed neighboring nations, denied its people basic human rights, and under Stalin, had engaged in ethnic genocide as far-reaching as Hitler's—made ample use of America's hypocritical racial inequalities in their campaign to stoke distrust and fear of

Western democracies. A 1961 Herblock cartoon captured it this way: Russia and the United States are in a neck-and-neck race to win international respect and the Cold War, but Uncle Sam lags slightly behind, burdened by carrying a menacing demon on his back—racism.

The bizarre juxtaposition of diametrically opposed banners and slogans along Berlin's East-West border is fact. So, too, are the final chapter's scenes depicting the calculated cruelty of August 13, 1961, when overnight the GDR unfurled 330 tons of barbed wire over 27 miles to cage in East Berliners. I found those details in eyewitness accounts and foreign correspondents' reporting—potent reminders of the importance of journalists working in foreign lands, braving arrest and physical harm, to bear witness to events in repressive regimes.

The photos and captions at the start of each chapter should give you a good grounding in what led up to the Berlin Wall being planned in secret and erected so suddenly—Soviet Russians taking over Eastern Europe after World War II; their attempts to push out American troops through the 1948–49 Berlin Blockade; their crushing the 1953 protests by East Berlin workers begging for decent wages, working conditions, and the right to vote; the escalating arms race; the tension between JFK and Khrushchev; and the flood of East Germans trying to escape the tyranny of communism.

A little more about Nikita Khrushchev, Russia's combative leader from 1953 to 1964: a disconcerting bundle of bombast and contradictions, Khrushchev would lead

Russia's de-Stalinization after the dictator's death. Yet he also suppressed the Ukraine's attempts at independence, crushed Hungary's revolt in 1956 (killing twenty-five hundred Hungarians during street fighting), and authorized the Berlin Wall. He would allow the printing of Aleksandr Solzhenitsyn's *One Day in the Life of Ivan Denisovich*, an unblinking look at the horrors of Soviet Gulag camps, but send nuclear missiles to Cuba to secure first-strike dominance over the United States.

Khrushchev pushed Russia into modern global politics by building up Soviet technology that resulted in his country's launch of the first satellite (*Sputnik*) as well as the first dog, first man, and first woman into space. At the same time he ordered secret surveillance and barbaric questioning of his people, plus clandestine disinformation campaigns to sow division within the United States. He didn't hide his contempt for JFK or his hatred of Nixon and bragged about manipulating the outcome of our 1960 presidential election. In 1956, he famously threatened, "We will take America without firing a shot. We do not have to invade the U.S. We will destroy you from within."

Vladimir Putin, who leads today's Russia—the nation credibly reported by all seventeen U.S. intelligence agencies and the Senate Intelligence Committee to have interfered in our 2016 presidential election—seems to adhere to Khrushchev's philosophy that ginning up conspiracy theories and smear campaigns will unravel a rival society. Putin was well schooled in such tactics, having served as a KGB secret police officer for fifteen years. Stationed in

East Germany for six of those years, Putin worked with the Stasi to monitor the thoughts and movement of its citizens, arrest dissenters, and recruit informers to steal Western technology and NATO military secrets. When Putin rose to power in 2000, Russian dissident writer Felix Svetov said he was a typical KGB type. "If the snow is falling," said Svetov, "they will calmly tell you the sun is shining."

Independently reported and corroborated truth, a free press, individuality and self-expression, the dignity of self-direction, respect for others and differing views—these are all liberties that communist regimes fear, because such freedom of thought exposes the lies of political fanaticism and authoritarian leaders. East Germany, under the thumb of Soviet Russia, sought to stop any trickle of such "poison." Music was the most dangerous, because it could float free through the air on radio waves into communist territory. The GDR waged war on what its party leaders decried as decadent Western songs, the "wiggle-hip" and dangerous "free dancing" presented by rock 'n' roll singers like Elvis Presley. The GDR's weapons ranged from ordering the creation and teaching of the Lipsi dance to prosecuting youth like Matthias for *Kulturbarbarei*—a charge akin in seriousness to sedition—for the innocent and age-old teenage desire to listen to music celebrating youth and perhaps advocating a little rebellion against adult authority or the status quo.

For many behind the Iron Curtain, AFN (the American Forces Network) and RIAS (Radio in the American Sector) were lifelines to the outside world, providing news, American music, and radio dramas, a proverbial window into a world they were supposed to hate and fear. RIAS broadcast carefully crafted Voice of America programs, while AFN's primary function was to provide entertainment for American servicemen and their families. But AFN commentators were well aware that many other people were listening as well.

Starting in 1956, the State Department sent American performing artists into the Soviet Bloc and underdeveloped countries at risk of falling into communism, calling it "cultural diplomacy." The hope was that concerts by jazz legends Louis Armstrong, Duke Ellington, Benny Goodman, and Dave Brubeck would spread firsthand awareness and appreciation of American music to lands saturated with anti-America rhetoric. The State Department also believed these performances would combat overseas perceptions of America as racist, since these groups were integrated and jazz music was such a wondrous combination of diverse American musical influences. Dizzy Gillespie's big band, for instance, performed in Iran, Pakistan, Lebanon, Turkey, Yugoslavia, and Greece. An American ambassador reported, "We could have built a tank for the cost of this tour, but you can't get as much goodwill out of a tank as you can out of Dizzy Gillespie's band."

The featured musicians often had more complicated experiences on these tours, however, painfully aware that while they were being sent out to improve the United States' image regarding civil rights, racism prevailed back home. Celebrated in Ghana as a demigod when he played there, Armstrong had a very public run-in with President

Eisenhower over Ike's handling of school integration during the 1957 Little Rock Crisis at Central High School. In 1962, Dave and Iola Brubeck wrote a satirical musical, *The Real Ambassadors*, and Armstrong sang anguished lyrics, asking: *If all are made in the image of Thee, could Thou perchance a zebra be?*

I hope that you, as readers, will take from Drew and Matthias's story the importance of thinking for yourselves, of listening and opening up your hearts to others who differ from you, and of our responsibility as a free people to not simply stand by when witnessing others advocating for their rights, whether in a foreign nation or in our own. I hope the cousins' hard-won friendship helps you marvel at the astounding resilience of the human spirit, our longing to imagine and to cry out against darkness. The saga of the Berlin Wall proves free speech and the arts can indeed change minds and chip away at barriers.

Use your voice. We'll be listening.

ACKNOWLEDGMENTS

As always, if you find value in this novel, it has everything to do with my adult children, Megan and Peter, who are themselves professional creative artists. Their ideas, questions, and sensitivity to hard issues and the conflicting nuances within the human spirit, plus their astute edits of my drafts, honed the narrative's voice, pacing, clarity, breadth, and themes. Megan also took on the enormous task of researching and then tracking down the most compelling images to punctuate and heighten the book's impact. Peter helped keep my teenage boy protagonists authentic—aggravating and endearing, blustery and vulnerable.

I'm very grateful for Elise Howard's courage in publishing a highly researched novel for teens on such a serious, complicated era, and her meticulous editing that made it far better. Thanks, too, to Laura Williams, for her masterful art direction and jacket design; Kayla Escobedo, for deft handling of the photo essay's complex material; Ashley Mason, for painstaking attention to detail; and Susan Schulman, for her literary taste and belief in my voice.

George Gilmore and Jim Branson graciously spent hours talking with me about their memories of being "military brats" in Berlin in the early 1960s and led me to other wondrously rich first-person resources. I honestly would not have been able to write this novel without their generosity and vast knowledge. Thanks, as well, to Daniel Grave, a talented theater artist and Berliner, who went to multiple museums and archives to research the city during the Cold War for me.

SELECTED SOURCES

There are reams of academic studies of the Cold War, but I found these to be particularly accessible and immediate in detail:

BOOKS

Agee, Joel. *Twelve Years: An American Boyhood in East Germany*. Chicago: The University of Chicago Press, 1975.

Cates, Curtis. *The Ides of August: The Berlin Wall Crisis 1961*. New York: M. Evans and Company, Inc., 1978.

Donner, Jorn. *Report from Berlin*. Translated by Albin T. Anderson. Bloomington: Indiana University Press, 1961.

Gilmore, George H., Sr. *A Cold War Soldier*. A memoir of service in West Berlin and elsewhere. Self published: July 2005

Kempe, Frederick. *Berlin 1961: Kennedy, Khrushchev, and the Most Dangerous Place on Earth*. New York: Berkley Press, 2011.

Lowe, Yoshika Lofti, and Trisha A. Lindsey, editors. *Cold War Memories: A Retrospective on Living in Berlin*. Middletown, DE: Brats Overseas Books, 2014.

Taylor, Frederick. *The Berlin Wall: A World Divided, 1961–1989*. New York: Harper Perennial, 2007.

ARTICLE

Bainbridge, John. "*Die Mauer*: the Early Days of the Berlin Wall." *The New Yorker*, October 19, 1962.

DOCUMENTARIES

Bellows, Susan, dir. *American Experience: JFK*. PBS, American Experience Films, 2013.

Berkeley, Hugo, dir. *The Jazz Ambassadors*. BBC, Normal Life Pictures, Antelope South Limited, Thirteen Productions LLC, Arte, and ZDF, 2018.

Isaacs, Jeremy, prod. *The Cold War*. CNN and BBC-2, 1998.

Musil, Donna, dir. *BRATS: Our Journey Home*. Brats without Borders, 2005.

DRAMA SERIES

Dierbach, Alexander, dir. *Line of Separation (Tannbach)*. ZDF miniseries, 2015. (in German)

FEATURE FILMS (PG-13)

Hadrich, Rolf, dir. *Stop Train 349*. Allied Artists Pictures, 1963.

Hamilton, Guy, dir. *Funeral in Berlin*. Paramount Pictures, 1966.

Herbig, Michael Bully, dir. *Balloon*. Distrib Films, 2020. (in German)

Johnson, Nunnally, dir. *Night People*. 20th Century Fox, 1954.

Michaels, Richard, dir. *Berlin Tunnel 21*. CBS-TV Movie, 1981.

Reed, Carol, dir. *The Man Between*. United Artists, 1953.

Ricciarelli, Giulio, dir. *Labyrinth of Lies*. Claussen Wöbke Putz Filmproduktion, 2015. (in German)

Spielberg, Steven, dir. *Bridge of Spies*. DreamWorks Pictures, 2016.

PHOTO CREDITS

page 191 (bottom): Everett Collection Historical / Alamy Stock Photo; page 192 (bottom): Library of Congress

CHAPTER 10

Page 210 (top): INTERFOTO / Alamy Stock Photo; page 211: NASA; page 212 (top): Everett Collection Historical, Inc. / Alamy Stock Photo; page 212 (bottom right): Everett Collection Historical / Alamy Stock Photo

CHAPTER 11

Page 234: Keystone Press / Alamy Stock Photo; page 235: Library of Congress; page 236 (top): RGR Collection / Alamy Stock Photo

CHAPTER 12

Page 260 (top): Werner Kreusch, Associated Press; page 261 (top): NATO; page 262 (top): Library of Congress; page 262 (bottom): Album / Alamy Stock Photo

CHAPTER 13

Page 284: dpa Picture Alliance / Alamy Stock Photo; page 285: Hum Images / Alamy Stock Photo; page 286: dpa Picture Alliance / Alamy Stock Photo; page 287 (top): dpa Picture Alliance / Alamy Stock Photo; page 287 (bottom left): National Archives; page 287 (bottom right): National Archives; page 288: CIA; page 289: National Archives; page 290: Patrice Habans, Paris Match / Getty Images

EPILOGUE

Page 320 (top): dpa Picture Alliance / Alamy Stock Photo; page 320 (bottom left): dpa Picture Alliance / Alamy Stock Photo; page 320 (bottom right): Imago Europe Collection / Alamy Stock Photo; page 321 (top left): National Archives; page 321 (top right): Everett Collection Historical / Alamy Stock Photo; page 321 (bottom): dpa Picture Alliance / Alamy Stock Photo; page 322 (top): dpa Picture Alliance / Alamy Stock Photo